The Best Laid Plans

RUSSELL GOVAN

© Russell Govan 2021.

Russell Govan has asserted his rights under the Copyright, Design and Patents Act, 1988, to be identified as the author of this work.

First published in 2021 by Sharpe Books.

For Chris.

CONTENTS

Chapters 1 – 31

Chapter 1

The scream dies almost immediately, barely lasting a couple of heartbeats. But it's enough to pull me up short. The hairs on the back of my neck are at attention, like squaddies on parade.

I'm aware of the adrenaline rush as my brain switches up several gears. Definitely a female scream. The sudden suffocation of the sound – *definitely* the intervention of a second party. ***Definitely*** someone in danger – my experience and instincts combine to confirm these certainties in a nanosecond. The damping effect of the torrential rain and the surrounding tall buildings suggest it came from a distance maybe just a couple of hundred metres ahead in the same northerly direction as I'm facing. Probably from one of the alleyways on the opposite side of the road.

My instructions are clear and absolute. *Keep your head down. Focus on your mission to the exclusion of all else. Do not get involved in anything that you do not have to.* But those instructions contradict most of my basic training and all of my core instincts, and I'm already running at full tilt. My PB for 100M is 11.1 and, despite the conditions and my six-foot three frame being drenched through, I reckon I'm moving at pretty close to that rate. I stay on the balls of my feet and take care to avoid splashing any puddles so that I don't alert anyone to my approach.

After twenty seconds I hear the sounds of a struggle and an indistinct male voice coming from an opening just ten metres ahead to my left. I slow down, then stop and peer around the corner to recce the situation. The alley is no more than two metres wide and unlit, but there's sufficient illumination from the streetlight behind me for me to see all I need.

Just twenty metres into the passageway three figures are clearly identifiable. A young woman is being pressed against a large wheelie bin by a tall, powerfully-built male. He's got his left hand across her mouth, with his right arm across her chest, pushing her backwards. There's a flash of reflected light from where his right hand should be which means he's holding a blade. Another male, shorter – maybe five-eight – is bent forward, hitching the woman's skirt up with one hand and roughly tugging at her knickers with the other. The woman is trying to kick out with both legs, although there's a weariness to her resistance like you see on wildlife documentaries when mortally wounded prey continues to struggle instinctively, but feebly.

I step forward into the alley. My faint shadow is sufficient to alert all three to my presence and each of them turn with squinted eyes to try to pick details from my silhouette. The shorter of the two men rather ridiculously removes his hand from the woman's knickers and smooths her skirt downwards. He addresses me, "On yer way, mate. Nothing to see here." His voice is reedy and nasal, cutting through the sound of the rain splattering the tarmacked ground.

I've got surprise on my side and I have control. I look right past him and talk directly to the woman. I affect a broad Glaswegian accent, "Are you okay, hen?"

"Didn't you hear me, mate? I said there's nothing to see here. On yer way!" He's calling me his mate, but there's nothing friendly about his demeanour. A quick glance back over his shoulder confirms that his partner has released the woman and stepped behind him, his right hand gripping the knife. It's either a MAC 695 or 700 military survival knife, with an 18cm blade – a serious bit of kit. Emboldened, the short-arse takes a pace forward.

I look past the pair of them. "I said, are you all right, hen?" She tilts her head so that she is looking in my direction. She mouths something, but no words come out, or they are drowned out by the monsoon.

"Are you fucking thick or something, you stupid Jock bastard?" He's taken another step towards me. "Just fucking walk on by."

He's at exactly the right distance. I sprint, then leap feet first at head height. The sole of my right boot makes contact with his jaw with sufficient force to propel him backwards into his accomplice's midriff, knocking both off their feet. I'm on top of him instantly and use both hands to crash the back of his skull satisfyingly against the ground. I know that's him sorted.

His oppo is hauling himself back to his feet, using the

wheelie bin for leverage. I launch myself at his back, grabbing a shoulder in each hand and pulling him down. The wheelie bin tips over and spews out ripped bin bags. Despite the rain, the sulphide and ammonia stench of rot almost makes me retch. I steel myself against the reflex, but my opponent is less resolute. As he gags, I rabbit punch his Adam's apple and he rolls backwards, clutching at his throat. I rise to my feet and administer a ferocious kick to the side of his head, which jerks violently. He is lying prone so I check whether he is unconscious or dead. It's the former, and the same for the other guy when I check him. The thought occurs that I could do the world a favour by snapping both of their necks. But two killings would draw far too much unwelcome attention to the incident, so I don't act on the impulse.

I turn towards the woman, who is standing with her back and arms pressed hard against the brick wall on the other side of the alley. Her head is turned sideways, looking right at me, eyes frozen wide. I step towards her and she mouths something that I can't make out. I lean in closer and she whimpers, "Please, don't hurt me."

Although I'm pumped, I've got sufficient wits about me to remember the pretence of being Scottish, and to recognise that she is seriously traumatised. "Don't worry, hen. You're safe. That pair are unconscious and are not going to hurt you. Are you all right?"

She nods. I think she trusts me. She surprises me by speaking again. "Who are you?"

"My name's Jamie Mackie," I lie easily. "Do you have a phone?"

She casts around, looking for something and points at a handbag on the far side of the toppled wheelie bin. I vault over and retrieve the bag. The torrential rain has damped the stink from the spilled contents of the bin and I tiptoe through the debris past the prostrate knife-man, before handing her the bag. She takes it in two tight fists and clutches it firmly against her chest, head bowed. Several seconds take a decade to pass while she remains stock still and silent.

"Is your phone in your bag?"

She looks up at me. She's got huge eyes and I think that she might be on something. Her cheeks are streaked with mascara. She doesn't speak.

"What's your name, hen?"

More years pass and I'm about to repeat the question when she saves me the trouble, "Amelia."

"Amelia, is your phone in the bag?"

She doesn't answer, but opens the bag, dips her right hand inside and brings out the very latest top-of-the-range Samsung model. She offers it to me and I see that she's wearing a ring on her middle finger that matches her expensive-looking earrings.

"No, Amelia. I don't want your phone. I need you to make a phone call to the police."

She extends her hand towards me, still proffering the phone. I take a step backwards. Amelia tries to close the gap by taking a pace forwards, but the heel of her left shoe has broken off and she stumbles. I prevent her fall by catching her and immediately feel her go rigid. Her mouth is clamped tight and she is breathing hard through her nose, but she doesn't drop the bag or phone. I manoeuvre her as gently as I can so that her back is against the wall again, and then I take a step away. Her eyes are locked on mine and, despite her vulnerability, there's a ferocity there that I didn't expect.

"Amelia, I need you to telephone the police. Do you understand?"

A nod.

"Good. You have to dial 999 and ask for the police." I'm speaking slowly and pause now. It's important to allow her time to process. "Then you need to tell them that you have been attacked and that the attackers are still present. You need to tell them that you are..." I look backwards and up to read the sign. "Tell them that you are in Baker's Passage, off the Tansey Road. Can you do that?"

Another nod. She's still looking at me. "Jamie?"

"Aye, what is it?"

"Will you stay? Stay until the police come?"

"I cannae do that. I'm sorry, but I have to go now. Will you phone the police?"

"Okay."

I go over to the two unconscious bodies and give each a powerful kick to the ribs. The complete lack of response confirms that they are both totally sparko, and no threat to Amelia. She's still looking right at me and I nod pointedly towards her phone, then I head back out on to Tansey Road. I pause just around the corner to hear Amelia say the word "Police", so that I know she's making the call, and then I'm running back in the direction I originally came from.

I take the next narrow alleyway on the right, parallel to Baker's Passage, and sprint-weave between the bins and puddles. This route is going to take me more than a mile out of my way, but I know that it avoids the CCTV cameras at Dixon's Cross and the traffic cams along Hoxley Drive. I can hear the sirens that confirm Amelia's call is being answered already. I'm trying to think if I've left any traces. I never touched her phone, so no fingerprints. Same for the wheelie bins. Unlikely that Forensics would find anything linking me to the scene, especially with all this rain. Except the handbag – shit! I'm trying to remember how I held it – I don't think I'll have left any prints. What about before that? The junction of Howard Street and Tansey Road, there's a camera there. Shit! It's less than half a kilometre from the scene, so it'll get checked. If Moll sees it, she'll clock that it's me straight off. Shit, shit, shit! I'll either have to brazen it out or just completely deny it. I can decide nearer the time.

I cross Brook Street and turn right on to Holmesmeath Avenue, a half-mile stretch of Victorian terraces and semis. The rain has eased to a drizzle that gives each streetlamp an

other-worldly orange aurora. I break into a gentle jog which I keep up as I marshal my thoughts. Moll couldn't have been clearer - *do not get involved in anything that you do not have to*. Just my bastard luck that less than an hour later I'm flattening two fucking creatures. My best hope is that Moll never hears about Amelia's case – but my luck's not *that* good. I play it all over in my mind again – I'll deny everything officially, and take my chances with Moll. The jog means that I cover the distance home in double quick time, before slowing to walking pace as I round the final corner. The lights in the flat are still on – the only one in the street. Vi must be waiting up for me. Double shit.

The communal front door is propped open by a bin bag that a cat or a fox has already made short work of. The mess is nearly as bad as the smell. I hold my breath and tiptoe through chicken bones, rotted fruit, soiled nappies and greasy paper towards the staircase. By the time I reach the third floor I judge it safe to breathe again and turn my mind to what I'm going to say to Vi. As I turn the key in the door, she surprises me by pulling it open. She's a mess – hair all over the place and eyes swollen. I see mascara tracks on cheeks for the second time tonight. "Vi, what is it? What's wrong?"

She's struggling to breath, and I'm not sure she's going to answer me. "It's Mummy." No more words are necessary. I wrap my arms around her and hold her tight.

Chapter 2

Vi's mother had been ill – seriously ill – but there hadn't been any indication that death was imminent. I keep her clasped close to me on the threshold for over a minute, until her breathing becomes more regular. She looks up into my eyes, which I use as a cue to nod towards the couch. We take a step in that direction, and I free my right arm to push the door closed behind us.

We sit down beside and half-facing each other, with my left hand resting between hers on her lap. "Do you want to talk about it, Vi, or would you like me to get you something. A cup of tea or coffee, maybe?"

She nods, "Yes, a coffee, please. Thanks."

I stand up slowly, trying to somehow transmit sympathy, warmth and love as I do so, keeping my eyes fixed on hers until she breaks the contact by lowering her head. I can see as I enter the kitchen that there's enough water in the kettle, so I flick it on and fetch two mugs. The clock on the cooker shows it's ten past one. The kitchen is spotlessly clean and immaculately tidy, just like the rest of the flat – a tribute to Vi's OCD. Even though she's not allowed in there, my own bedroom's the same, partly to fit in with the rest of the flat, but mainly because I prefer it that way.

I finish making the coffees, return to the living room and place the mugs on the table before resuming my previous position. Vi picks up the mug closest to her and takes a sip, winces, then puts it back down.

"Too hot?"

"A little. I'll let it cool for a bit."

I know a bit about grief – the force gives really top training – and I'm weighing up whether to speak next or to wait for her. Is she still in the denial stage, or is she already moving on from that? Vi reaches forward and picks her phone up from the table. She presses a couple of buttons and scrolls, then passes it to me in silence. There's a text exchange on display.

Mummy: *I am genuinely sorry to have to tell you that your mother died at twenty-seven minutes past midday today. Mallingford.* The text is timed at 2.04 pm.

Reply: *What the hell is going on? Is this some sort of sick joke? What are you doing with Mummy's phone?* Time 2.06 pm

Mummy: *There's no need for that sort of language, Vivienne. Your mother's condition worsened significantly last week and she agreed that I should have the use of her phone to tell you when the inevitable happened. There was sufficient morphine that she felt no pain at the end. I will make the necessary arrangements and inform you of the time and location of the funeral. It would be good to see you there. Mallingford.* Time 2.09 pm.

That's the entire exchange. I've encountered some shit in my time, but this is off the scale. I turn back towards Vi, her teary eyes lock on mine and we lean into each other's embrace. I'm processing as I hold her close. Viscount Mallingford is Vi's estranged father who she refuses to talk about, other than to say how much she hates him. I don't know what happened between them, but it beggars belief that any father would let his daughter know about her mother's death via text message. The tiniest shift of Vi's body signals that she's ready to break, and we disentwine. Before I try to understand more, I need to check where she's at. "Vi, is this really true?"

"Depends what you're asking." Her voice is calmer, steadier than I anticipated. "If you mean is Mummy dead, then yes, that's true. I phoned the hospital. I spoke to Doctor Veerasamy, the one I met when I visited Mummy the time before last." There's a pause as she struggles to draw a deep breath and suppress a sob at the same time. "She told me it was true. She said that Mummy had been unconscious for the last forty-eight hours, and that she had no pain at the end."

Vi's resistance crumbles as she is consumed by a series of sobs. I'm holding her once more, cooing comfort as best I can. A minute, maybe more, passes before it subsides and she again draws free from me. "Thank you, Josh."

"You're welcome."

She looks away, eyes fixed on the blank wall opposite for the briefest of moments, then turns back to me. "Or were you asking about the text messages themselves? Maybe you were wondering whether they could possibly be real." She looks at me, checking my reaction.

"I know they're real, because I saw them. But, if I'm honest, I can hardly believe what I saw."

"Oh, believe it, Josh. That…that bastard is capable of anything." There's a calmness to her that's surprising. "He knows how much I love Mummy." Her voice catches, and she pauses. "He knows how much I *loved* Mummy. He knew that I would have wanted to see her again. To be with her again, just one last time." She inhales slowly and deeply, keeping control. "And the bastard would have known that Mummy would have wanted to see me." There's a tremble in her voice when she says her mother's name, but she holds it together. She gets to her feet. "He would have enjoyed the thought of how I would feel when I found out."

"Good God, Vi. I know you hate him, but he can't be *that* bad, surely?"

I regret my words instantly as Vi takes a step back, eyes wider than should be possible, and screeches. "How the fuck would *you* know? How the absolute fuck would you know?" For a second I think the fury in her eyes might be a signal that she's actually going to attack me. Then she dissolves into tears once more, and slumps back down on to her seat.

"I'm sorry." I reach forward to push her mug nearer to her and pick up my own.

She contemplates hers for a second, then picks it up using both hands, inhales the coffee aroma, and takes a sip. There's a pause before she repeats the cycle. She's looking straight ahead at nothing in particular that I can see, while I'm sitting again at a ninety-degree angle to her right, waiting for her to re-engage eye contact. I take a mouthful of coffee and she turns her head towards me. "This is *my* fucking flat, Josh. It's *my* Mummy who's dead, and it's *my* bastard of a father that we're talking about. *Mine!* Don't fucking presume to know anything about what's mine to know." Her voice is cold, but her eyes are ablaze as she stares me out, challenging me. She's past denial and full square in anger mode. I bow my head and nod gently to confirm I understand.

"Wait there." Vi gets to her feet and strides towards her bedroom, returning immediately with something in her right hand – a photograph that she places on the table in front of us as she sits back down beside me. I know immediately that the couple in the picture are her parents. The woman's beauty is striking and the resemblance to Vi is so marked that it would be easy to believe that it was the same person. The great big eyes, wide mouth, high cheekbones – she could be Vi's twin. But there are differences too. The woman in the picture is smiling – her expression radiating a joy that I've never seen in Vi during all the months that I've known her. The woman in the picture looks whole, happy and fulfilled. Vi is a pale shadow by comparison. Looking at the mother and then at the daughter is like looking at a vase of flowers when they're fresh and then a month later.

The man is tall and slim, clean shaven and grinning. His blond hair is swept back. The flash of the camera reflects off his forehead above close-set eyes and an aquiline nose. The word that springs to mind is *aristocratic*, and I wonder whether that's because I already know that he is. The couple are arm-in-arm and waving towards the photographer with their free hands. The woman is wearing a yellow skirt suit with matching heels. The man is wearing a conventional navy lounge suit with collar and tie. Both outfits are beautifully tailored and obviously expensive.

I realise that Vi is studying me as I study the picture. She's waiting for me to say something. "So, these are your parents." A feeble statement-cum-question, but sufficient to trigger a response.

"On their wedding day. They'd got changed for going off on honeymoon and that's them waving goodbye to their guests at the reception. Mummy told me that was the last day she was truly happy."

She wants to talk. Her eyes are beckoning me for an acknowledgement, permission to continue. I oblige. "What happened?"

"They'd had a whirlwind romance. He was on the judging panel when she won Miss East Midlands and he was besotted by her." I glance at the photo again and register for the first time that Vi's mother has more curves than her daughter. "He pursued her daily after that. Calls, flowers, wined and dined her, professed his undying love and proposed three times before she finally said yes."

I pull a quizzical face.

"Really. That's how Mummy always explained it to me. I believe he must have genuinely fallen for her, because he faced some opposition from his parents and others in his social circle.'

"Why?"

"Mummy was a legal secretary from a working-class family. His friends and parents thought she was far too common for him. They believed it was just infatuation on his part and that marrying Mummy was completely crazy. But his stubborn streak meant he was determined to prove them wrong, so they were married just four months after they first met."

"What went wrong?"

"He was violent. He hit her. It was always worse when he'd been drinking. He'd had a lot of champagne at the wedding reception, and that night he punched her in the ribs."

"On their *wedding* night?"

"And probably every other day or night after that."

"Dear God. Why did she put up with it? Why didn't she just leave him?"

"She was terrified. He told her he'd kill her, and that he'd kill her family too. She believed him and, if you ask me, she was probably right to. That man is the incarnation of evil. There's nothing he wouldn't do." Vi stops, leans her head slightly to the side and looks straight at me.

"And that's why you hate him so much."

She surprises me by qualifying my statement of the obvious. "Partly."

I throw her the puzzled look again.

"He raped me."

I feel like I've been kicked in the stones and, fleetingly, I think I might be sick. I can hear the blood hissing in my ears. I draw breath, slowly. "When?"

Vi breaks eye contact and turns, then looks towards the floor. There's a pause before she resumes speaking, and when she does her voice is different, a semitone deeper and speaking more softly. It's like she's spying on someone and reporting what she sees to somebody else behind her. "So many times, that I eventually lost count."

She pauses and I feel drugged, unable to speak or move – somehow hypnotised by the horror.

"I was thirteen the first time. It was the second night of the October half-term holiday. My second night home from boarding school. I used to go to a *very* posh boarding school - appearances meant everything in our family. He came into my bedroom about half an hour after I had gone to bed and climbed in beside me. I could smell the drink on him and I tried to get out of the bed. But he pinned me down with his body and placed one of his huge hands over my mouth. *Daddy wants a kiss*, he said. I tried to bite him but he slapped me so hard I thought he would loosen my teeth. Then he put his hand back over my mouth, hitched up my nightie with his other hand and raped me. I tried to squirm, to wriggle free, but I was paralysed by fear. I knew exactly what was happening and I was powerless to stop it. When he finished, he kissed me on the forehead – like he had done ever since I was a toddler – and he told me that if I told anyone what had happened, he would kill Mummy and then he would kill me."

Vi pauses, but I can tell she hasn't finished. She starts pulling at a lock of her hair using her left thumb and the first two fingers, then starts to twist it tightly round the forefinger. She begins to tug it gently, rhythmically at first, then faster and faster so that I fear she'll pull it out. I've seen her display this tic before, but never with quite the same intensity. Her shoulders hunch and her body seems to tense every muscle, then very suddenly she stops and her whole body seems to relax.

Her head is still tilted downwards. "He would have killed us. I never had any doubt about that. That's why I let him keep doing it and doing it and doing it. For years."

The last two words almost cause me to gasp, but I contain it.

The story just get worse and worse. Except that it isn't a story, and Vi is reporting rather than telling. It's almost as if, by relaying what happened as dispassionately as she can, she doesn't need to engage with it. I've seen some witnesses behave like this in court – giving their evidence in a manner that insulates them from re-living the pain.

"When I was sixteen, at the start of the school summer holidays, I just couldn't take it any more. I told Mummy what he was doing. I'd always believed she must have had her suspicions, but I don't think she did – perhaps she simply didn't want to contemplate the fact that he was even more awful than she already knew."

There's another pause and this time I can't resist the need to fill the vacuum. "What did your mother do? What did she say?"

"She didn't *do* anything, except cry. She only said two things – that I should run away, and that I must promise never to tell anyone what had happened to me."

"That was it?"

"Yes. I packed a suitcase, stole a number of his things that I thought I could pawn easily, and left. I stayed with a school friend for the first two weeks, and after that in a B&B for a few days. Then I hooked up with a guy and moved to Paris. Pretty soon the bastard had me working the streets, strung out on smack most of the time. The whole thing is pretty much of a blur. I remember I thought at the time that, no matter how shitty a life it was, it was better than being back at home. Then, after a few years, he got killed and it was clear to me that I had to get out of Paris, out of France altogether. So, I came back."

"When was all this?"

She looks up and turns to look at me. "Four years ago. I came back and got on a programme. Got myself clean." The spell is broken, she's not reporting any more – she's re-engaged in conversation.

"So, you were in France for six years?" I knew from previous conversations that she'd been a working girl, and that she's had a couple of terminated pregnancies. But I didn't know where, when, or how she'd got there – until now.

A nod of the head, "Uh-huh".

"And you've never told anyone about what happened with your father."

The slightest shake of her head. "I promised Mummy I wouldn't." There's another pause and her eyes are welling up. "But now Mummy's…"

She falls into my arms for what seems like the thousandth time tonight, head on my shoulder, body shuddering gently, and cries silently. We stay like that for several minutes, until her breathing becomes regular and shallow, and I am reminded of just how quiet the night can be.

A sudden, persistent, distant bawling splinters the stillness and signals that it must be nearly two o' clock. Vi leans away and squints at me quizzically.

"It's the baby downstairs. It cries at almost exactly the same time every night. I expect it wants to be fed."

Vi looks doubtful. "I never hear it during the day."

"There's so much other ambient sound during the day that it probably gets lost amongst it. I expect that the mum probably gets to it more quickly then too."

"And you hear it every night?"

"For the last six weeks." The crying stops as abruptly as it started. "That's it. We won't hear it again."

"Good. Look at the time. I need to get to sleep – and you too. Thanks for being here for me, Josh."

"No problem. You should have a lie-in tomorrow. I'll get in touch with Ryan to let him know what's happened. I'll ask him to postpone Saturday night."

"No."

"Sorry?"

"You heard me perfectly well, Josh. I said *no*." I can see that all thought of sleep has vanished. Her voice is firm and her eyes steely.

"I just thought, with your mother and everything…"

She doesn't flinch at my mention of her mother, as she cuts across me, "That's the right motivation, Josh, but the wrong solution. I joined the group because of Mallingford." She almost spits his name. "Because of what he is, and what he represents. Society, the state, it's all structured for the benefit of bastards like him. So that he and his kind can do whatever the hell they like, and know that they'll get away with it." The steel in her eyes glows white hot. "Well we'll fucking show them. They're going to get what's coming to them and it'll be us who delivers it." There's a pause as she inhales mightily. "So, we're not postponing Saturday, okay?"

"Okay, you're right. I get it." And I do get it. I understand this lovely, stupid, kind, screwed-up woman much more clearly now. "I think we were meant to be getting some sleep, weren't we?"

She tosses me the weariest smile and mini-waves her hand, "You're right. Night, night."

"Night, night, Vi." I turn and head towards my room. I know that Vi will be in her bed soon too, but not before she's washed and dried the coffee mugs and put them back in the cupboard.

Chapter 3

Molly Leishman frowned. "Okay, Tom, I can be with you in about half an hour. See you then. Bye." She continued to scowl at the phone screen after it went black. Old Tom Wilson had been her first ever desk sergeant, and he'd always had her back.

She'd smiled instinctively when the familiar voice had introduced himself, then wondered why he was calling as the ritual exchange of pleasantries progressed. *I think that there's something here you might want to see.* That was how he'd introduced it. *There was an incident last night in an alley way off Tansey Road. We've been reviewing CCTV footage.* Then he'd left it hanging, forcing her to prompt him to go on. *One set of cameras picked up a figure who could have been involved in the incident.* One of Tom's less endearing features was his propensity to string things out and to dramatize them. Memories of how irritating that habit could sometimes be almost prompted her to rebuke him, but she'd bitten her lip, knowing that he would feel compelled to fill the silence. *I can't be sure, Molly, but I think there's a chance that the figure could be Josh Gray.* There had been another pause as she'd digested his words, before she'd given him the satisfaction of instructing him to "Go on."

We've got two ne'er-do-wells, he'd paused and corrected himself, *two **alleged** ne'er-do-wells in the Royal Infirmary*.

Molly finished replaying the conversation in her mind, closed her eyes and inhaled deeply. Surely, he wouldn't have been so stupid. She'd seen him only last night. Told him to keep his head down. Been explicit about focusing on the job to the exclusion of all else. Surely, *surely*, he wouldn't have been stupid enough to get involved in an incident. Not immediately after she'd warned him. Except of course he *is* that fucking stupid. Now she's got to cover his arse. And once she's done that, she's going to hand him his cute little arse on a plate.

Molly leaned forward, switched her desktop off, then used her feet to propel the office chair backwards from her desk. "I've just got to head over to Walton Street Station."

"Be gone long?" Johnny Duke didn't break from gazing studiously at the spreadsheet on his screen.

"Half an hour's drive each way, and maybe up to an hour there. So, probably a couple of hours."

"Any chance you can pick me up a cappuccino and a Chelsea bun on the way back." His head still hadn't moved.

"Get your own coffee and cake, lard-arse."

"Can't blame a man for trying."

Molly exited both the office and the building smiling. She'd once fetched Johnny a coffee almost two years ago and, ever since, they'd gone through the ritual exchange that had just played out any time she left the office. Although he was always deadpan, she knew that being called lard-arse needled Johnny, so she was quite happy to play along with his stupid game. The smile faded as she opened the door to her Golf and her mind returned to the call from Tom Wilson.

The late morning city traffic was unusually light and she found herself entering the front door and approaching the reception desk at Walton Street less than twenty-five minutes later. She introduced herself to the young officer behind the desk who called Tom Wilson to alert him that he had a visitor.

Less than thirty seconds later a door in the far corner of the reception area opened and a familiar figure strode towards her. She'd calculated during the drive over that it must be more than two years since she'd last seen him, and his previously salt-and-pepper crew cut was now shockingly white. That, and a noticeable thickening round the waist, made him seem much older to her. But the broad, sonsy face, with its cheery grin and affectionate eyes was as recognisable as ever. "You made very good time, Ma'am." The Cornish burr was less prominent than it had sounded on the phone.

"Less of the Ma'am, Tom. Just call me Molly."

"Perhaps in private, Ma'am. But…" he flicked a theatrical glance in the direction of the desk officer, "in front of the other ranks…"

Molly squeezed her lips together to suppress a smile. "Of

course, sergeant. I must say that you're looking well."

"I'd like to borrow those glasses of yours the next time I use a mirror. Now, if you'd like to follow me through." Sergeant Wilson waved his security card at the reader and pushed open the door he'd come through just a moment before. Molly followed him along a wide corridor with numerous doors, all open, and passageways off to either side. Two thirds of the way along, Tom ushered her into a room on the right where a civilian member of staff was seated one third of the way along a console, watching three separate computer monitors while simultaneously demonstrating a prodigious keystroke rate on the keyboard in front of her. On the wall behind the monitors was a bank of eight large television screens arranged in two rows of four, one above the other. Each screen displayed a grid of nine separate views feeding in from different traffic, surveillance and security cameras.

The CCTV operator was wearing an all-in-one earphones and mic headset. She smiled her acknowledgement as Tom gave her a mini wave to indicate that he and Molly were going to move to the other station further along the console to her right. Tom fetched a very basic wood and gunmetal chair from the far corner of the room and placed it beside the vacant operator's chair. "Do you mind taking that chair, Ma'am? It's just that I find the tech easier to operate from this one."

"Of course." She took her seat, adjusting its angle slightly as she did so, while Tom did the same. "Okay, Sergeant, can you explain what this is all about?"

Tom Wilson leaned forward very slightly towards her, almost conspiratorially. She found herself reciprocating instinctively. "There was an incident last night Ma'am. 999 call at half past midnight to an alley way off Tansey Road. Called in by a woman, Amelia Harris – 26 years old, reporting that she'd been the victim of an attempted rape." He paused briefly, to look Molly in the eye. "She said that the perpetrators were still with her at the scene."

The bizarre twist had the desired effect as Molly's face contorted in bewilderment. She clocked the fleeting satisfaction in Tom's eye and realised this was rehearsed for her benefit and that he was enjoying himself. "Go on, Sergeant."

"We had a car there within two minutes of receiving the call. The officers attending found Miss Harris at the scene in a state of some confusion and distress." Tom's attempt at another pause was cut short by a frown from Molly. "There were also two men, the alleged assailants, both unconscious at the scene."

"You mentioned them on the phone call earlier. Do we know what happened?"

"An ambulance was called and all three were taken to the Royal Infirmary. One officer accompanied the alleged assailants in the ambulance and the other drove Miss Harris there in the squad car. The two men were admitted and are still in there. We have a guard in place for each of them. Miss Harris was checked over and found to be physically unharmed, apart from a few scratches and bruises. She said that she believed her drink had been spiked and the hospital ran tests, looking for traces of benzodiazepine or something similar. We've not heard the results yet, but if I had to bet on it, I'd say she's right."

"Okay, Tom, that's fine. But do we know what happened?"

"Miss Harris insisted that she was well enough to attend the station and provide a statement."

"Really? In that state, and possibly still drugged. Was that wise? What do we know about her?" Molly had stiffened somewhat, although her voice remained calm.

Tom took the cue to get on with it. "The officers involved seemed to think so, and Sergeant Downing was on duty when she came in. She was offered the appropriate support and counselling services, and that offer will be repeated in the follow-up meeting." He knew that the reputation of the much-respected Downing would provide reassurance.

"Good." Molly's voice softened. "And the woman? Miss Harris?"

"26 years old and single. Had gone to Club Monserrat with three of her friends for a night out. She remembers drinking, dancing and chatting to someone we believe to be one of the alleged assailants. Then nothing until she was in the alleyway being assaulted by two men. She had the presence of mind to scream at the top of her voice when she realised what was happening."

"So how do we get from there to having two men in The Royal?"

"It seems her screams alerted some sort of highland hero."

Molly's patience was being tested, and it showed in her tone. "Explain."

"A man arrived on the scene. She describes him as very tall – well over six feet – slim but powerfully built, piercing eyes, prominent nose, thick black hair and full beard. He was wearing jeans, trainers and some sort of zip-up jacket."

The description confirmed Molly's fear that the mystery man was indeed Josh, but she knew the importance of being poker-faced. "You mentioned a highland hero?"

"Yes. The man spoke with a Scottish accent. He called himself…" Tom paused as he struggled to recollect the name. "Mackie, that's it. He told her that his name was Jamie Mackie."

"What else?"

"Seems like he took the two men out with some sort of flying kung-fu kick. Then made short work of them by cracking one fellow's head off the ground, and kicking the other guy in the head. Then he told Miss Harris to dial 999 and made off."

"That's it?"

"I can get her statement for you if you like, but that's pretty much the gist of it."

"No, that won't be necessary just yet. There's quite a bit of detail in what you've just said. More than I'd expect from someone who'd been drugged and then traumatised. Are we sure about Miss Harris? Is she reliable?"

"I've not spoken to her myself, Ma'am. I'm relying on reports from the officers involved. But she's a journalist with The Herald, so that would maybe explain why she was so good when it came to observing and recalling details."

"Maybe. How credible do we think she is?"

Molly's eyes were fixed on Tom, challenging - almost interrogating him. He shifted slightly uncomfortably, as the recollection surfaced of how demanding a boss she had been before. "Apparently she's highly educated and very well spoken. She's reported as wearing very expensive clothes and one officer described her as…" Tom hesitated, although it was clear to Molly that there was no artifice to this pause, before he continued in a quieter, smaller voice. "He described her as…very presentable."

The final word hung in the air as Molly silently and swiftly deployed anger management controls she'd learned years earlier. *Presentable* was the code used by male colleagues to describe a particularly physically attractive female. Tom's use of it just now was all the more incendiary because of the incident almost ten years previously, when she'd mauled him after overhearing him use the same word to describe her in a conversation with a senior officer. It had reinforced her determination to play down her own looks when at work ever since. Whenever on duty, her hair was scraped tight back, she wore glasses rather than contacts, and never any hint of make-up. Although always smart, her clothes were chosen for function rather than fashion or to flatter.

Despite its claims otherwise, the force had always been dauntingly sexist and still was. It was more subtle now than when she had been more junior, but she still encountered it frequently enough to know it hadn't gone away. She also knew that if she challenged Tom on its use again now, he'd have some bullshit reason about how it was relevant to the case. He'd defend that claim despite the fact there had been no comment on the attractiveness or otherwise of any of the males involved in the incident. However, that war was going to be a very long campaign, and Molly had learned which battles were worth taking on. This wasn't one of them. "Does she intend to press charges?"

"Yes, Ma'am. But her case isn't that strong. She's got a few minor cuts and bruises, and there'll probably be confirmation of drugs in her system. There was also a knife recovered from the scene that she's mentioned in her statement. But the rain at the time of the incident was so heavy that Forensics are likely to draw a complete blank. It looks like it will boil down to her word against the two in hospital, unless…"

"Unless there is a witness who can corroborate her version of events."

"Yes, Ma'am. We examined every single frame of footage from the surrounding area from the time the 999 call was received, but there was no trace of anyone matching the description of Jamie Mackie. Then a further examination of footage from the half hour before the call was received threw up this individual, captured by the camera at the junction of Howard Street and Tansey Road." Tom leaned forward and clicked the mouse to bring it to life. An image of a man comprised considerably less than 10 per cent of the entire street view on the screen and, other than the suspicion that he might be bearded, it was impossible to recognise him. "I'm afraid it's only a really basic picture."

Molly was well aware that some installations run sophisticated facial recognition software on an extended trial basis. Otherwise surveillance cameras, when used by the police, are governed by the same rules as when an officer wants to approach an individual on the street. Just as an officer needs a reason to stop an individual and ask them to account for their movements, so a CCTV operator must have a sound reason for using a camera to zoom in on a particular individual. Consequently, all cameras operating automatically are set sufficiently far back that identifying someone unknown is improbable. Molly craned her neck forward and narrowed her eyes in concentration. The individual on screen could be seen walking, slightly stooped against torrential rain. The footage captured him for nine seconds and reaffirmed absolutely for her that it was indeed Josh.

"I know that Josh Gray was at Bolton Street nick at the same time as us and I can see why you thought it might be him, Sergeant. That individual certainly looks the right height and build, and seems to have a similar gait. But I can confirm that definitely isn't him." Molly's role had helped her perfect the skill of deploying convincing lies when she deemed it necessary, but she knew how well Tom Wilson could read people, particularly her. She tilted her head quizzically.

"Ah okay, Ma'am. I thought it was worth a shot, but if that had been him then you would have known." A pause and a smile. "I know how busy you must be, Ma'am, but have you a few minutes for a cup of tea and a chinwag?"

"I've always got time for a cuppa with you, Sergeant." Molly followed Tom's lead as he got to his feet and headed back out into the corridor they had previously entered from.

Stopping in front of a vending machine positioned near the foot of a flight of stairs, he inserted his card in the reader then punched a selection. "Still milk with no sugar, Ma'am?"

"Yes please. Impressive that you remember after all this time."

"One of the few benefits of beginning to resemble an elephant is developing an excellent memory." Tom passed the plastic cup to Molly with his left hand as he punched in the code for his own drink with his right. "There should be an interview room vacant upstairs, if you'd like to follow me up."

A minute later they were seated opposite each other across a basic Formica table in a characterless rectangular room that might accommodate six people at a squeeze. The only feature was a large clock on the wall, obviously chosen for functionality rather than aesthetics. "So, Molly, how are you?" Tom's smile was as wide as it was sincere.

"Not so bad, Tom. I keep myself busy." Molly took a sip of her tea and grimaced.

"Sorry, I should have warned you. The tea and coffee all taste like TV static – doesn't matter whether you have milk or sugar, they all taste the same. The only one that's different is the soup, which tastes of cabbage and socks." Tom made mock-apologetic big eyes.

"And how are you, Tom? And the family?"

"I'm grand, thanks – and so is the missus. Our Kate's expecting again. We'll have our seventh grandchild next February."

"Seven! You must be looking forward to retiring to spend more time with them."

"Quite the contrary. That sounds like too much hard work, compared to staying in the job." He flashed her a smile, then brought his closed left hand in front of his face and tilted his head to study his fingernails. Molly was immediately on her mettle as she recognised the unconscious signal. "You were very certain that the individual on that footage wasn't Josh."

The Met, like every other force, suffered from infiltration by corrupt officers. Everyone knew it, but the problem was identifying who they were. Organised crime sponsored the appointment and nurtured the careers of its placemen and women in return for key intelligence. A by-product of Josh's previous undercover op – his first – had led to the identification of one such senior officer working on the Fraud Desk at the Economic Crime Department. Molly was as confident as possible that Tom was old-school straight, but protocol – and basic common sense - dictated that she protect her officer. "I saw Josh just the day before yesterday. Unless he's managed to grow the full set of whiskers described by Miss Harris since then, I'm pretty confident he's not your man."

"So…" Tom studied his fingernails for a second time, "…you're running Josh?"

"Yes." She couldn't deny it. Molly silently cursed herself for her stupidity.

Tom scratched his left thumbnail with his right. "And how's that working? I mean for you."

"It's working fine. Josh and I finished when I got my promotion. We agreed that was the sensible thing to do. We have a purely professional relationship now, and its working fine." She repeated the phrase for emphasis, and hoped that the knot she felt in her stomach wasn't reflected in her voice.

"Glad to hear it." He stopped playing with his hands and smiled. "And I don't suppose you're able to hint at what kind of op Officer Gray is working on?"

Molly certainly couldn't hint that Josh had infiltrated a group of malcontents that intelligence had flagged as potentially preparing to engage in acts of violence. "You're right, Tom. I couldn't possible hint that Josh is working on an op involving an ongoing and long-running insurance scam."

It was nonsense, and she was aware that Tom would know it was nonsense. But it was sufficient. Police stations are the best-wired places on earth. Already everyone in the building would know that she was visiting Tom, and speculation would bubble up like autumn mist on the Thames. Tom would be able to feed the hunger for gossip - explaining with a knowing wink that there couldn't possibly be any covert op investigating an insurance scam – absolutely no way.

"Anyway, that's enough shop talk, Tom. Have you got any photos of your grandchildren?" The conversation meandered harmlessly and comfortably for another ten minutes to a natural conclusion of goodbyes and insistences that they mustn't leave it so long next time. Molly left Walton Street grimly determined that she wasn't just going to hand Josh his arse on a plate, she was also going to have his bollocks on toast.

Chapter 4

Less than four hours sleep, but it's 5.50 am and my body clock auto-wakes me. The bedside alarm will sound in five minutes, just in case I'm not already awake. Inventory time.

I need to look after Vi. Confirm that she really is okay for tomorrow.

I should clean up round the communal front door, otherwise Vi will freak out.

Recce tomorrow's target again – make sure nothing's changed.

The Howard Street camera will have caught me. I need to change my appearance now - today - rather than wait until Monday.

I roll out of bed and make my way quietly to the bathroom. The fierce mint of the toothpaste heightens my sense of wakefulness. Vi is a fairly heavy sleeper so I judge that it's fine to take a quick shower. But, if I'm going to clear up downstairs, I'll do that first before showering and having breakfast. I head back to my room, throw on yesterday's clothes, then go through to the kitchen and fetch two heavy duty black bin liners and a pair of rubber gloves from the cupboard below the sink.

The smell is unlikely to have improved overnight. I fetch a scarf from my room and return to the bathroom. I squeeze a pea-sized blob of toothpaste on to the end of my right index finger and smear it through my moustache, then wrap the scarf round my head three times to cover my nose and mouth. Apart from the big Chinese-looking guy from the flat below, who has a regular job and leaves every morning at quarter past seven, no-one else uses the stairs before eight. I'm not likely to bump into a neighbour and terrify them.

I leave the door on the latch, cross the landing and begin descending the bland staircase – cream walls, beige stairs and a battle-worn wooden handrail atop black metal railings. Despite my precautions, the smell intensifies as I descend, while at the same time the characterless walls become increasingly disfigured by graffiti. At ground level it's hard to know whether the smell or the extreme right-wing graffiti is more offensive. "Political" slogans, racial slurs, crude pornographic images and two sizeable swastikas deface the walls, all intended to cause distress to the multi-ethnic residents of the block.

It looks like the strewn rubbish has suffered further animal attack overnight – probably by a cat after the chicken carcass – and I curse to myself as I pick up the debris and stuff it into one of the bin liners. One particularly rancid bag of food waste causes me to gag, and I struggle to control the heaving feeling in my stomach. It was a good decision not to have eaten breakfast.

It's actually a quick job to gather everything into the bag and tie it up, before double-bagging it for good measure. I pull the large swing door open and carry the rubbish all of twelve metres to the large communal bin in front of the block. It defies belief that somebody who lives here can't be arsed to carry their garbage those last few metres. I'm pretty sure it must be the young east European woman who lives on the ground floor, as she's the only person in the block with a child still small enough to be wearing the nappies that made up a significant proportion of what I've just cleared up. The wired glass window above the door is propped wide open, so the lingering smell should clear up pretty quickly.

I head back upstairs, clean and disinfect the rubber gloves in the kitchen, then head for a shower. Soap, water and shampoo banish any sense of lingering smell along with the sluggishness from my diminished sleeping time. I dress in fresh, anonymous clothing then make a breakfast of porridge turbocharged by oat milk and leavened by salt and crushed walnuts for taste and texture. I do the calculations as I eat. Vi rarely wakens before 10.00 am, and might well sleep later given how late it was when she went to bed last night.

It's 6.35 now. Three and a half hours should be plenty time to scout tomorrow's target and get myself a new look.

An eight-minute walk to the train station, half an hour on the train, twenty-five minutes on the tube and another five-minute walk deliver me to the target. The site is secured by two-metre-tall blue hoarding. There are safety notices placed at regular intervals but, because of the relatively low footfall along this road, only one advertisement: *Extraordinary homes with amenities that inspire – READY TO MOVE INTO NEXT SUMMER*. Every time I see it, I struggle to imagine that someone was paid to come up with it. The gate that Jonno is charged with getting the key for is almost directly opposite the side street where we'll park the van.

The site is in full swing already, even though it's not yet eight o' clock. The insistent hammering of a pneumatic drill plays out in staccato bursts over the low, throaty growl of several heavy vehicles manoeuvring beyond the blue barrier. There are occasional shouts from workmen, but no words are distinguishable. The sounds aren't from immediately behind the hoarding – more like fifty to a hundred metres beyond. That would make sense given the location of the sixty-metre-high tower crane, like an emaciated yellow Eiffel Tower that some giant has bent at a right angle halfway up. Nothing at all seems to have changed in the adjacent area – three blocks of derelict buildings scheduled for demolition and redevelopment once the site next door completes. The dilapidated buildings are swept weekly by a security team with dogs, so the probability of squatters who might become witnesses is remote – but I still walk the pavements on both sides of each street to check for signs of occupation. All clear.

I've seen enough, and don't want to be dawdling around here, possibly attracting attention. I walk back to the tube station and only have to wait a couple of minutes for the train. I get off after only two stops, exit the station to the left, walk a couple of hundred metres and then jump on a bus travelling in the broad general direction of Vi's flat. I understand the importance of varying my route and avoiding the danger of developing a routine. The rush hour traffic is frustratingly slow, so when I see the *Traditional Turkish Barber* sign above a shop on yet another anonymous parade, I decide to take the opportunity.

I disembark from the bus and pretend to read a text on my phone, leaning casually against the bus stop. This location seems a good choice as there are no cameras obvious anywhere, I've never been here before and am unlikely ever to be again. The shop is brightly lit and modern, with two cutting stations on either side and a waiting area to the right rear corner with bench seats in an L-shape around a low coffee table bedecked with magazines. There's a flat screen TV on the back wall where a serious-faced man seems to be trying to convey anguish as he performs what I presume is a Turkish ballad. There's not a single hair in sight on the immaculate laminate floor, which suggests I will be the first customer of the day.

I stand just inside the threshold, holding the door open with my right hand, and address the fellow behind the counter in the back-left hand corner of the shop, who is quickly getting to his feet. "You are open?" I deploy my best Dublin brogue.

He's out and walking towards me, five-foot six, around thirtyish, thick black hair swept back with a side parting, neatly trimmed beard, welcoming eyes and a wide smile. "Yes sir, yes. Open 8.00 am to 8.00 pm seven days a week. The others will be in later, but at this time it only requires one of us." He's already taken my jacket and placed it on a hook in the waiting area and is beckoning me to the chair nearest the counter where he emerged from. I take my seat, let him put the paper collar round my neck then fold it neatly round the smock that he's flourished over me. "What can I do for you today, sir?"

I'm gay for the purposes of my assignment, and I'd briefly considered getting the Freddie Mercury moustache to reinforce the stereotype, but it's way too distinctive a look. I catch his glance in the mirror. "The lot. I'd like a Number Two all over, and a traditional wet towel shave." I see cartoon dollar signs in his eyes.

"Certainly, sir. I'll do hair first and then the shave. You want square neck or tapered?"

"Square please."

"Yes, sir. You stay around here?"

"Bartholomew Road." The name of a long side street of terraced houses the bus passed shortly before I got off elicits a nod from him. "I'm visiting my sister."

"That's nice. I could tell from your accent that you're not from around here."

"I'm from Ballyfermot, in Dublin."

He smiles, but I can see from his expression that it means nothing. I'm pleased that he already seems to be on autochat while he concentrates on the task in hand. "Any special reason for the visit, sir?"

"An old school friend is getting married tomorrow on the other side of the city, so it gave me a chance to catch up with my sister beforehand." People remember you if you are difficult or awkward – bland chit-chat increases the speed with which he's likely to forget me.

"And that is why you are going for the whole smart new look? The wedding?"

"That's right."

The conversation meanders harmlessly as the clippers perform their serious cropping. A call on his mobile phone interrupts his handiwork. He apologises, saying he must answer, then becomes quite animated with whoever is on the other end of the call. I don't speak Turkish, but I'm willing to bet there are plenty of swear words. He looks right at me a couple of times and, momentarily, I imagine I am the topic of conversation before dismissing the notion as obvious nonsense. The call ends and he apologises again, then he resumes cutting and chatting harmlessly. Our conversation comes to a necessary end when it becomes virtually impossible for me to talk as he tackles my beard. I respond positively to every option offered – eyebrow trim, ear burning and aftershave rub. Just thirty-five minutes after sitting in the chair I'm looking at a guy in the mirror with fiercely short hair and a face that is clean-shaven for the first time since New Year's Day, over nine months ago. We go through the ritual of him angling a small mirror behind me so I can approve the reflection of the back of my head. "Yes, that's fine. Thank you."

"Thank you, sir."

I retrieve my jacket, slip it on and step up to the till on the counter. "How much is that?"

"That will be fifty pounds please, sir."

I take three twenty-pound notes from my wallet and hand

them to him. "Just give me five pounds back." It's a generous tip, but not overly so. Really large tips – or particularly mean ones – are more likely to be remembered. This is a good but unremarkable tip. Besides, he's done a good job and I'm pleased.

"Thank you, sir." We both turn at the sound of the door opening as his next customer arrives. "Enjoy your wedding." He smiles, but his eyes are already on his next job. We share polite leaving noises and I step outside the shop. A quick glance back through the window shows him already engaged in conversation as he sweeps up my shorn hair. I'm all but forgotten already. The air is cold and I feel a chill around my face, head and neck. I pull a soft acrylic beanie hat from my pocket. It's reversible, like my Harrington jacket, and I elect to go with the solid navy look.

A brisk twenty-minute walk brings me to an overground station. An unremarkable journey with one change then a leisurely stroll brings me back within sight of the four-storey block of flats that Vi and I call home. My watch tells me that it's five to ten, and I can see the curtains in Vi's bedroom window are still closed. The front door swings inwards and, even though it's nearly three hundred metres away, I recognise the young woman from the ground floor. She's propping the door open with another bag of rubbish!

I resist the urge to run, although my pace does quicken. I don't want to cause a scene – any unnecessary attention would be both stupid and unwelcome. Part of me is wondering how on earth she can have generated another bag of rubbish in so short a time, the other part is bewildered as to why she just doesn't take it to the communal bin. The answer to the second conundrum reveals itself as she disappears back inside then re-emerges awkwardly trying to manoeuvre a double-width pushchair through the doorway. She needs something to prop the heavy door open. I hadn't realised she has twins – that might explain why she's able to produce quite so much trash. Once she negotiates the exit, she heads off down the street in the opposite direction to me. The door behind is left propped open, presumably to make her return straightforward. When I arrive at the propped door I pass through, leaving the arrangement untouched, and head upstairs.

I turn the lock, push the door open, then close it behind me virtually silently. The more sleep Vi can get, the better. I slide my shoes off and leave them beside the door then tiptoe toward the living room. Vi is seated on the couch and has just placed her coffee mug on the table, which is just as well – as she would surely have dropped it otherwise. The shriek startles me, although it dies almost before it starts as it metamorphoses into an urgent cascade. "Josh? Josh! What the hell! Jesus bloody Christ, Josh! What are you trying to do to me? I almost shat myself! What the hell have you done to yourself?"

I don't know if she's more furious or bewildered. "I didn't realise you were up. I was trying not to wake you."

"Of course I'm bloody up! You can see I'm up. What's the idea sneaking around like that? And what the hell has happened to your hair? Where's your beard? I nearly didn't recognise you. For God's sake, Josh."

"Okay, okay! Calm down. I'm sorry. I didn't mean to startle you." I can see from her eyes that the anger has subsided and that it's curiosity that needs to be satisfied now. "I wanted to go out and recce tomorrow's target and get back before you were awake. I wanted to be here when you woke up in case you needed anything."

"And your hair? Your beard?"

"I'd been thinking about doing it for a while. I saw a barber open this morning with no queue and decided to go for it."

"So now you'll be pulling guys that go for the clean-cut boyish look, rather than the caveman type." She says it with a smile and I know she's relaxed. It won't last once the grief kicks in again. Today's going to be a long day of looking after her, rehearsing her for tomorrow and deciding whether or not she's really going to be up to it.

Chapter 5

Vi is going to be fine for tonight. I don't know whether it's displacement activity to keep her grief at bay, but she's been properly focused and I'm confident she's ready. There was a wobble yesterday when Mallingford got in touch. Her phone rang and caller ID showed it was her mother's phone. She refused to answer it. He tried again twice and she let it ring out.

Finally, he texted: *Vivienne, you are not answering your phone. Call me. Mallingford.*

She replied: *I do not want to speak to you. EVER.*

He responded: *As you wish, Vivienne. Your mother's funeral will be at 10.00 am on Tuesday. St. John's Church and afterwards at The Claremont Hotel for luncheon. I expect that you will attend. Mallingford.*

That had definitely thrown her for a while. She explained that she loved her mother even more than she hated her father and so she must attend. But would I go with her – there was no-one else? I had to say yes.

When we got back to prepping for tonight, she explained that Mallingford has significant holdings in a couple of property development companies, albeit not the one that we're targeting. An attack like the one we have planned will impact the whole sector. Apparently, his appetite for money is as great as for deviant behaviour, and Vi clearly relishes the thought that our actions tonight will impact Mallingford's pocket - however slightly or temporarily.

She has memorised the route from Ryan's place to the target and back. I'm impressed by her thoroughness – she's reviewed the route on both Google Maps and Street View so many times that she can answer any question I ask. The most direct route can be covered in just half an hour at that time of night, but we'll be driving for twice that long to minimise camera coverage and suggest a false trail in the event that someone does think any footage of the van is worth investigating.

"Are you ready to go?" I ask, already knowing the answer.

"Why else would I be dressed like this?" She extends her arms sideways, clad from head to toe in a combination of navy and black. The blue beanie hat constraining her hair makes her head look smaller, a notion accentuated by her charcoal puffer jacket.

I smile instinctively. "Okay. Let's go."

The train is exactly on time. We alight after four stations and catch a bus quickly, so that we are nearing Ryan's house just fifty minutes after leaving the flat. As we get closer, I scan the approach. It's the most anonymous semi on the blandest of streets in the most humdrum of middle-class suburbs. There are lights behind virtually every downstairs curtain as families crowd around TV screens, and dinner parties grow increasingly loud on the back of too much supermarket special offer wine. The slight drizzle when we set out has now developed into a steady downpour and even close-clipped garden hedges seem to strain as they are buffeted by urgent gusts of wind.

Aside from Vi and me, there's no-one about on foot. A solitary car passes. There are only two cars actually parked on the road – all of the houses have driveways and garages.

The two parked cars are unoccupied and the only houses on the entire street with security cameras, apart from Ryan's, are further along on the other side of the road. We, and Ryan's house, are not in range of them. Vi and I enter through the open driveway gates and approach by the paved driveway that runs alongside a neat lawn. Ryan inherited his parents' house when they were killed in a car crash years ago. I occasionally wonder whether the trauma of their death had anything to do with him being the way he is now.

The motion sensor has alerted Ryan to our presence and he's already opening the door before we get to it. He ushers us into the hallway while he peers out to check whether or not our arrival has been observed. "Jonno's through there." He points to the sitting room. I'm familiar with the layout of the house as I've been here at least a dozen times. There are almost thirty in the wider group that meet in the room above the pub, but Ryan has only ever invited seven of us back here. The eight of us are the core group – the most committed.

Jonno is sitting in an armchair facing the door and grunt-nods a greeting to Vi and me. He doesn't get up, probably because he's self-conscious about being a short-arse and Vi is five-nine, while Ryan's the same height as me. He's almost as broad as he is tall, doesn't have any apparent neck and breathes exclusively through his mouth. His mousey hair is short-cropped, eyes wide-set, and his nose small but bulbous. His lips are slightly lopsided on the left, and a stud earring in each lobe completes an appearance that is more inoffensive in its sum than its parts. He's thick, but harmless. I once had a dog that was more eloquent than him, and it used to lick its own arse. I sometimes wonder why Ryan includes him in the inner sanctum, and presume it's because of his unquestioning loyalty.

Vi and I both sit on the sofa that backs on to the wall beneath the closed curtains masking the window. Ryan is towering over us. "What's with the clean-shaven suede head look, soldier boy?" Though he's my height he's about ten kilos lighter and consequently gaunt. His thick dark hair is swept back and hooded, piercing brown eyes give the impression of intense scrutiny. High cheekbones, Roman nose, thin lips and a tapered jawline complete an appearance that Vi tells me she has always found attractive.

"I recce'd the target again yesterday. That's the ninth time in the past six weeks. I don't think anyone clocked me, but I wanted a different appearance for the job tonight."

My answer is obviously satisfactory, because he makes a brief hum and moves on. "I take it you two are both set?"

"Yes, Vi has memorised the route in minute detail." I glance at her and she nods affirmation. "What about you guys?"

Jonno reaches into his trouser pocket then presents the key to a mortice lock with a slight flourish. I know from yesterday's recce that it's the right kind of key for the lock on the gate. "I had a copy made and kept the original."

I need to make sure my voice doesn't betray any tension. "Where did you get the copy cut?"

"Calm down, soldier boy." Ryan intercedes to protect Jonno from interrogation. "He got it cut in a little cobbler's miles from the site. And before you ask, he paid cash and he wasn't wearing his guard's uniform."

"Good." I give Jonno a conciliatory nod.

"Everything is set. The Transit's in the garage – solid blue and unmarked." I nod approval – anyone spotting it under fluorescent street lighting would struggle to identify the colour. "I used it to take a pile of old junk to the dump earlier. The next-door neighbour saw me loading up and leaving, and the surveillance camera at the dump will have picked me up. I'll drop it back at the hire company tomorrow and post the keys in the box. So, I've obviously got a rock-solid reason for having hired the van – not that anyone should be asking."

Ryan is a bright guy, now he's animated and in full flow. I'm relieved he's talking about practical issues rather than harping on and on about politics like he so often does. He takes a seat in the other armchair and leans forward. "I've changed the plates and can switch them back again when we bring the van back. I've strapped two kitchen chairs to the sidebars inside the back of the van for you two to sit on."

He glances at me and then at Jonno to underscore who he means. Jonno makes a puzzled face, which isn't that different from his usual expression.

"We can't have four bodies in the cab, Jonno – it'd attract too much attention. There's already a question about having a woman driving a van."

"With this hat and jacket, and the darkness, no-one will spot I'm a woman. That shouldn't be a problem." Vi's tone is insistent.

"You're probably right. Anyway, I've loaded the charges into the back along with the rest of the gear, so we're good to go."

"Any chance I could see them before we head off?" I'm keen not to challenge his authority. "I wouldn't want to make an arse of things when we get there. My training stressed that you can never be too careful."

"Very sensible, soldier boy." There's no sarcasm in his voice as he gets up. Getting this right tonight matters, but I can see that for Ryan it *really* matters. He heads out of the room to fetch the charges.

"How thick do you think I am?" Jonno's leaning forward,

frowning at me. I resist the temptation to answer. "I'm not gonna march into a key cutter in my uniform and tell him I want a key cut so that I can break into the site I'm meant to be guarding. Fuck's sake, soldier boy." He tries to imitate the way Ryan says it, but he misses the condescending note and it doesn't land properly. Jonno got a job with Clipadrus Security almost seven weeks ago. The developer is enormous, but not averse to saving money wherever it can. Clipadrus is an unlicensed outfit who quote cheaply and provide the service quality that goes with that. Their less thorough vetting procedures enabled Jonno to be recruited easily.

"You did really well to get the key." Vi's diplomatic intervention causes the tension to evaporate immediately, as Jonno smiles at her. She knows he's got a soft spot for her, and she's played him beautifully here. I know that she's a screwball like the rest of them, but she does have something about her too.

Ryan returns, carrying two heavy-duty canvas tool bags, olive green and three-quarters of a metre length, which he places carefully on the carpet in front of me. "Knock yourself out, soldier boy." His dismissive tone belies the faintest note of anxiety. He cares what my opinion will be.

I lean forward and unzip the first bag carefully, then push the opening wide apart. There are a pair of two-hundred-metre spools of detonating cord, half a dozen boosters and a clear plastic bag containing detonating cord clips. The detonator and toolkit are tucked at one end of the bag.

"There's another couple of spools of detonating cord in the van, in case we need them." Ryan's voice is low, measured and earnest.

"This should be plenty," I reassure him, "although it's always better to have too much than not enough." I zip the first bag closed and open the second. The inside is lined with thick towels which provide a bed for the charges, each individually wrapped in a separate smaller towel. I remove one of the charges – a copper cylinder with a ninety-degree V shape cut from it. The length and weight appear to be exactly as I specified. These Linear Shaped Charges are custom made. I'm impressed. The charges are accompanied by a steel tube precisely the right size to accommodate an LSC. The tube has a narrow slit running its length, a steel mesh at one end to allow the detonating cord through and a hinged cap at the other. It has a steel collar welded to the rear surface midway along its length behind the slit, with either end of the collar extending straight out, like a pair of welcoming arms, perfectly parallel and equidistant from the aperture. "I presume there are more of these." I catch Ryan's eye and nod at the tube.

"There's another bag that's got the rest of them in the van."

"Okay, that's good. There are five charges in here. I only asked for four."

"Like you say, soldier boy, better to have too many than not enough."

I can't really argue with that. "This is top quality kit. It's been engineered to a very exacting standard. It won't have come cheap." I'm fishing, hoping that he'll have a nibble.

"Don't worry about the cost." Ryan's tone confirms he is pleased that I'm impressed. "And put it this way, if we pull this off tonight, there will be plenty more where this comes from."

I pause a moment, inviting him to say more, but he clams up. Instead, I take the fixing tube and hand it to Jonno. "What do you think? Will you be able to weld these to the crane steels?"

He supports the tube in one hand and runs his index finger along the edge one of the arms of the collar. "This has been chamfered properly, a right good job. Burn away the paint from the other surface and I'll weld this tighter than a Scotsman's wallet." He glances towards Vi and a satisfied expression spreads over his face in response to her smile and nod of approval. "The welding gear is in the van already, so I think we're good to go." He checks himself as he realises that that he has overstepped his position, and casts a wary look in Ryan's direction.

But Ryan is in uncharacteristically benign mood this evening and doesn't even flinch at Jonno's presumptuousness. Instead, he simply agrees. "You're right, Jonno. Let's get this show on the road."

Chapter 6

An hour later and the van stops. The ignition is switched off, confirming that we've arrived rather than stopping at lights or a junction. Vi drives really well and the journey was as smooth as we could have hoped for. Nevertheless, the motion of the van meant that Jonno and I had to straddle the chairs facing backwards so that we could hold on to the same sidebars that the chairs are strapped to in order not to slide off. My back and arms are stiff, but the lack of sound insulation means that the rain hammering on the roof throughout the journey has spared me the ordeal of making small talk with Jonno.

There's a click as the back doors are pulled open and the inside of the van is illuminated by the street lighting. "Okay, you two, the coast's clear. Let's go!" Ryan has to shout to make himself heard above the racket the rain is making. I can see it bouncing off the road behind him. He drags out two of the canvas bags, one in each hand, as I scramble out with the other two. Jonno follows me, carrying his portable welding kit. Vi is twenty metres in front of us, on the pavement at the corner of the junction between our side street and the road along the side of the site. She is beckoning us forward, confirming that we are still good to go. We splash past her, Jonno in the lead with the welding kit in his left hand and the key, already retrieved from his pocket, in his right. As we pass her, Vi sprints back to close the van door and get back into the cab. So far so good.

Jonno has the door unlocked and we are all through with the door closed behind us less than thirty seconds after we started our sprint from the van. There is sufficient ambient light from the streetlights on the other side of hoarding for us to be able to see clearly, despite the rain. The site is vast and open, and dominated by the monumental structure – already emerging five storeys tall from the earth – some 150 metres ahead. The crane is almost a hundred metres from us and there's a small fleet of construction vehicles parked between it and the building. Heras fencing runs from the right-hand corner of the structure in a straight line all the way up to the hoarding behind us. To the left there is an open expanse about seventy metres wide between the edge of the building and further hoarding that has dog-legged to enclose that end of the site. At the far end of the structure, to the left, there is a large portacabin surrounded by more Heras fencing. I know, from what Jonno has said, that is the compound where the high value tools and equipment are secured. To the right, out of sight on the far side of the building, are numerous other cabins, including the one where the security guard is based.

Glances are exchanged between the three of us and, on a nod from Ryan, we make our dash for the crane. Except it's not a dash, as some steps see us sink almost shin-deep into mud as we traverse the sodden landscape. Carrying heavy equipment doesn't help, but at least we are all wearing boots rather than shoes, so the risk of footwear being sucked off is minimal. Keeping momentum in conditions like this is vital and I keep ploughing ahead as steadily as the underfoot conditions allow. Eventually I get to the crane and place my two canvas bags on the concrete base, just as Ryan does the same.

I look in the direction that the security guard would come from to check that we've made it this far without being spotted. There's an urgent tapping on my shoulder and I turn and follow Ryan's outstretched arm pointing to Jonno, some thirty metres behind us, mud more than halfway up each shin, obviously stuck. Shit! I lean in close to Ryan and shout, so he can hear me above the howling wind and crashing rain. "Wait here. I'll go and fetch his equipment. Then we both go back and pull him out together." Ryan nods his agreement.

I squelch my way to Jonno, trying to pick out footing that looks the least treacherous. He hands over the welding gear as I explain the plan, then I turn and plod my way back. His kit is actually lighter than what I was carrying, so he was just unlucky that he stepped in the wrong place. I explain to Ryan the plan I outlined to Jonno and we head back out together, making our way three metres beyond Jonno, where we stop and turn on my signal. Jonno's back is towards us, arms outstretched, cruciform. I nod to Ryan and we both start our charge. He grabs

Jonno by his right underarm and I take the left. There's a split second of resistance before our momentum propels us onwards, sucking Jonno with us. Ten metres forward the conditions underfoot are firmer, and we drop Jonno to let him complete the race under his own steam. When we reach the concrete, both Ryan and I are heaving for breath. Jonno gives us both a big thumbs up signal and a nod of gratitude.

We manoeuvre our kit into position, then Jonno takes his right glove off and begins tapping on his mobile phone, as planned. Ryan and I hover as he fires off the pre-prepared text, then the three of us wait with an increasing mixture of impatience and concern. Jonno has cultivated a friendship with the security guard on duty tonight and his response to the text is key. After a million-year two-minute wait, Jonno's phone glows bright and he peers at the screen as he scrolls through the reply. His face breaks into a grin as he holds the phone towards Ryan and me so that we can see the exchange.

Jonno: *Yo Tourettes! Howzit going? I'm just chillin with a few beers watching Match of the Day. Laughing at the thought of you patrolling that shit hole. Ha ha. Lol.*

Tourettes: *Fuck you, you fucker. I'm fuckin wotching MOTD too you shit. Got my Thermos and a monster fuck-load of sarnies. Wotching the fucking movie after. Not leaving the fuckin cabin in this bastard weather. Gonna punch your fuckin lites out next time I see ya. Fuck you bastard.*

Jonno had been confident that his colleague's reputation for being the worst and laziest employee was as well-deserved as his nickname, and that there was zero chance of him patrolling the site and catching us. Still, it's good to get this confirmation. I lift the bag containing the tubes and put it next to the crane legs on its jib side. Jonno is in close attendance with his welding gear, while Ryan is a few metres behind keeping watch. The weather is still filthy – getting even worse if anything – but being underneath the crane tower offers at least some protection. I fetch a second bag closer and retrieve a tape measure and file from the toolkit within it. I measure the steel crane leg carefully and use the file to scratch a mark on one corner. Jonno is watching intently and, on a nod from me, fires up his torch and makes quick work of the paint on the far side of the leg, before cleaning the exposed metal with a small wire brush.

Jonno puts his torch and goggles down, removes his gloves and fetches a short-shafted mallet and an iron clamp from another of the canvas bags. I offer up the tube to the crane leg such that the collar arms are flush against either side and extend ten centimetres beyond. I steady it in position and Jonno locks it in place with the clamp. I continue to hold the tube firmly to provide additional support for the clamp and brace myself as Jonno swings the mallet. His aim is fantastic. There's a clang of metal on metal that chimes with the vibration through my shoulder, but I'm confident the sound won't travel far given the awful weather conditions. That single blow has bent the arm seventy degrees, as it wraps round the back of the crane leg. I give Jonno a quick thumbs up and he signals that strike number two is on its way. After the third strike the arm of the collar has bent the full ninety degrees and is flush against both the side and back of the crane leg.

Jonno dons his welding gear and sets to work on fixing the collar in place at the rear of the crane leg. Once he is satisfied that the job is well done, we repeat the entire process with the second collar arm on the other side, before removing the clamp. Ryan approaches us and taps furiously at his left wrist with his right index finger. I look at my watch and realise that it's taken us twenty-five minutes to secure the first tube in place – more than twice the time we had anticipated. Galvanised by that realisation, and becoming more efficient with experience, we crack on and fix the other three tubes in pace in fifty minutes.

It's my show now and I set about installing and wiring the charges. Ryan takes the fifth charge from its canvas bag and hands it to Jonno, who places it into a backpack, alongside a spool of detonating cord. "What the fuck are you doing with that?" I'm yelling, partly to be heard and partly because I'm furious.

"Jonno's taking it up the tower." Ryan has stepped right in front of me and is yelling back. "He's going to pack the charge into the gap between the slewing ring and mast top. He's watched how you wire it up. All you'll need to do is connect it at this end."

The bastard truly is as mad as I thought. "I've done the maths, Ryan. These charges at ground level will be plenty to bring the whole thing down and have the jib crash down on top of the building."

"Not the point, soldier boy. I'm going to film this beauty as she goes and I want another explosion at the top."

Mad. Mad. Mad. He's fucking demented. "I don't think you understand, Ryan. We don't need to do it. We don't need the additional risk!" I'm almost screaming.

He moves forwards, putting his face right into mine, and prods me hard in the chest. "I'm the fucking officer in this set up, squaddie! You do as you're fucking told!" His face is contorted and as punchable as any I can remember.

I tilt my head back slightly, in preparation for headbutting his nose to a pulp, and see that Jonno is already halfway up the tower. Fuck! Deep breath. "Okay, Ryan. You're the boss." The superior expression on his smug face almost causes me to revert to Plan A, but I resist the temptation. We move out from under the tower to get a better view of Jonno's progress. He's already reached the operator's cab, but he's not stopping. He's crawling out on to the counterjib. "What the hell is he doing?" I'm screaming at Ryan again. He shrugs his shoulders and gives a *search me* look.

The scene is both hypnotic and surreal. I'm standing with Ryan on a piece of ground that looks like The Somme, watching Jonno behaving like some half-arsed trapeze artist two hundred feet up in the air. God only knows what the wind speed must be like up there. A sense of the inevitable about to be fulfilled is rarely satisfying. There's a sudden movement, and the next three and a half seconds pass in ultra-slow motion as Jonno plummets earthwards. His face smashes off a concrete mixer, snapping his neck and bouncing his body some three meters away into a deep puddle.

I know he's dead and so does Ryan, who takes a step in the direction of the body, before I pause him with a hand on his shoulder. "I'll sort the body. You start moving all the stuff back over to the hoarding." I'm still shouting to make myself heard. Ryan's eyes are glazed at first, but then he seems to register what I'm saying and nods, before heading back below the crane tower. When I get to the body there's not much left of the front of Jonno's head. Identifying him from dental records will be a challenge, if not impossible. I check each of his pockets methodically to see if there's anything that might be used to determine who he is. There's nothing, apart from his phone, which now has a shattered screen, and the key. I pocket those and retrieve the backpack and its contents – the charge and the spool are still inside – and head back under the crane tower to re-join Ryan. He's already moved two of the canvas bags and Jonno's welding kit back across to the door in the hoarding.

I check each of the charges and the detonating wire connections to satisfy myself everything is still go. I turn to Ryan who seems to be studying what I'm doing. "Do you still want to go ahead? After what happened to Jonno?" I'm almost hoarse with all the shouting.

"Definitely! I'll grab the final two bags. You follow me with the wire." His voice is strong and clear, authoritative even. I pick up the spool and follow him. Rather than take a straight line, he arcs to the left – he's worked out a route that has less treacherous footing, and I'm glad of it.

When we get to the rest of the gear the hoarding acts as a windbreak and it's easier to hear. "Josh." He looks at me. "Are you sure that this will work?"

"100 per cent." That's probably one of less than half a dozen times he's called me by my name.

"Good. Which bag has got what you need in it?"

I point to the bag that I stuffed Jonno's rucksack and phone into – the one with the detonator and toolkit. I've already slipped the key into my pocket.

"Right, let's get everything else back to the van. Then we can come back and finish off here." Ryan doesn't pause for discussion. He opens the unlocked door, grabs one of the bags and the welding kit, and sprints towards the van. I grab two other bags and head after him.

Vi is already out of the van and opening the rear doors. By the time I get to the back Ryan has already slung his kit inside and has both of his hands on Vi's shoulders. I chuck my two bags in and turn to the others. Tears rather than rain are glistening on Vi's cheeks. "I saw him fall." She sobs. "I watched him climb up there and then I saw him fall."

Ryan grabs her shoulders with both hands and shakes her. She stops, eyes fixed on him. "Pull yourself together! It's happened and we're all upset. But that's not going to help. We need to complete this job. It's what Jonno would have wanted." He shakes her hard by shoulders. "Do you understand?" She nods.

I'm impressed. She's in shock and he's handled it well. A load of clichéd old bollocks – *it's what Jonno would have wanted* – but it seems to have done the trick. Hats off to him. He steps back and addresses both of us. "Vi, get back in the van and be sure you're ready to get us out of here. We…" he nods in my direction, "…are going back over to finish the job."

"Okay." Vi has found her voice again, surprisingly strong and clear. She turns to close the van doors.

I follow Ryan back across and through the hoarding. I make the final connections to the detonators as he sets his phone to camera mode. I raise my left hand, with all four fingers and thumb extended. I lower my thumb. Then my index finger. Then my middle finger. Ryan turns his attention to filming. I finish the silent countdown and press. There's a split second of silence before an almighty flash and crash, as though the gods have hurled a thunderbolt at the base of the crane. As the rumble subsides it is replaced by a hideous creaking sound and I am off and running. I don't care how dilatory Tourettes is, even he will have to investigate this. I climb into the cab of the van and slide along to the middle seat beside Vi, who is staring through the windscreen at the crane disappearing backwards from view. There is another mighty crashing sound and Ryan is visible dashing towards us. He clambers in beside me and yells at Vi, "Go, go, go!"

"Did you see that? Did you see that? What a fucking beautiful sight!" He is absolutely pumped. "We did it! We fucking did it. Man, I am buzzing."

"Did you manage to get it all on camera?" I'm trying to bring him down.

"Every second! Did you hear it? Boom!" He makes explosive jazz-hands. "You did well, soldier boy. Top marks. This will be the first of many."

Vi is silent, concentrating on the road.

Ryan is wired to the moon. He is as mad as they come. And he doesn't seem to give a shit about Jonno.

Chapter 7

Molly's mouth was dry. Not the arid dryness you get when you've had way too much to drink the night before. Not the thirst, so often accompanied by a thick head, that confirms a proper hangover. This was the dryness that results from a couple of cocktails followed by a shared bottle of wine – then going to bed without a precautionary glass of water. Of course, pausing to drink a glass of water would have interrupted the spontaneity – and she had been just as eager to go to bed as Freddie had.

Now, however, she regretted both decisions. She'd first met Freddie when he came into the station three months ago as a duty solicitor. He'd been persistent in asking her out until she finally agreed. Last night had been their fourth date and, as usual, he had been good company – funny and attentive. The week before, on their third date, she'd ended up back at his place. Despite the excitement of going to bed with someone for the first time, the sex had been mediocre, to the extent that she had seriously considered ending the putative relationship as soon afterwards as etiquette reasonably permitted. But hope had triumphed over experience and last night's date had seen them end up back at her flat.

If anything, Freddie's performance between the sheets had been even more disappointing than the first time, and she knew that this was a relationship that was already over. She felt his presence behind her in the bed and could tell from the rhythm of his breathing that he was still asleep. She decided that getting up and dressing quietly before he wakened would spare her the disappointment of another unsatisfactory carnal exchange. She could manufacture some work-related pretext to evict him from the flat with his dignity intact, then end things properly with a phone call a day or two later. Freddie was the sixth guy she'd been out with since she finished things with Josh, and the sixth disappointment. Either they were inadequate lovers, unstimulating company, or – in one instance – both. She still believed that breaking up with Josh had been the right thing to do, probably, but there were occasions – and this was one – where she ached for the mutual satisfaction that they used to provide for each other.

Molly eased gently out of bed, slipped on her dressing gown and exited the bedroom silently. She used the toilet without flushing and waited until she reached the kitchen at the far end of the flat before washing her hands. Having closed the kitchen door, she switched on the portable TV, with the sound low, and started eating her muesli. The news channel was leading with the General Election campaign, still with three and a half weeks to run but already feeling to Molly that it had been going on since the dawn of time. She was contemplating switching channels when the article ended. *Back to our main story, there was a major attack last night on a construction site in the capital. Details remain sketchy, but it is believed that explosives were used to bring down this tower crane at the Brightwater View development.* Jerky images, presumably drone footage, showed a floodlit scene. There was a tangled yellow structure collapsed, with one end smashed into a building, clearly causing considerable damage. *We understand that a man's body was discovered at the scene, but it is not known whether he was involved in the attack or if he is an innocent victim. So far, no-one has claimed responsibility for the incident. We hope to bring you more details on this story as it develops.*

Molly's half-chewed mouthful of muesli seemed to swell in inverse proportion to her constricting throat. Her head felt like it was floating, detached from her body, and for a second she feared that she might actually be sick. *The Brightwater View development.* She swallowed what was in her mouth and inhaled deeply. *The Brightwater View development.* She silently repeated the name to herself like a mantra, as another part of her mind processed what she had just seen and heard on the television. In their meeting on Thursday Josh had again identified Brightwater View as a potential target for the group. And now on Sunday morning it was a national news item as the location of a terrorist attack. *It is believed that explosives were used.* Not only must Josh have known what was planned, he was fundamental to its execution. What the hell is he playing at?

Molly drained the excess milk from her muesli into the sink, scraped the semi-solid remains into the food waste bin and put the bowl and spoon into the dishwasher – all on automatic pilot as her mind pored over the last briefing session she'd had with Josh. She reached for her phone, left on the worktop charging overnight – switched to silent, so as not to interrupt the 'passion' in the bedroom. Another mistake. There were three missed calls and a text message. *Check the news regarding Brightwater View and get yourself into the station as soon as you get this. Text to let me know you are en route.* The calls and text were all from the AC. The text was timed at 6.38 am, two minutes after the last missed call. The kitchen clock confirmed it was now 7.40, causing Molly to curse under her breath.

She headed back to the bathroom and straight into the shower, determined to wash away all traces of Freddie, and conscious that the sound of the running water would probably wake him. She was in and out in barely more than five minutes, and was towelling herself dry when her eye was taken by the reflection in the misted mirror. The bathroom door eased open behind her and Freddie's head appeared, beaming a smile she had previously considered engaging but that now seemed gormless. She mentally chided herself for the unnecessarily cruel thought.

"Good morning gorgeous. You're up bright and early. Freshening yourself up before coming back to bed?" His tone and expression confirmed that this was expectation rather than mere hope.

Molly suppressed her irritation. Experience had taught her that it was simply her mind's way of girding itself to ditch someone, and that allowing the emotion to vent typically made the process even more painful for both parties than was already inevitable. "I'm really sorry, Freddie. There's been some sort of terrorist incident and I've got to go in to the station."

"Oh."

His disappointment at the unexpected thwarting of his libidinous ambitions banished any thought of asking if anyone had been hurt or injured in the incident, a fact that further fuelled Molly's suppressed annoyance. "Honestly, I'd like nothing better than to be able to stay here this morning." She gave him a look that she hoped masked the insincerity of the platitude. "I really don't have a choice."

"Right."

"I have to go in immediately."

"Okay." Freddie's face was that of a small boy realising that Santa Claus hadn't brought the gift he yearned for.

The demon in Molly's head was reminding her that Freddie's only truly appealing feature had been his quick wit – now evaporated and replaced by monosyllabic utterances. She brushed past him and headed to the bedroom where she picked her way through hers and Freddie's discarded attire from the night before with a sense of mild distaste. She dressed quickly in fresh clothes and by the time Freddie came back into the room she was seated in front of the dressing table mirror, using a doughnut to fix her scraped back hair into a bun. He approached her from behind, comfortable in his nakedness despite her being fully clothed, and leaned in to try to nuzzle the back of her neck. The attempt at an affectionate gesture only had the effect of bumping Molly's arm, causing her to drop a hair grip. "For God's sake, Freddie. Not now!"

"Sorry."

Molly watched Freddie in the mirror as he slunk back into bed and pulled the sheet up over himself. She completed fixing her hair – it would finish drying in the car – put on her glasses, stood up and turned to look at him. She held his wounded puppy-dog gaze. "I've no idea when I'll get back, so just let yourself out."

"Fine."

There was something about the way he said it – not with any malice or belligerence, but something she didn't have the words for – that made Molly realise that Freddie understood things between them were not fine.

Five minutes later Molly got in the car and texted the AC that she was on her way, before setting off en route to the station. Her mind was racing, and she was grateful that it was Sunday morning meaning that the light traffic didn't demand too much concentration. She didn't like admitting it to herself, but she found breaking up relationships hard. Even short-term relationships like the one with Freddie. Part of it was because she didn't want to cause upset. But she knew a larger part of it was because it picked at the scab of her breaking up with Josh. Even now, nearly three years after the event, it still tormented her. It had been her own doing. She instigated it, having decided to prioritise her career ambitions over their relationship. She remembered Josh's incredulity and incomprehension. She remembered his strong, invulnerable face streaked with tears. *But I love you* he said. He had never said it before. And he had never said it again. It knifed her soul when he said it because she realised that she loved him in the same instant that she knew she had blown it forever.

Molly gave herself a mental slap. Allowing the break up with Freddie to trigger memories of the end of her relationship with Josh was painful and pointless. It served only to distract her from what was important in the here and now. She replayed the Thursday meeting with Josh again. He had talked about Brightwater View, just as he had in their previous two meetings. He had said that it was a potential target for the group. He had been very clear about that. *Potential.* They had discussed flagging the need for a raised level of alert to the firm responsible for site security, but decided that doing so also risked alerting the group that something was amiss. She had included all of that in her report, diligently written late on Thursday night while everything was still fresh and filed online. She knew that Josh had said something else that she couldn't quite recall, and it was gnawing away at her.

The fact that the AC herself was on the case underscored the profile attached to it, and made Molly feel uncharacteristically nervous. She admired the AC more than anyone else in the force and regarded her as a role model. She remembered asking the AC at their first ever mentoring meeting whether she had found it more difficult to rise through the ranks because she was a woman. She also remembered the reply. *Is it harder for an officer to progress because they are female, or black, or disabled, or gay, or clearly identifiable as belonging to some other minority? Maybe. Probably. Is that fair? No. But the important thing is to regard any additional difficulties as challenges to be overcome rather than excuses for failure.* Molly contemplated the prospect of the AC being directly hands-on involved in her case as inspiring and terrifying in equal measure.

Chapter 8

Molly pulled into the car park, put on the parking brake and checked the time on the dashboard clock - 8.22. The journey had provided useful thinking time, and she felt ready to face whatever was required of her in the hours ahead.

She made a dash from the car to the station, hunched against the continuing rain, picking her steps to avoid the puddles. Once through the front doors she paused in the foyer as she searched for her purse inside her handbag.

"Good morning, Ma'am."

"Oh, good morning, Sahil. Sorry, I didn't see you behind that screen."

"No problem, Ma'am. I see it's still raining cats and dogs out there." The desk sergeant smiled at her. "Do you need me to buzz you through."

"It's okay, thanks." She waved her pass and smiled. "Got it now." She walked around the desk, presented her card to the reader and pulled the door towards her. She made her way along the brightly-lit corridor and wrinkled her nose at the almost overwhelming smell of bleach. Some poor sod must have had to clean out a cell after a Saturday night drunk had thrown up. She turned into her office and was slightly surprised to see Johnny Duke turn his head towards her.

"Been expecting you. I don't suppose you picked me up a bacon bap from Rico's on your way in?"

"As a matter of fact," she flicked her eyes towards her handbag, "I did, actually." She had to struggle to suppress a grin as she watched his eyes switch to the bag. "But it smelt so good I decided to eat it myself."

"Bitch."

"Only looking after your heart, lard-arse." She could no longer resist the temptation to grin in triumph at her victory this latest petty skirmish. "Why were you expecting me?" She was trying to work out the reason that Johnny's face had taken on a wary expression as he tensed on his seat, but a familiar voice from behind her answered the question before it had fully formed in her mind.

"Because I came in here earlier and asked him to send you to me as soon as you arrived."

Molly turned to see the immediately recognisable five-foot six figure of the AC, in full uniform minus hat and jacket, framed perfectly by the doorway. Slim, with sharp features that included a prominent hooked nose, and a striking pair of deep-set mahogany eyes that brooked challenge from no-one. Her olive skin was complemented by make-up, expertly applied with a light touch, and her raven hair was tied back in a short pony tail. Molly had never been sure if the AC's nickname, The Hawk, derived from her eyes or nose, or both. What she did know, from overheard comments, was that the fifty-two-year-old senior officer was still considered very 'presentable' by many colleagues – both male and female.

"Good morning, Ma'am."

"Good morning, DI Leishman. Can you come with me, please?" The AC didn't wait for a response and Molly found herself scurrying after her, without a backward glance at Johnny. She followed along quickly and into one of the small, characterless interview rooms to the left of the corridor. "Close the door behind you, please." The AC turned to look back at Molly as she sat down on one of the two metal-framed wooden chairs on the far side of a matching rectangular table. She indicated with a nod that Molly should do the same on the opposite side. The table and all four chairs were screwed to the floor, a necessary precaution given some of the exchanges that took place in the room. Molly knew that the selection of this particular space, functional but not particularly comfortable, presaged a focused briefing rather than a cosy chat.

"Okay, DI Leishman – tell me what you know, and what you think."

The AC's choice to continue address her by title rather than her given name, even in private, confirmed the formality and gravity of the situation. "Yes, Ma'am. What specifically do you want to know?"

Molly felt a slight shudder of apprehension, almost bordering on fear, as she saw the AC's eyes harden.

AC Carswell leaned forward, placed both elbows on the table and cupped her hands together, before resting them on the same surface. She inhaled slowly, paused, and then spoke quietly in a low voice. "We are in the midst of a General Election campaign. Terrorists have attacked a high-profile construction site. The press are demanding to know what is going on from both the Home Secretary and the Commissioner. The Commissioner is demanding to know what is going on from me. And I am demanding," she enunciated the word slowly and with particular care, "*demanding* to know what is going on from you." The AC leaned just the tiniest fraction further forward, and her eyes lasered Molly's. "I have read every report you have filed on DC Gray's current operation, including the one detailing your meeting with him on Thursday. I know everything that's included in those reports. What I want is to hear it from the horse's mouth and to know *everything* else that you know, and what you think." She leaned back slightly, her eyes still firmly fixed on Molly's. "Now, drop the naïve little plonk routine and answer the question."

Molly could feel her palms becoming clammy. "Yes, Ma'am. Ryan Watson had been on the radar as a person of interest for a few years. He studied Politics and Economics at Leeds and was active in left-wing politics, something that continued after he graduated. Politics was his passion, to the extent that he was happy to take a succession of low-paid menial jobs. When his parents died in an automobile accident, he inherited their house and a sizeable investment portfolio. He flirted with a few far-left organisations, but was drawn to the Labour Party when Jeremy Corbyn became leader. The subsequent failure of the Corbyn project saw Watson become deeply disillusioned with mainstream politics, and rekindled his interest in more extreme organisations or movements."

Molly paused for breath and the opportunity to gauge the AC's mood. The senior officer sat stock still, even her breathing imperceptible, unblinking eyes fixed on Molly – who recognised the unspoken command to continue.

"Watson became increasingly interested in anarchism and

started to hold his own meetings, open to the public. Over a two-year period he attracted a solid following of thirty-odd attendees at his monthly meetings, where he promoted an increasingly radical agenda. Just over eight months ago he began meeting more frequently in private with a subset of his followers. We had credible sources that suggested the sub-group contained the more radical members and that extreme direct action was on their agenda. That was when we got agreement to try to get someone on the inside."

As Molly paused briefly again, she felt a sense of relief when the AC responded. "I know all of that from the files, thank you." The tone was level, with no hint of chiding. "What is our man on the inside able to tell us about Watson?"

"Watson is intelligent, which we knew, and articulate – which we also knew. It seems that he is also very charismatic, when he chooses to be. He has an eye for the ladies and has probably had intimate relations with most female members of the group at some point."

The AC arched one eyebrow quizzically.

"I know Ma'am. One might imagine that could cause petty jealousies and interfere with cohesion within the group. But, apparently it's not at all uncommon for individuals in Watson's position – specifically men – to behave in that way."

"Is that conjecture on your part?" The AC's eyes were subtly different, reflecting that her interest was piqued.

"I've been doing some independent reading, Ma'am. There's a surprising amount of writing and research about contrarian groups out there."

"I see. Very good. Now let's get to the crunch. Your man – Josh Gray – met with you on Thursday, and didn't give any hint of what was planned for last night. I really want to know what went wrong."

"I understand Ma'am, I…" Molly was cut short by the intrusive chimes of the AC's phone.

AC Carswell glanced at the screen, and then at Molly. "Sorry, I have to take this." Molly made *do you need me to go* gestures but received a gentle shake of the head in response. The AC pressed the phone to her ear, stood up and took a pace.

Hello Derek.
Pause. Another couple of paces.
I'm actually with DI Leishman right now. We were starting to review things when you called.
Pause. The AC turned on her heel and retraced her paces. Molly again mouthed an offer to leave, only to receive a slight shake of the head and a wagging finger.
Yes. Yes, I understand that.
Pause.
Absolutely. I understand. Brief pause. *That's very clear. I'll get back to you as soon as possible.*
AC Carswell ended the call, put the phone back in her pocket before pausing to take a deep breath, then returned to her seat opposite Molly.

"Is there a problem, Ma'am?"

"That was the Commissioner. There's a press conference scheduled for eleven." She checked her wristwatch. "That's just over two hours. We need to conclude this meeting as quickly as possible so I can report back and give him and his comms folk as long as possible to decide how they want to spin it."

"Spin it, Ma'am?"

"Report it – you know what I mean. The press don't care what the story is, just so long as there's a story. But it needs to be something that can be followed up over the coming days that doesn't offer the chance for headlines like *Clueless Cops* or *Police Baffled*."

"I understand." Molly leaned forward just a few degrees. "Shall we continue?"

The AC met her eyes and held them. "Yes, please."

The interruption had allowed Molly extra thinking time, and she felt more in control. "I met with Josh Gray on Thursday evening. It was a pretty routine meeting where he briefed me on what was going on within the group, and particularly the behaviour and state of mind of Ryan Watson. He said that Watson was noticeably more excited than normal over the last few weeks, but that it wasn't evident why. Josh also reported, for the third time, that he had been keeping the Brightwater View development under surveillance for the group as a possible target."

AC Carswell's eyes narrowed, making her gaze impossibly more piercing. "And? That was it? Two days before a multi-million-pound attack on the site that has left a man dead, he described it as a *possible* target?"

Molly was unsure if the AC's deep breath was to stifle incredulity, anger or both. "Yes, Ma'am. That's what he said."

AC Carswell sat back in her chair, her eyes never leaving Molly's. "There's an obvious question. Gray has been involved with the group for over six months, and for half of that time he's been shacked up with another group member. Think very carefully before you answer this. Do you think he's gone native? Has he gone rogue?"

The question hadn't been obvious to Molly, and she found herself nonplussed. She did as she was instructed and thought hard, using the time to marshal both her thoughts and composure. "I don't believe that's the case, Ma'am."

The AC moved forward very slightly, eyes still lasering Molly's. "I think that you *do* believe that. So, here's another question for you to think about before answering. Are you compromised, DI Leishman? Does your previous relationship with DC Gray render you unable to be impartial?"

Molly was suddenly aware that she was wringing her hand below the table, an action that somehow seemed to help clear her mind. "It's possible, Ma'am, but I don't believe it is the case. Can I explain why?"

"Please do."

"Josh was able to integrate with the group quickly because Watson regarded his knowledge of explosives from his time in the army as useful."

"The skills that were developed during his time working in bomb disposal."

"Actually no, Ma'am. That was part of his cover story. The army refused his application to join bomb disposal. He had been given a late diagnosis of ADHD and was deemed unsuitable for a role in that team."

"ADHD?"

"Yes, Ma'am. Attention Deficit Hyperactivity Disorder.

It's…"

"I know what it fucking is!" The AC banged the desk with her right fist. "You thought it was a good idea to appoint someone diagnosed with ADHD to go undercover? What in the name of God were you thinking?"

Molly felt her stomach somersault. She had never heard the AC swear before. "Ma'am, Josh has a verified IQ of 138 – he is very, *very* intelligent, although that's not linked to his condition. When he was diagnosed with ADHD it was classified as mild, manifesting in a degree of impulsiveness, a willingness to take risks, and an occasional tendency to become angry. Following his diagnosis, he studied everything he could about the condition as well as getting therapy, both of which he says helped him manage it. As an aside, he studied everything he could about explosives and bomb disposal anyway. I think he did that prove to himself he could, even though he accepted that the army couldn't take the risk with him." All of this was delivered with a calmness of voice that didn't reflect her inner turmoil. She paused to gauge the reaction.

The AC placed her hands together, as if in prayer, and brought them to her face, thumbs tucked under her chin. A long breath, both in and out, was clearly audible. She placed her hands back on the table in front of her and tilted her head slightly to one side, whilst maintaining focus on her junior officer. "Molly, are you still in love with Josh?"

The switch to the use of her first name and the directness of the question disarmed Molly. "I don't know." She had said it before she had a chance to think. She had said it because it was true, unless she was still kidding herself. There was an uncomfortable few seconds of silence that lasted for all eternity. "But I do know that Josh hasn't gone rogue."

"You seem very certain about that."

"A moment ago, when you were on the phone with Commissioner Thorburn, I managed to remember something that Josh had said. I didn't pay any attention at the time, but I think now that it might have been significant." Molly registered a flicker of impatience in the AC's face. "When we were talking about Brightwater View, he said that sometimes you need a sprat to catch a mackerel."

"Not exactly cryptic, but tell me your interpretation."

"I think that he meant Brightwater View wasn't the main thrust of what the group are about. I think he must have meant it was test run, or a sighting shot of some sort."

"That's a bit of a leap, Molly. There's somebody dead and massive damage, but you think it's just some sort of trial run?"

"Ma'am, I understand you're concerned that my judgement might be clouded." She brought her hands up and clasped them in front of herself on the table. "I accept that the situation – my history with Josh – isn't ideal. But it really *is* history, and I'm as sure as I can be that Josh Gray is still working on our behalf, and that he's playing a longer game than I'd previously realised."

AC Carswell took yet another deep breath, and held it. "This isn't good, Molly. If you're right, then Gray hasn't been keeping you fully in the loop – that's not acceptable. Him deciding to behave like a maverick and ignore protocols that dictate he keep you *fully* briefed cannot continue. On the other hand, this group does now clearly constitute a genuine threat to public safety, and might be planning much bigger incidents. Having someone on the inside in those circumstances could prove invaluable."

The AC paused and broke eye contact with Molly for the first time, other than when on the phone, since they had started their discussion. She closed her eyes and dipped her head for several seconds, before sighing and looking back towards Molly, with eyes that seemed somehow much softer. "Molly, this is all about trust. People up and down the chain of command – right from the Home Secretary down to the most junior officer – have to know that they can rely on the link either side of them." She leaned forward and placed her hands on top of Molly's, before continuing in a voice that was both earnest, yet just above a whisper. "I believe that I can rely on you, and I'm going to base my report to the Commissioner on that belief. But you need to get a grip of Josh Gray. Understand?"

"Yes, Ma'am. Thank you."

AC Carswell removed her hands from Molly's and sat back up straight in her seat. "Now, DI Leishman, this meeting is finished. We both need to be getting on with things. You must," she paused, "***must*** keep me personally appraised on any and all developments. Do I make myself clear?"

"Yes, Ma'am." Molly took her cue from the AC's nod, rose to her feet and exited the room at a pace barely below a slow jog. She had been unhappy with Josh being involved in beating up two alleged rapists – something the AC hadn't touched on, thankfully – but this had taken everything up to a whole new level. Now her reputation, probably even her career, were on the line. Josh Gray had a lot of explaining to do. A lot.

Chapter 9

It's 5.50 am and I'm well-rested and fully alert. I reach across and switch off the alarm as there's no chance I'll need it this morning. Inventory time.

Yesterday – Sunday – was a write-off. Vi and I caught the night bus back from near the drop-off point on Saturday night and got home just after 4.00 am. We were both on too much of an adrenaline high to sleep. We spent most of the day watching rolling TV news about the attack, or talking about Vi's mum and the funeral. Vi eventually crashed and went to bed at 7.00 pm. I folded an hour later.

Ryan called Vi during the morning – he obviously couldn't sleep either. He said he wanted to see the two of us today at 9.00 am. Unusually, he said that he would come here.

Vi is, naturally, concerned about tomorrow's funeral – and the prospect of seeing Mallingford again. I need to get my hands on a suit.

I'm going to have to make contact with Moll. And I'm going to have to be able to give her something tangible.

Ryan's decision to come at 9.00 means that there is little else that I can achieve before then, other than go for a run.

It's ten to nine, and there's a knock on the door. Vi doesn't even look in my direction as she darts down the corridor. I can hear her making *welcome, come in* noises and I'm briefly confused by the sound of a second female voice, before I recognise it as Ruthie's. Ryan comes into the room, followed by Ruthie, with Vi bringing up the rear. He grins at me – seemingly warm and sincere, which I'm not used to – and takes a pew on the two-seater sofa. "Morning, soldier boy…" there's a hesitation and an expression that suggests he's making a calculation, before correcting himself, "morning, Josh." And another smile.

Ruthie has plonked herself on the sofa beside him. She's early thirties, about five foot five, average build and fair-haired with a pale complexion. She has perfectly symmetrical, unremarkable features that Vi has described as neither pretty or beautiful, nor plain or ugly. I agree with Vi's description, but there is something indefinable about Ruthie that is attractive, even though she's not my type at all. She's the most recent member of the inner group, having been invited in just three months ago by Ryan. Vi and I are both certain she's sleeping with him, and their joint arrival at this relatively early hour would seem to bear that out. Vi thinks that there's something suspicious about her, but I wonder if that's maybe just a little bit of jealousy.

Vi offers teas or coffees, but Ryan declines – more graciously than I would expect him to do normally, and Ruthie does the same. I'm sitting in the only chair and, given the sofa is fully occupied, Vi takes a position cross-legged on the floor beside me, opposite the others.

"Thanks for letting me…us…come round so early." His uncharacteristic politeness is complemented by a sense of positive energy that I've only seen before when he's rabble-rousing at a meeting. I'm sure that he switches it on for effect then, whereas now I'm pretty certain that what I'm seeing is genuine.

"No problem." Vi's tone suggests that's she's as surprised at Ryan's demeanour as I am.

"I wanted to come round to discuss a couple of things. We clearly need to talk about Saturday night, and there's also news that I need to update you on." Ryan pauses and checks Vi's and my face to gauge our reactions. "Obviously the operation at Brightwater View leaves us all with mixed feelings. On the one hand, we did what had to do brilliantly – and we got fantastic coverage. On the other hand,…" he pauses again, before resuming in a more sombre tone. "…on the other hand, we lost Jonno." He stops and looks at me, then turns his attention to Vi.

"The TV this morning says that he's still not been identified." There's a catch in Vi's voice as she speaks, and I'm worried that tears might not be far away.

"I know. I heard that too." Ryan's voice is gentle, measured. "We all knew the risks when we became part of this group,

Jonno included. We each agreed to take those risks because we all believe that our cause is more important than any one of us. That doesn't mean we aren't upset at losing him – of course we are. We are all grieving his loss, and we'll all remember him. But the best tribute we can pay him is to continue with our work. Carrying on is the best way of honouring his memory."

Ryan pauses again, and I can see a distant look in both Vi's and Ruthie's eyes as they digest his words. I can't believe that they just swallow this bullshit. It's a reminder that, apart from Ryan, the members of this group have dogmeat for brains. That said, I have to tip my hat to a master manipulator.

He continues, noticeably more business-like now that he's discharged the formalities demanded by decency. "The fact that they haven't been able to identify Jonno is good news as it will delay them making a link to us."

"I think there's a way we might be able to extend that advantage." Ryan looks at me, and I can see he's mildly irritated that I've interrupted him. However, he's also clearly intrigued by what I might suggest and nods permission for me to continue. "I picked up his phone on Saturday night. We can use it to text a message to his supervisor saying that he's ill, and unable to come into work. That's bound to delay them identifying him."

Admission into the inner group is completely at Ryan's discretion. Apart from impeccable credentials that confirm absolute commitment to the cause and loyalty to him, he also insists on some very sensible security precautions. Aside from our addresses, dates of birth, full names and NI numbers, we all have to provide him with our phone passcodes and a list identifying who our favourites are. He occasionally asks to see someone's phone and checks text messages, as well as incoming and outgoing calls. The thoroughness of his vetting process either means that he's paranoid, or that he has access to resources that enable him to conduct detailed checks. I believe it's the latter, which is one reason my operation was approved and why so much was invested in securing my background story and trail.

Ryan's focus is on me now. "That's not a bad suggestion at all." He continues to look me in the eye, and I get the sense that

– although he is probably comfortable that I am loyal – he is still trying to calibrate how smart or otherwise I really am. "If you fetch it, I can take it and send in exactly the message you suggest. I'll make sure that I send it from outside his address so that, if anyone were to triangulate to get the location, it won't arouse suspicions. Good thinking, Josh. Can you get it now?"

"Sure." I go to my room and return quickly with Jonno's phone, which I hand to Ryan. He presses the power button, and the screen lights up.

"Still got 37% power." He takes out his own phone and scrolls until, I presume, he gets to Jonno's passcode. He types that into Jonno's phone and scrolls through it, pauses to read some texts, then presses the screen and holds the phone to his ear for around thirty seconds, before switching it off. "He's got a message from the fellow he texted on Saturday night, which is nothing to worry about. He's also got another text and a voicemail from his supervisor asking if he can cover the nightshift tonight. That confirms that they haven't identified his body I can easily reply to them both later to avoid them getting suspicious." He looks at me again. "Good initiative there – must come from your military training." His smile makes my stomach turn.

"You said that there was news that you need to update us on." Vi shuffles her backside as she speaks, clearly not comfortable on the floor.

Ryan's eyes spark, and he leans forward. "Yes. You know – obviously – that I have links to others outside of our group who sympathise with our beliefs."

"The people who supplied the LSC's we used on Saturday." I'm making a statement and asking a question at the same time.

"Yes, they supplied the explosives. And they are very," he pauses for emphasis, "*very* pleased with the results we achieved." He looks at each of us in turn before continuing. "Our friends clearly needed us to demonstrate that it was worthwhile for them to deepen their partnership with us. I'm delighted to tell you that, after Brightwater View, they are totally convinced."

He's unable to contain his grin. I want to ask him so much more, but I need to be careful.

Fortunately, Vi has no reservations. "What does that mean for us?"

"What that means for us..." Ryan leans forward from the sofa on to one knee in front of Vi and plants a kiss on her forehead before returning to his seat. I register the briefest hint of a frown crossing Ruthie's face. "...what that means for us is that we are now poised on the brink of bringing down the whole corrupt shitty system." He's jubilant. But not like a lottery winner is jubilant. This isn't just luck, it's more like a tennis player who has won through to a Wimbledon final. This is something Ryan has put a lot of time and effort into, and it's paid off for him.

Vi's tone is quizzical, "What do you mean? How? Jesus, Ryan – put us out of our misery and tell us what you actually mean."

Normally an interjection like that wouldn't be well received by Ryan, but he is absolutely flying and doesn't seem to mind. "Okay, okay. Let me explain." He shifts forward on the sofa. "We are less than four weeks away from a General Election in a campaign that has shone a light on how useless the system is. The two main parties are utterly polarised and their supporters despise each other. No-one is standing on a positive manifesto and the polls are showing that over 40% of people are no longer sure that democracy is the best way to organise things. The self-proclaimed "voices of reason" are being marginalised or no-platformed, and there are even rumours that both the police and military are considering their positions."

I've heard a lot of this tripe before, but Ryan's tone is different this time. Rather than sounding like something he's wishing for, it sounds like something he believes is actually happening right now. He can't contain his excitement, and he's up on his feet pacing as he continues. "Everything is on a knife edge. Democracy, parliament, financial institutions, the armed forces, the police, the monarchy – everything. It's the opportunity that we've been waiting for. It's all at the tipping point – and we can help topple it over."

He pauses, but his eyes are ablaze. I look at Vi and Ruthie, then back to Ryan. He absolutely believes what he's saying, and so do they. "So, how, Ryan? *How* are we meant to make that happen?" I need to get him to give me more.

He looks right at me, takes a mighty breath and smiles. "Practical as ever, eh, Josh?" His smile is accompanied by him climbing down from his soap box and returning to the sofa. I can see that he's still pumped, but I also sense that he's dialled it down a bit.

When he continues, he speaks more deliberately, although the urgency is still struggling to return to the surface. "Josh is right." He's addressing all three of us. "There are three and a half weeks until the election, which doesn't give us long to undermine it."

I can feel my heart leapfrog. This is it.

Ryan continues. "Our partners are co-ordinating a number of different organisations and groups like ours. The plan is for us to carry out a number of attacks on high-profile targets in London. Other groups will do the same thing in various parts of the country. The intention is to cause the maximum amount of carnage and then to publish a warning that the next wave of attacks will all be on polling stations on election day."

"Jesus." Ruthie's blasphemy captures all of our reactions. There's a long silence.

"What we need to do is to identify four or five targets, and exactly what we need to make the maximum impact at each of them. If we do that then our partners will make sure that we are supplied with whatever we need, just like we were on Saturday night."

"You said the maximum amount of carnage. You're talking about killing people?" Vi's arms are cuddling her knees and she's looking straight ahead, not making eye contact with anyone. Ruthie is as silent as she's been for most of the time since she got here.

"We're all familiar with the term collateral damage. It's not pleasant, but it's what's necessary. The more dead there are the bigger the fear of going to cast a vote. The election gets undermined and whoever is declared the winner has no legitimacy. You can't have a democracy where people won't go out and vote. Where law and order has broken down and people don't feel safe to go about their normal day-to-day business."

The mad bastard has totally lost touch with reality. For

someone who must originally have been motivated by egalitarian aims and a desire for social justice, he has completely lost sight of what first inspired him. He is totally consumed by pure rage and a power-crazed thirst for chaos. I'm willing to bet that, if all the planned attacks went ahead and the warning is issued, we'd see the biggest General Election turnout ever. But that doesn't matter. What matters is what he believes, and the attacks proposed on innocent people. "How do we identify the targets, Ryan?" I tilt my head quizzically. I know that he's crazy – they all are – but he's not stupid. He's been more forthcoming than ever before, shared more than he ever has previously. Part of that might be because he's so pumped up. Part of it is because it's necessary. But I'm sure he's done the calculation. He knows that, because of Jonno's death, the equation has changed. We are all complicit in Jonno's manslaughter, and that changes the dynamic. That's why he is taking us into his confidence.

"More precisely, how do *you* identify the targets, Josh." He's smiling right at me. "We can all identify places where there will be crowds of people – maybe famous landmarks or locations that are significant to the establishment. But none of us have your expertise. None of us can calculate the amount and type of explosive required to have the maximum impact in any given location."

I know that my response is critical. "Timescales." I leave the word hanging for a second. "Our biggest challenge is timescales. We need to generate a list of potential targets, recce them, then narrow the list down to what is achievable. Then we need to specify exactly what kit we require for each site and agree how we are going to deliver it."

"Deliver it?" Ruthie's attention is total.

"Who is going to plant each device. When and how. How each one will be detonated. It all needs to be worked out, and it needs to be credible. Do we have any dates?"

Ryan has been listening intently. "The intention is that we should hit the targets exactly one week before the election."

I sigh theatrically. "Shit! I was hoping you'd say we'd hit the targets 48 hours before the election. This means we've got three weeks, instead of three weeks and five days."

Ryan leans forward. "You can do this, Josh. *We* can do this." He nods, and I nod back the confirmation he wants. There's a moment of hush, as everyone digests what has just been discussed. Vi has continued to maintain her arms-round-knees posture and is still staring into space, and Ryan has picked up on it. "Are you okay, Vi?"

"I'm fine."

"You don't sound fine." Ryan sounds like he's about to start an interrogation. I catch his eye and shake my head gently. He throws me an inquisitive look and I mouth the words *later - outside*, the latter accompanied by a tilt of my head. Thankfully, he decides not to press Vi.

I need to move this on. "You've given us a lot to think about, Ryan. Can I suggest that the next step should be for me to give some thought to generating a target list? Input from all of you is welcome, of course. But I need to get my mind around this pronto." I press my luck by making less than subtle *time for the meeting to end* movements in my chair. "Did you guys come in Ruthie's car?"

Ryan is clearly surprised by my abrupt commandeering of proceedings. "Yes. We parked just round the corner."

"Great. Any chance I can hitch a lift? I've got some things I need to go into town for." I get to my feet, making it clear that I'd like to leave now.

Chapter 10

Having said our goodbyes to Vi, with me reassuring her that I'll be back by mid-afternoon, Ryan, Ruthie and I are making our way downstairs as we head towards the car.

"Vi didn't seem all with it back there." Ryan's behind me and taps me lightly on the shoulder. "What is it you wanted to tell me? Are you worried that she might not be up to it anymore? Has Saturday – Jonno – put her off?"

I reach the entrance vestibule on the ground floor, then turn to face the others as they catch me up. "You don't need to worry about Vi's commitment." I'm surprised at how genuinely defensive I feel about her. "She's just a bit pre-occupied right now. It's her mother's funeral tomorrow."

"Shit! No." Ruthie's face is a mixture of disbelief and concern.

"The funeral's tomorrow?" I can see Ryan thinking. "So, when did she die?"

"On Thursday last week."

"Unbelievable. And no-one thought to tell me?"

"I wanted to tell you, but she was insistent. She was determined that Saturday night should go ahead, and that she should play her part." I pause. "And she did."

"Is she okay to be left alone? What, with the funeral being tomorrow, and everything?" Ruthie's face is a mixture of concern and compassion.

"I think she should be okay. I shouldn't be too long – I just need to pick up some clothes so that I'm presentable at the funeral tomorrow."

"Honestly, it's no bother. I can drop you in town, drop Ryan home and then come back to be with her until you return."

"You heard what Josh said. He'll probably be back here before you could make it." I can see that Ryan has other plans for Ruthie today.

Ruthie shrugs and nods, then when she thinks I'm not looking, returns the lascivious glance that had accompanied Ryan's kyboshing of her proposed mercy mission to Vi. We make our way to the car, and twenty-five minutes later I'm walking down the High Street, deciding whether to buy something new, or to head over and collect something from my own actual flat. With my cover being as a gay man, the flat is a useful base if I hook up online with someone and she doesn't want to go back to her place.

If I collect a suit from my flat, I'll have to explain where it came from. Why would someone who ostensibly earns a living by taking cash-in-hand casual shifts in hotel kitchens own an expensive tailored suit? But trying to buy a new suit that actually fits me and doesn't break the bank is a challenge.

Ten minutes later I'm at the junction of the High Street and Leicester Road, and I can see that *Sky High's* capacious "emporium of all things odd and outsized for the discerning gentleman" is open. I know, from my time on squaddie's wages, that they will be able to kit me out and that it'll be cheap. Less than half an hour later I'm back outside the shop, still slightly bewildered by the window display that includes a seven-foot-tall model of a green-faced Frankenstein's monster garbed in full top hat and tails, à la Fred Astaire. I have a large bag in each hand, and now own a new charcoal grey suit, white shirt, black tie and classic black Oxford shoes, all for the princely sum of £235. I'll keep the receipts in case I can claim for this stuff on expenses.

I check my watch. 10.35. I can catch a bus just a couple of hundred metres from here that will get me to the storage unit in about fifteen minutes, so I head towards the stop. I agreed with Moll last Thursday that our next meeting would be on Wednesday afternoon at the greasy spoon on Milton Street, but that was before the balloon went up. The fact I didn't make contact yesterday means that she'll be full-on Adolf-in-the-bunker by now.

10.55, and I'm entering the code into the pad to gain access to the huge warehouse. Three minutes later I'm on the first floor outside my unit, keying in the second code and gaining entry to the totally anonymous 6-foot by 4-foot space. I open the suitcase – the only thing in there – and retrieve the phone and charging lead. The suitcase also contains absolutely everything that could link me to my job. There's been no call for me to take anyone from the group back to my own flat, but it might conceivably happen so it's a sensible precaution to make sure there's nothing there that could blow my cover. I press the on button and the screen flashes to life long enough for me see I have missed calls and a message, before dying. Reception in here is very hit-and-miss, and there's nowhere to charge the phone, which I slip into my pocket. I put the charging lead into one of the bags and exit the cell, pulling the door closed behind me. The clang of metal on metal echoes along the sterile corridor, not entirely drowning the click of the electro-magnetic lock re-engaging.

It's only a three minute walk to the coffee shop and I'm pleased to see that that there are barely any customers in. I secure my favoured seat in the corner by the window before purchasing a cappuccino, then plug the charging lead into the nearby socket and connect it to the phone, which beeps gratefully. The proximity of my own drink amplifies the heady aroma of coffee and sweet pastries, and I breathe it in hungrily. This is the best seat in the shop – private, affording a view of both everyone inside and those passing outside, as well as free power to recharge the phone.

I switch the phone on. Five missed calls, all from Moll – one on Friday, two yesterday and two this morning. The single text message simply reads *Call me immediately you get this*. She hasn't left any voice messages. I take a swig of my cappuccino and cradle the phone in my other hand. No point in putting this off. I dial Moll. Six rings and then it switches to voicemail *This is Molly Leishman. I'm sorry I can't answer the phone right now. Please leave a message with your name and number and I'll get back to you as soon as possible*. Shit! I ring off without leaving any message. That was the last thing I was expecting. I'm surprised at the relief I feel – after all, it's only a stay of execution. I decide that I'll ring back and leave a message, saying I'm sorry to have missed her and confirming that I'm still okay to meet on Wednesday at Milton Street.

I'm just about to dial when the phone vibrates in my hand. Molly.

"Hello."

Where the hell have you been?

"Where were you when I called just now?" Counterattack might work.

Don't try that shit with me, Josh. It's thirty five hours since that crane came down and total radio silence from you.

"I couldn't get away."

Well, you're away now, so get on with it. And, trust me, this better be very, very good. I've got AC Carswell all over me, demanding answers. My whole career is on the line because of you.

"Do you want me to update you, or do you just want to keep ranting?"

There's a second's silence and I can picture her, flushed from the neck up, like she always is when she is furious and trying to contain it. Another second passes.

Give me your report, DC Gray.

I start talking, voice low so that I'm not overheard, despite there being no-one within four metres of me. I talk about the attack on Brightwater View and how Ryan and Jonno deviated from the agreed plan, leading to Jonno's death. I report on the link to Ryan's "partners" and how the group is part of a bigger operation intent on causing mayhem across the country the week before election day. I explain that the "success" of Saturday night's operation seems to have cemented my credibility with Ryan, and that I now enjoy more of his confidence. She lets me deliver my briefing without interruption, and when I finish I'm starting to wonder whether she's still there. The suspicion that we've been cut off grows with the silence.

Let me get this straight. The group you have infiltrated is one of a number of similar groups, co-ordinated by some indeterminate network or organisation. All of those groups are going to carry out multiple terrorist attacks simultaneously on Thursday the 27th. And you have been tasked with identifying the targets for your group in London.

"That's a good summary."

Shit. Are you absolutely certain about this, Josh?

"Definitely. I got it from the horse's mouth – Ryan – just this morning. It seems that, by carrying out the attack on Saturday, we've passed some sort of audition. Whoever is co-ordinating this is incredibly well resourced."

And we don't know who is co-ordinating things, or anything about the other groups?

"Nothing. You're going to have to put Ryan under intense surveillance. But it will have to be ultra-subtle, as he's totally paranoid. If you identify his 'partners' you might track down the other groups."

Understood. Are you still able to operate pretty freely?

"Yes, at least for the moment. As I say, I seem to have Ryan's confidence. That said, it could be that his 'partners' might be scrutinising me, so I'll need to stay alert."

There's another pause in the conversation. I've dumped a lot on Moll, and she'll be reviewing her notes to see if there's anything else she needs to ask.

Josh, why didn't you tell me about the plan for Saturday, and the explosives? We met two nights before, so you obviously knew.

"My gut told me that Saturday was a rehearsal for something bigger. If I'd told you what was planned for Saturday you wouldn't have sanctioned it. You'd have aborted the op and we wouldn't have got the intel about the 22nd."

Ends justify means, eh? Misleading your senior officer is okay, is it? How do I present that to the AC? How can we trust you going forward?

She's presenting a perfectly valid point of view. Undercover work relies on being able to trust the officer absolutely. There's a list as long as your arm of those that have either overstepped the mark, or even gone rogue. The people in charge understand that we have to be allowed some leeway in order to operate, but ultimately they need to believe that they can trust us.

"I've told you the truth now, Moll. It's up to you to decide whether you can trust me."

It's not just me, Josh. It's AC Carswell, the Commissioner and the Home Secretary. They all need a reason to trust you.

"The biggest co-ordinated series of terror attacks on the UK is just weeks away, and I'm your only man on the inside. They'll have to trust me. You'll have to trust me."

There's another pause. She's weighing up what I've said. Deciding whether she can trust me. Whether she can sell trusting me to the great and the good. She's also considering the impact of all this on her career prospects. Ultimately, that's what it boils down to with her.

Okay, Josh. I'm willing to run with that. But, so help me, if you hold anything else back...

"You don't need to worry about that."

I better not. But we're not finished. We need to talk about Thursday night.

"What about Thursday night?"

Don't push it! You know exactly what I'm talking about. You were given a direct order that you chose to disobey within an hour of receiving it.

Shit.

"The camera at the junction of Howard Street and Tansey Road?"

Old Tom Wilson spotted you. I had to go to Walton Street nick to agree a cover story that he knew was bullshit, but was still willing to buy.

"Old Tom..." I find myself smiling at the very mention of his name. "...he's one of the good guys."

It doesn't fucking matter that he's one of the good guys! You disobeyed a direct order and that could have compromised the whole operation.

"A woman was being raped! What was I meant to do? Walk on by? So what if two fucking puddle-drinkers ended up in hospital? Anyway, that's all irrelevant now. You can't report it up the line or it will undermine your argument that I can be trusted."

I can hear her breathing. I can almost hear the cogs whirring. I can picture her top teeth biting her lower lip, her neck flushed raspberry.

You disobeyed a direct order. If all of this gets resolved…when this is all over, there will be a reckoning DC Gray. I will see you at Milton Street on Wednesday, as previously arranged.

She's gone – hung up. I've got away with one there, for now. I check the phone – it's 88% charged. I disconnect it from the charger and put it in my pocket, and place the charging wire in one of the bags. I'll return them to the locker and head for home. I need to start identifying targets, and I need to be there for Vi.

Chapter 11

I adjust the knot, then check it in the small wall mirror to the side of the wardrobe. My tie looks perfect, the midnight satin sheen contrasting sharply with the punishing white of my collar. The shirt is a cotton mix, and not too unpleasant to wear. I shrug my shoulders to test the fit of the jacket, and I'm pleasantly surprised that it still feels as good a fit as it did in the shop. If I was having made-to-measure I'd have gone for slightly wider lapels, but given the price I can hardly complain. I've got a belt on, although the trousers don't need one as they rest at just the right length on my shoes. I'm as ready for this as I can be so, after a final check that I've got two fresh handkerchiefs in my pockets as well as my wallet and phone, I leave my bedroom.

"Wow! You scrub up pretty well. If I didn't have a funeral to go to I'd be tempted to try and turn you straight." Vi is all over the place this morning. Four weeks after I moved in we both got very drunk one night and ended up having messy, unsatisfactory sex – something we both regretted afterwards and promised would never happen again. The only positive thing to come out of it was that it reinforced Vi's belief that I was gay. The fact that she's saying something so completely inappropriate just shows how fragile she is. She needs me to support her.

"You look pretty fantastic yourself. There's no need for you to waste your time chasing a gay man – you could have any straight guy you want." She does look good. She's wearing a black blouse with a cardigan over, black pencil skirt and black tights, with knee-length black boots. She's straightened her hair and is wearing make-up, which is very much a rarity for her. I have honestly never seen her look better. "Genuinely, Vi, you look beautiful and elegant."

She comes towards me and wraps her arms around my waist, resting her head gently on my chest. "Thank you. Thank you, Josh." She holds the pose for fully twenty seconds, before her arms loosen and she steps back. I can see that her eyes are moist.

"Whoa! Stop right there, missy. What did we agree? No tears

today. Isn't that what we promised?"

She sniffs and blinks twice in an exaggerated manner. "You're right." She looks straight at me. "Do you really think that I look elegant?"

"Yes. And beautiful."

"I want to look good for Mummy. I want her to be proud of me."

"She'll be proud of you, Vi. Of course she will." She's wearing a tiny gold cross on a fine gold chain around her neck and rubs it between her thumb and forefinger. "That's lovely. I've never seen it before."

"Mummy gave it to me. I've never worn it, but I want to wear it today."

"It looks perfect." A car horn sounds outside. "That'll be our cab." I head over to the window to check. I can see the illuminated 'taxi' sign through the gloom below. "Yes, that's it. Better get our coats on and go."

Vi slips on her charcoal puffer jacket. It doesn't exactly complement the rest of her look, but it's all she's got and at least it's the right colour. I slip on my grey herringbone Crombie. Vi's background meant that she knew how expensive an item it was when she first saw it after I moved in, and I'd had to lie that I'd picked it up in a charity shop.

We are just ahead of the rush hour traffic, so the cab delivers us to Paddington in plenty of time to catch the 7.55. The taxi journey was completed in near silence, but as the train carries us closer to Pinkley Vi becomes much more talkative and fretful. She doesn't know who else will be at the funeral – apart from Mallingford, obviously. Her mother was an only child, and both maternal grandparents are dead, so she's not expecting anyone from that side of the family. She's fearful that the attendance will be tiny and that somehow that will reflect badly on her mother. Then she's concerned that perhaps there will be a vast number of strangers present, and that will make her feel uncomfortable. She wonders whether the vicar will be same one as when she used to attend church as a child. What form will the reception take – buffet, formal sit-down, or what? On and on, round and round, the same anxieties that she has been repeating for days.

But it always comes back to the same thing – Mallingford. Will she have to sit beside him in church? What are the seating arrangements, if any, likely to be at the reception? Will she be expected to speak to him? What if he approaches her? She doesn't want to create a scene and risk tarnishing her mother's funeral. She makes me promise – again – that I won't let Mallingford get her on her own.

Just after ten past nine the train comes to an unexpected stop in the middle of nowhere. I press my head against the window and squint towards the front of the train, where I can just make out that there's a signal at red.

"What's the matter? Why have we stopped?" It's not as if Vi needs anything untoward to wind her up even more.

"I can see a red light up ahead. I'm sure we'll be going again shortly."

Two minutes of peering through the filthy windows at rain falling on to a field of winter barley is unexpectedly interrupted. *Good morning, ladies and gentlemen. This is your guard speaking. We understand that the engine on the train ahead of us has failed. Engineers are already on board working to resolve the problem. We hope to be on the move again soon.*

Vi looks at me with an expression that the word bereft could have been coined for. "We're not going to make it."

"Don't worry, he said we'll be on the move again soon."

"He said he *hoped* we'd be on the move again soon."

I check my watch – almost quarter past nine. Vi has told me that the church is a ten-minute ride from the and I've got a taxi booked to collect us, assuming that it will wait. I estimate that we're probably fifteen minutes away, so this train needs to get going sooner rather than later.

Another quarter of an hour passes at near lightspeed as I feel Vi's increasing despair, and rising frustration at my own sense of impotence. Then there is a sudden, gentle jolt and the carriage begins to move. *Ladies and gentlemen, this is your guard speaking. I'm pleased to report that the issue with the train in front has been resolved and we are able to proceed. We expect to arrive at our next station, Pinkley, in…*there's a pause and Vi and I lock eyes, waiting…*in just over twelve minutes time*. I look straight at my watch as Vi checks the time on her phone.

The train pulls into Pinkley Station at exactly twenty to ten. It's a small countryside village and, apart from Vi and me, there are only two other passengers who get off – a well-dressed elderly couple. We half-run along the platform, through the unmanned station building and out to the front where, to my relief and mild surprise, there's a black hackney – its rattling diesel engine audible, despite the relentless wind and rain.

I dash to the cabbie's half-open window. "Is this the cab for Ambrose?" I booked the cab in Vi's name – she uses her mother's maiden name rather than the despised Mallingford. I'm shouting to make myself heard over the weather. "To St. John's Church at Wantwell?"

"St. John's at Wantwell - yes. But the booking is in the name of Waterson-Jones."

Before I can say anything, there are three firm taps on my shoulder. I turn to find the man from the elderly couple right behind me. "I'm Waterson-Jones." His voice is directed at the driver, loud and firm. Then he addresses me. "I take it that you're going to the funeral too. Jump in with us, there's plenty of room for four." There is no time for polite debate, and seconds later the taxi is en route with four of us inside.

Vi and I are on fold down seats with our backs to the driver, directly facing Mrs. and Mr. Waterson-Jones respectively. He leans forward to shake hands. "I'm Martin, and this is my wife Sara." He's a big chap, almost my height and with the build of someone well-fed and largely sedentary. I reckon he's sixtyish, with thick salt-and-pepper hair and a prominent nose whose burst veins testify to an over-fondness for drink. Sara is tall, slim and pretty, easily ten years his junior – possibly more. Both are beautifully and very expensively dressed, and his Received Pronunciation accent strongly suggests he is from a moneyed background. Sara sounds equally refined, although I'm sure I can detect the trace of an accent. Vi and I respond by confirming our own names.

Martin has the easy manner often found in privileged people

comfortable in their own skin. "So, we're all obviously going to Margaret's funeral. I'm an old colleague of Charlie's," I sense Vi tense slightly at the mention of her father, "and I...we had to come today to show our support." He lets the information land, before continuing. "And you?" He looks toward Vi. "Are you related to the family?"

"Margaret was my mother." Vi's voice is calm and clear. She is looking straight at Martin.

"Oh, you poor dear." Sara leans forward and takes Vi's hands in hers. "I am so, so sorry for your loss." Her voice is warm and sincere.

Vi smiles, "Thank you."

"And you, Josh?" Martin directs his question to me. "I take it that you're Vi's partner?"

Before I can respond, Vi cuts across me. "Josh shares a flat with me, but we're not a couple." She flicks me a sideways glance, before returning her attention to Martin. "He's gay, so we're obviously not a couple. But he is a very, very good friend." Her right hand reaches across and hold my left.

Sara and Martin are classy enough people to simply take Vi's completely incongruous declaration of my sexual orientation in their stride. I can see in Sara's face that she realises Vi is struggling to keep her emotions in check, and that the social faux pas warrants only sympathy. She smiles gently, "It's important that you have such a good friend, particularly on a day like this."

I smile my own thanks back to her.

The rest of the journey passes amidst innocuous conversation about the horrible weather, and the shared sense of dread all four of us had felt when the train stopped so unexpectedly. At ten to ten the taxi arrives at the open gate in a stone wall outside what appears to be a very old church, disproportionately large for the village we've just driven through. There are other people walking along the side of the building towards the open doors, umbrellas tilted into the wind and rain. I presume that they're coming from a car parking area nearby. Martin diplomatically declines my offer to pay for the cab, settling it himself with the inclusion of a sizeable tip, before we spill out and scurry towards the shelter of the church.

We enter the capacious south porch, which is thronged with dark-garbed people making their way further inside. Vi had told me it was a 15th century building and, over the aroma of burning candles and wet clothes, the most distinctive smell is that of age. Soft organ music fills the air. Unlike with so many old churches, I can see that this one benefits from being part of a particularly prosperous community. It is warm, the décor seems fresh enough that it cannot be more than twelve months old, and the parish noticeboard is sufficiently busy to suggest a sizeable and active congregation. Sara waves at Vi and me, and nods towards Martin, who points towards a double row of heavily-laden coat hooks, where they have just hung up their own outer garments. The bodies in the porch area are thinning and we cross easily and force our own jacket and coat onto the heaped pegs.

"Vivienne! How marvellous to see you." The dark suit and clerical collar remove any guesswork about the man who has gently pressed his hand on to Vi's wrist. "It's so lovely that you managed to make it. And it's good to see you looking so well."

"Oh, thank you, Reverend Alworth. I'm so glad you are still here." I know she's sincere when she says that, and I'm pleased to see the warmth of the smiles she exchanges with the small, balding, bespectacled man. Not blessed by his God in the looks department, with flushed features reminiscent of a cartoon owl, the vicar nonetheless has an indefinable quality that makes him immediately engaging. "I'm sorry it's been so long, Vivienne. But now that you're all grown up, I insist that you call me Jeremy." He smiles again then turns to me. "And who is this?"

"This is Josh, Rev...Jeremy. He's a friend."

Jeremy shakes my hand enthusiastically. "Welcome, Josh. Any friend of Vivienne's is a friend to us all. He switches his attention back to Vi. He hands her a white card-bound A5 pamphlet with a picture of her mother and some dates, presumably birth and death, embossed on the front. "Here's an Order of Service for you, Vivienne." He smiles benignly. "And now, my dear, I'm afraid that we must all go inside. The pews at the front are for family. Your father and some other family members are on the right hand side. I believe the pew on the left is empty." I wonder if he knows something about Mallingford's treatment of Vi when she was younger. He places his hand on her shoulder and leans in, whispering, "Stay strong, Vivienne, and follow me."

Jeremy leads the way, with Vi and me a couple of paces behind. We enter at the back of the south aisle and make our way behind the rearmost pew on that side, until we reach the nave, where we turn right. Vi hesitates as her mother's coffin comes into view at the other end of the nave, in front of the altar. I squeeze her hand gently and toss her a fleeting glance of reassurance. She smiles a watery smile, nods then draws herself up straight and we follow Jeremy along the channel that divides the congregation. As we walk slowly forwards I do a headcount. Somewhere between ninety and a hundred – many more than Vi had feared. The arrival of Jeremy, followed by Vi, sends a frisson through the gathering. The library-whispers and shuffling of feet mingle with the melancholy notes of the organ, while heads turn to get a look at Vi.

We reach the end of the nave in front of the chancel. Vi takes a step forward, places her right hand on the coffin, and bows her head. There's the briefest of pauses before she steps back, head held proud, then turns and leads me to the empty pew on the left. She takes her seat gracefully, gaze fixed firmly in front of her. I take my place on the ancient, hard wooden seat by her side, right by the nave. I feel proud of her. I turn to the right. Mallingford is seated two along on the pew on the other side of the nave, leaning forward and staring past me at Vi. His features are marginally more gaunt and the hair a more faded blonde than in the picture Vi showed me, but it is unmistakably the same man. His focus switches to me and, although his features remain expressionless, his glacial eyes radiate disdain. He leans slightly further forward, briefly trying to get a better look at Vi, then sits back and turns to whisper something to the person on his right.

Chapter 12

The music fades as though perfectly rehearsed, and Jeremy climbs up into the pulpit. He places an Order of Service on top of the massive bible on the lectern in front of him, and leans forward to the microphone. "Thank you all for coming, particularly when the weather is so bad. I know that some people here have travelled considerable distances, and I also know how grateful the family are that so many of you have made the effort to be here today. We are, of course, gathered here…"

I've attended a number of Christian funerals, and this one follows the expected pattern. There are religious tracts, and four separate hymns – thankfully the congregation is sizeable and familiar enough with them that we avoid the excruciating pain of the vicar, the organist and a handful of doughty souls carrying the tune while the majority mumble and hum along behind. One woman, a close friend of Margaret's, pays a particularly moving tribute to her and I have to pass Vi a handkerchief for her tears. I don't particularly enjoy funerals - who does? Equally, nor do I mind them, as they're just part of the cycle of life. But I'm uncomfortable in this funeral. There are the best part of a hundred people that I do not know from Adam behind me. They can see me and I can't see them – it is completely at odds with my instincts, which are telling me that I am being scrutinised from behind. I feel genuine relief as Jeremy draws the service to a close.

"We will now proceed outside for the interment. It sounds as though the weather has eased somewhat during the service, but there is a supply of umbrellas available in the porch for anyone who needs one. After the committal of Margaret's body, the family will be hosting a luncheon reception at The Claremont Hotel. They would be pleased to see as many of you there as possible." He gives the subtlest of nods and four pall bearers materialise from the ether and lift the coffin. As they begin the procession up the nave, Jeremy steps behind them and nods again to indicate that those in the front two pews should take their place behind him. I get to my feet and turn ready to follow, as Vi steps up beside me. Mallingford steps forward opposite us and his eyes lock with Vi's. He extends his hand, offering to take hers for them to jointly lead the mourners following Jeremy and the coffin. The next moment, I see his face contort in fury as Vi turns past him to take the position of lead mourner, pulling me alongside her. The thought that Mallingford will be looking daggers at us from behind gives me a sense of satisfaction.

I pick up an umbrella as we pass through the porch, although I can see that the rain has indeed eased considerably. When we arrive at the open grave the pall bearers place the coffin on the putlogs and lace the webbing for lowering it through the handles on the sides. The grave is in the shadow of a mature, leafless sycamore, and Jeremy positions himself at the head of the grave, with the tree behind him. As those of us following catch him up, I find myself standing beside him. He is on my right and Vi on my left. Mallingford takes his position to the left of Vi. She tugs at my elbow and we swap places. She does not look at Mallingford.

The rest of the mourners gradually form a three-quarters circle around the grave, and I finally have the chance to have a proper look at them. A fairly even split between men and women, all clothed in funereal shades – many in expensive-looking attire, under a small forest of umbrellas providing shelter from rain that seems undecided about whether or not to stop. Unsurprisingly, given Margaret's age, the majority in attendance look to be aged from their mid-fifties upwards, and what hair is visible is predominantly grey or white. There is one woman holding an umbrella, to the rear and the right of the group as I look at it, who is standing by herself, on the very edge of the proceedings. She catches my eye because she is much younger than most others present – I would guess late twenties – and because she is strikingly attractive. And she is looking directly at me. As I glance in her direction she switches her focus, but not quickly enough to avoid me clocking her.

Jeremy raises both his hands to shoulder height and the minimal chatter and shuffling of feet ceases, so that only the wind and his words are audible. "For as much as it has pleased Almighty God to take out of this world the soul of our sister

Margaret Mallingford, we therefore commit her body to the ground..." The pall bearers have removed the putlogs and are slowly lowering the coffin. Jeremy steps towards the grave, a small wooden box in his left hand from which his right picks a pinch of soil, "...earth to earth..." He tosses the soil on top of the lowered coffin, "...ashes to ashes..." He turns and proffers the box of soil to Vi, who follows his example. "...dust to dust..." Jeremy intones as he repeats the ritual with Mallingford. Vi pointedly steps back to be as far out of range of her father as possible. "...looking for that blessed hope when the Lord Himself shall descend from heaven with a shout, with the voice of the archangel, and the trump of God, and the..."

As Jeremy continues I take the opportunity to lift my eyes. Every head is bowed, save for that of the mystery woman who is, once more, looking straight at me. As I catch her eye again she glances past me and fixes on Vi, whose head remains bowed. The women does not bow her head, but continues to look towards Vi as Jeremy concludes the committal, "...and so shall we ever be with The Lord, wherefore comfort ye one another with these words. Amen."

The spell is broken and the first whispers of conversation begin.

Vi turns through ninety degrees so that her back is towards Mallingford who, whether deliberately or not, reciprocates. "Thank you, Jeremy – that was a beautiful service." He nods his gratitude and then takes a step backwards as a small, bird-like woman forces herself between Vi and him.

"Miss Vivienne, I'm so glad you were able to come. It's so lovely to see you again, and to see how grown up you look." She has clearly made an effort in terms of what she's wearing, but – not unlike Vi and me – her clothes are obviously considerably less expensive than those worn by most others present. She appears to sense that Vi is unsure, and tilts her head slightly to the side, smiling broadly. "Surely you remember..."

"Tillie!" Vi pulls the woman into an embrace that I fear might snap her. "Oh, Tillie! Tillie!" The hug lasts for several seconds before Vi lets go. I'm not sure whether Tillie's continuing grin is pleasure at being recognised, or relief at being able to breathe again. "Josh, this is Mrs. Tillerson – she used to help Mummy out around the house. Tillie, this is my friend, Josh."

We exchange hellos, and Tillie insists that I call her Tillie, rather than Mrs. Tillerson. The cluster of people around the grave has thinned rapidly as people make their way to their cars. When Tillie learns that Vi and I had arrived by train and taxi she insists that she give us a lift to The Claremont Hotel. The rain has stopped completely and the wind has lost its ferocity. I follow behind Vi and Tillie, diverting briefly to return the borrowed umbrella, then catch them up at the car.

The journey to the hotel lasts just over five minutes, during which time the two women chatter and laugh away. I'm pleased that Vi has the opportunity to let some of the tension she's been feeling ease. Tillie manoeuvres the vehicle into one of several empty bays in the extensive car park. The hotel is a vast regency affair, with a significant modern extension visible to one side, set in acres of parkland, and with the feel of a country club. The degree of exclusivity and the expense of staging any sort of event here is self-evident.

Once inside we are directed toward the Banqueting Hall by well-scrubbed hotel staff, all immaculately turned out in crisp white shirts with black satin bow ties and black trousers or skirts. The directions are hardly necessary as we simply need to follow others we recognise from the funeral, but I assume the level of service on display comes with the price tag. It transpires that Tillie still helps out with cleaning at the Mallingford home and is plugged in to the arrangements for the funeral. She was able to set Vi's mind at rest in the car when she explained that the luncheon was to be a formal fork buffet, but with no arranged seating plan. The intention is that mourners should be free to move from table to table as they wish, in order that they might catch up with other attendees who they might not have seen for some time.

The Banqueting Hall looks to be about twenty metres wide and fifty metres long, with very high ceilings, ornate cornicing running at three-quarters height all the way round the pale yellow walls, and a spectacular crystal chandelier below a rococo ceiling rose. The left hand wall consists of a series of tall sash windows, affording a view over a huge rolling lawn that falls away to what I imagine must be a man-made lake. On the opposite side is a long row of serving tables covered in white linen tablecloths and laden with plates and a long line of highly polished serving dishes. There are half a dozen men and women in full chef's outfits stationed irregularly behind the tables, serving food to people in a queue of a dozen or so in front of us.

Down the middle and right side of the room are two rows of eight circular tables, also with white linen tablecloths, each with eight chairs and table settings. The majority of the tables are already occupied by diners who didn't dally by the graveside like we did. The tables are variously full, almost full, sparsely populated or empty. The room is filled with the sound of soft chatter, the clinking of cutlery and a heady aroma of various dishes competing to tempt the hungry. Four waiting staff flit between tables serving drinks, taking orders and, in one case, clearing away dishes.

Mallingford is at the table farthest away on the right, sitting beside Martin and Sara who shared their cab with us. He is watching Vi as we enter. At a table half way down on the right, with her back to the window so that she can observe most of the room, is the woman who was staring at Vi and me at the committal. She turns her head to speak to the fat man sitting to her right, but I sense she was watching us again until I looked in her direction.

There are half a dozen final stragglers who make up the tail of the food queue behind us. I refine my headcount calculation to one hundred and five, including us and Reverend Alworth – who is also seated at Mallingford's table. There's seating for 128, so there's plenty of room for everyone, without it feeling like there's been a poor turnout. Tillie's eyes are out on stalks at the choice of extravagant foods on offer. "It looks like there's been no expense spared here," I say.

Tillie turns to me and leans in conspiratorially. She whispers, "It's all show with the Viscount. This is to impress his friends. If his friends weren't here we'd be having meat paste sandwiches in the back room at the Red Lion. Do you know, he only pays me minimum wage?" The indignation in her voice means I have to suppress a smile.

Once the three of us have had our plates filled Vi turns to decide where to sit. An older couple are sitting alone at a table near the entrance, furthest away from where Mallingford is seated. The woman is half-standing, waving exaggeratedly and beckoning to Vi. "That's my Uncle Harry, my father's brother, and my Aunt Agnes. Father despises Aunt Agnes, so we should sit with them." Vi nods and waves her free hand to her relatives as she leads Tillie and me to join them.

At the table, Harry and Agnes Mallingford get to their feet to greet us. There are hugs and condolences for Vi from each of them, and polite handshakes for Tillie and me. Harry Mallingford has a look of his elder brother, but has lost his hair and carries more weight, as well as having a fuller, kinder face. Agnes is tall and slim, with shoulder length straight black hair so thick and shiny she might be mistaken for a teen from behind. Her face, however, betrays her age. Well applied make-up and an excellent bone structure hint that she was probably a real beauty once, but time and, I suspect, especially drink have taken their toll. Her dark brown eyes still flash with life and devilment. We take our seats beside them, and I make sure I am positioned so that I can view almost the entire room. I can see both Mallingford and the mystery woman stealing looks in our direction. Mallingford and Martin are engaged in an animated tête-à-tête, interrupted as they both lift their heads to stare in our direction, before resuming their collusion. There's no doubt that Vi, or perhaps both of us, are a cause of agitation.

The conversation at our table turns out to be surprisingly easy and entertaining, led almost entirely by Agnes. She is a font of amusing gossip, ribald jokes, and cutting sarcasm about Mallingford. Harry is content to take a back seat and enjoy the glow of his wife's social skills. Tillie seems slightly bemused, while Vi is clearly delighted by her aunt's company. Agnes is pleased to find that I am ex-army and regales us with a series of genuinely funny anecdotes about an army captain she dated before she knew Harry, who has clearly heard the tales before but doesn't seem to mind hearing them repeated. My suspicions about Agnes are confirmed as she orders a second bottle of wine only twenty minutes after the first, more than half of which she necked herself, as none of Harry, Vi or Tillie are drinking.

I'm caught off guard when a hand taps Vi's shoulder from behind and we both turn to see the mystery woman smiling down at her. She enjoys the rare good fortune of looking even better close up than from a distance. She has astonishingly bright big eyes, flawless skin and full, ruby lips - parted by her smile to reveal perfect teeth. For the second time today Vi's face betrays her confusion.

"Don't you recognise me, Veeva?"

Dawning recognition morphs quickly to absolute joy, as Vi lets out a squeal of delight, rises, turns and embraces her inquisitor. "Oh, my God! Meelie! Meelie, it's really you. The pair each have their arms round the other's shoulders, seemingly hypnotised by their beaming grins. After a moment Vi loosens her hold and turns to the rest of us. "Everyone, this is my old friend, Meelie. We've not seen each other since our schooldays. Meelie, this is my Uncle Harry, my Aunt Agnes and an old family friend, Tillie."

"I remember you, Tillie, from the two occasions when I visited." Tillie seems pleased by the acknowledgement as Meelie exchanges how-do-you-do's and shakes hands with Harry and Agnes, before turning to me. "And this is?"

"This is my very dear friend, Josh. We share a flat together in London."

Meelie takes my hand. "How do you do, Josh? I'm delighted to meet you." Her eyes hold mine for just a millisecond too long, and I'm not sure what it is I can read in them. Not quite scepticism, but perhaps a hint of puzzlement. Maybe. I can't be sure. I'm mesmerised by this woman and it's all I can manage to return her greeting before her attention is diverted by Vi.

"So, Meelie, how did you know about...this? About today?"

"Papa saw the notice about your mother in The Times and mentioned it to me. Even though I only met her a couple of times, I felt I should come. And really, I was hoping we might meet up again."

"I'm so glad you did. It's wonderful to see you again. Come, please sit with us."

I vacate my seat beside Vi for Meelie and move next to Agnes. The conversation resumes, although more splintered now, as Meelie and Vi reminisce while remembering to involve Tillie from time to time.

I continue to chat with Harry and Agnes, until Agnes announces that she is gasping for a cigarette. She tops up her wine glass, excuses herself and heads towards the door, handbag in one hand and drink in the other.

"Shit." Harry expresses irritation for the first time since I've met him.

"What's wrong?"

"It's just that, without Agnes here to ward him off, we're bound to be visited by my brother."

Vi overhears the comment and instantly I can sense her fear. I look to the faraway table and I can see Mallingford rising to his feet, his eyes looking in our direction. I can tell from his bearing that Harry is right.

"Would you please excuse me for a moment?" My request is directed to all of the company at the table, but my nod of reassurance is solely for Vi. I get to my feet and step into the aisle between the two rows of tables just as Mallingford reaches the same position at the far end. Our eyes lock like two Western gunslingers and I use mine to direct him to the serving table nearest to him, and farthest from me. I'm relieved when, after a brief pause, he changes direction and heads where I have indicated. The gamble that he wouldn't like any sort of scene, based on what Tillie said, has paid off. I make my way towards the rendezvous as swiftly as is possible whilst trying to avoid attracting interest from other diners. Fortunately, there are a few other people on foot moving between tables or returning from toilets and I reach Mallingford without attracting any attention.

"Viscount Mallingford, I wonder whether I could have a discreet word with you?" He is motionless as he looks me squarely in the eyes. He says nothing. "My name is Josh Gray."

"I know who you are. You begged a ride in my friend Martin's cab."

I ignore the barb. "I just felt that I ought to advise you Vi –

your daughter Vivienne – has made it clear that she does not want to talk to you."

There's a pause, during which his eyes continue to bore into mine. "You are telling me that Vivienne would prefer the company of my soft-headed brother, his lush of a wife, and a washer woman?"

"I'm sorry if that disappoints you, but she is quite clear about not wanting to talk to you."

His eyes run down and back up my full length, before returning to focus on mine. "And my daughter chooses to send you to deliver this insult?" He has lowered his voice, despite the fact that we are not in earshot of anyone else. "She chooses to send a sodomite in a cheap suit?" His voice is as harsh as his words.

I do not break eye contact, and barely blink. "I think you'll find that homosexuality has been legal in the United Kingdom since the Sexual Offences Act of 1967." I pause briefly. "I do not believe that is the case for either incest or paedophilia."

The merest flicker behind his eyes confirms that my words have landed. "Very well. Please pass on my regards to my daughter. As for you, sir, I hope that we meet again in circumstances that are less…constraining." He turns and heads towards the nearest table without looking back.

I make my way back to Vi's table. I lean down, mouth close to her ear and whisper, "Your father send his regards. He regrets that he will be unable to talk to you today." Then I slip past and return to the seat I vacated just a few moments before. Agnes returns a short time later, orders another bottle of wine and manages to down two thirds of it before the sounds and movements at other tables signal that the reception is ending. We say our goodbyes to Harry, Agnes and Meelie, and gratefully accept Tillie's offer to drive us to the station. Happily, there is no sign of Martin and Sara at the station, and Vi and I are soon enjoying the warmth of the carriage on the Paddington-bound train.

"Thanks for what you did back there. With Mallingford, I mean."

"Not a problem – I was only keeping my promise." There's a

brief pause, then the effect of the wine liberates my tongue. "So, who is Meelie exactly?"

"I told you – she's an old school friend. Actually, my oldest and best friend. Do you remember I told you that when I ran away I stayed with a school friend for the first two weeks? Well, that was Meelie."

"I see. And today was the first time you've seen her since?"

"Yes, first time. You seem very interested in her. I noticed when we were sitting at the table that you kept looking at her. I swear, if you weren't such a great big poof, I'd think that you fancied her."

"I certainly don't fancy her," I lie. "I think it might just be that she reminds me of someone."

I'm about to ask what more Vi learned about Meelie today when her phone pings. She takes it out and reads the message, her face increasingly clouded by fear as she does so.

"Vi, what is it? What's wrong?"

She doesn't say anything, but passes me the phone.

Caller Unknown: *Vivienne, your behaviour today was not acceptable and will have consequences. Be careful about what malicious gossip you share with your gay messenger boy, or there will be consequences for him too.*

Vi's tear-filled eyes seem half as big again as normal, dark pools of primal fear. "He's going to get me." Her voice is hoarse, barely above a whisper.

"No. No, he's not. He's an angry old man who's frustrated that you got the better of him today. He's just hitting out with idle threats to make himself feel better. He couldn't harm you even when he was in the same place as you, so he's no danger to you now." I hope my reassuring tone and smile don't seem as forced as they are.

"Yes. Yes, you're probably right."

Her eyes betray her words, but I can tell that this is not the time to pursue the conversation. I think that, if the opportunity presents itself, I will kill Mallingford. However, I have enough else on my plate right now that I can't contemplate engineering such an opportunity. Vi and I make the rest of the journey home largely in silence.

Chapter 13

Me: *Morning, Ryan. Sorry to text you so early, but I was wondering whether you had any time free this morning?*
Ryan: *Why?*
Me: *I've been thinking about what you shared with us on Monday. I've had a few ideas that I wanted to kick around with you.*
Ryan: *Sounds good. I'm free most of this morning if you want to come over.*
Me: *Thanks. I can probably be with you by half past nine.*
Ryan: *OK. See you then.*

Vi's still not up, so I drop her a quick text to let her know I've gone out and won't be back until this evening. I'm meeting Molly this afternoon, and that's likely to be tricky. If I can have a successful fishing expedition with Ryan beforehand it could provide intel that might make my session with her easier.

An hour later and I'm in Ryan's front room, sitting on the sofa below the window. Ryan is in one of the armchairs, nursing a mug of tea. Ruthie is framed in the doorway, wearing only knickers and what I presume to be a pyjama top of Ryan's. Her hands are holding the door frame on either side, her legs are long and toned, and the shape of her breasts is clear below the blue paisley material. I've not been laid for months and I find her overtly sexy pose arousing. "What can I get you?" She smiles at me.

"Sorry?"

"Tea? Coffee? Something else?"

"Oh, a tea would be lovely. Thanks."

"No problem." She turns to head to the kitchen and I can't help but notice what a fantastic arse she has. Fortunately, Ryan is looking in the same direction and misses me almost blowing my cover. He turns to me. "So, you've had a few ideas?"

"Yes. I've been looking at opportunities available to us a fortnight on Tuesday."

"Shit. When you say it like that, we really don't have long." He's leaning forward in his chair now, frowning slightly.

Ruthie re-enters the room and bends forward to hand me a mug of tea and I catch a flash of her breasts as she does so. I need to concentrate. She takes a seat in the other armchair and crosses her legs. "How is Vi? Did everything go okay at her mum's funeral?"

"It all seemed to go fine, thanks. A few issues with her father, but nothing unexpected."

Ryan is clearly impatient with what he regards as irrelevant chit chat. "Josh was just reminding me about how tight the timescales are. He's got some suggestions he was going to share." He nods for me to go on.

"We know from blowing the crane just how important thorough preparation is. I've identified four possible targets, but I wanted to sound you out to see if you think they're worthwhile before I spend any time investigating them."

Deferring to the egotistical bastard plays well with him, and all the normal non-verbal signals confirm that he is enjoying being treated as the alpha male. "Very sensible, Josh. So, let's see what you've got."

I take him through my list. Stratton Primary School in the East End. Pilton Community Centre south of the river. Drayton Park railway station. North Greenwich tube station. Ryan listens in silence, then makes a puzzled face. He turns to Ruthie, shrugs his shoulders extending his hands sideways, palms up. He swings back to focus on me. "A school and a community centre no-one's ever heard of, and two anonymous stations. It's hardly a grand statement, Josh. What are you thinking?"

"On Tuesday 22nd at 7.30 pm there are hustings taking place at both the school and the community centre. Both are in marginal constituencies and both are likely to be very well attended. In Pilton one of the candidates is Mary Montgomery – the one who resigned her seat in cabinet along with the party whip. She's standing as an independent. There's huge interest in her and that hustings will be packed with media. And…" I hope my pause for effect isn't overdone, "…both venues also double as polling stations on election day." I allow a few seconds to let this sink in, and I'm rewarded by the smile that spreads across Ryan's face.

"I'm listening now, Josh. Go on."

"At 8.00 pm Arsenal have a home tie at the Emirates Stadium in the Europa League, a game that will attract 60,000 fans. At the same time Dua Lipa is due to start her concert at the O2 Arena. That place can hold 20,000, and all the tickets sold out months ago. Between quarter and half past seven, both stations will be packed with people making their way to the two events."

I look Ryan straight in the eye and I can see that he's totally bought in. He's excited. "Good thinking, Josh. You've really been doing your homework."

"It's not that hard in all honesty. Just plug London and the date into a search engine and see what comes up. Then trawl the list for suitable candidates."

"Stop being so modest, mate. This is a work of fucking genius. Isn't that right, Ruthie?" He turns to enlist her approval, which she delivers with a nodded smile. My stomach is still recovering from the somersault it did when he called me his mate. His genuine delight at the prospect of blowing up so many innocent people cements my utter contempt for him.

"I don't know about that. These are only suggestions. There's no way we can be sure yet that they are viable targets – not without properly recceing them. And there's really not a lot of time to do that."

The chime of the doorbell interrupts whatever Ryan was about to say. He turns to Ruthie and indicates she should answer. He and I remain silent, listening intently as she opens the door. *Morning, love. This one needs a signature, I'm afraid.* Ryan casts me a relieved smile.

"There's something else to consider." I'm leaning forward, whispering. "Can I speak to you without Ruthie hearing?"

I lean back, trying not to look too much like a cartoon character caught out in a conspiracy, as Ruthie re-enters the room clutching a brown paper parcel. She places it on the sideboard just inside the doorway. "For you." she says to Ryan. "Probably that book your ordered."

"Thanks." He holds her gaze. "Do me a favour. Can you nip

down to the shop and pick up some bacon? I've got a sudden craving for it."

Everyone in the group knows that, even when he phrases something as a polite request, Ryan only ever issues instructions. There's a split second when confusion registers on Ruthie's face before it's replaced by a slightly forced smile. "Sure. No problem. Do you want anything else when I'm out?"

He shakes his head and she turns back out of the doorway. We can hear her making her way upstairs. Ryan leans towards me. "So, what do you need to tell me that you can't say in front of Ruthie?" His voice is lower than before, the tone earnest rather than threatening.

I pitch my voice to match his. "There are three key elements that will determine whether we're going to be successful. First is proper, thorough reconnaissance of the targets. I'm not being big-headed when I say that I'm confident that I can carry that out. Second is ensuring that we are supplied with the appropriate devices to attack the targets with. Again, I'm confident that you will deliver on that front." I pause as Ruthie's footsteps approach back down the stairs.

Her head appears round the door. "I'm just off now – shouldn't be more than ten minutes. Are you sure you don't want anything else?" I echo Ryan's shake of the head and she is gone. We hear the sound of the front door closing and her heels clacking against the paving stones.

"Go on, Josh. Get to it."

"The final element – the key one – is the people. The operation to bring down the crane was researched to the nth degree and the kit you supplied was perfectly on spec. When the op went wrong – I mean what happened to Jonno – we were able to recover and successfully complete the mission because there were enough of us there. Specifically, you and I were able to ensure everything went ahead."

I stop and look right at him. He holds my gaze, steadily. "And?"

"This time we're talking about as many as four separate operations running virtually simultaneously. We can't be personally involved in every one of them. *You* can't be involved in every one of them. The risk of something getting screwed up is most likely to be because an individual, or individuals, get it wrong."

His frown and the way he adjusts his position on the chair confirm that he's properly engaged with what I'm saying. "When you talk about the risk of someone getting something wrong, give me some kind of specific. Give me an example of what that could be. The one you think is most likely."

"That's virtually impossible to answer. We don't even know yet what the different variables are for any particular target – where to locate the device, what kind of device is most suitable, how to trigger it. We don't know what security is like…"

"For fuck's sake! I know all that. What I want you to tell me is your best guess of the thing most likely to go wrong." His voice has gone up an octave.

"Panic." I look him straight in the eye. "Individuals panicking. They find themselves in a high-stress situation that they have no experience of. They are fearful and sense danger. They feel isolated and the flight instinct kicks in."

Ryan is holding my gaze. "Go on."

"It's the reason that soldiers are drilled to death and conditioned to obey orders. So that when they are in combat or other extreme situations they don't panic, but do as they're told. Even then you still find some who panic." So far I'm telling him the truth. My cover is that I'm a gay soldier who quit the army because of bullying. Then I became a mercenary and was so sickened by the horrors inflicted on innocent civilians by governments of every political persuasion that I quit. My disenchantment made me a prime candidate to be taken in by Ryan's anarchist lunacy. "When you've got amateurs on the front line, no matter how committed to whatever cause they're fighting for, the number that panic then is massively higher. They often end up getting themselves and others killed."

"You're speaking from experience." He's making a statement, rather than asking a question. I nod to affirm the fiction.

Ryan suddenly gets to his feet and crosses the room to the window. He places his hands on the ledge and looks outside, saying nothing. He holds the pose for several seconds before turning and looking down at me. "What if I – we – kept control?"

"I'm not sure I understand. What do you mean?"

"You're the expert! I don't know. What if all of the devices could be detonated remotely? By me."

"You mean that four different people deliver the devices to the targets and then we detonate them remotely? That would be technically challenging, even if it's actually possible. And it still doesn't rule out someone panicking before they deliver the device to the target."

"Yes. Yes, you're right. But if we can see them or hear them we would know if they were panicking."

I can see the cogs whirring in his sick, twisted mind. I need to resist the urge to knock seven shades of shit out of him, and instead play along with his madness. "I suppose it's possible. We could use cameras like cyclists wear on their helmets, or something similar. We could use Bluetooth comms. It'd be tricky and we'd need to be careful to isolate the detonation frequency from the comms too. It'll take some working out."

He's only half-listening to me now, caught up in the crazy pictures inside his head. "We could tell them that we will detonate remotely at 7.45, but go earlier if they look like they are going to go apeshit."

"If we tell them that they need to get the devices into position by 7.30 and that they've then got fifteen minutes to get away they should be more relaxed. Particularly if all they think they need to do is to deliver the devices. No worries about setting triggers or detonating them. But, if one of them does still panic, well…"

"You could detonate their device before they get the chance to run. Turn them into a suicide bomber." I let the phrase hang in the air.

He's looking right at me, calculating before he says anything else. "Every single one of us has said they understand the risks that we might need to run if we are to achieve anything. Delivering a bomb to a target is just such a risk. But it's just the risk of getting caught, nothing else. There's no intention that we should become suicide bombers." His eyes don't waver for an instant as he delivers his homily. I tilt my head forward and look at my lap, signalling deference and making it hard for him to read my reaction. Every fibre of my being feels like there is electricity running through it. I ***know*** that what he intends is to blow up each of the poor sods in situ. The evil bastard doesn't give a shit about anyone.

"I need to recce the four potential targets ASAP – work out if they really are viable, and then spec what we would need." I pause, then look back up at him. "Is it wrong that I find this exciting?"

He visibly relaxes and smiles. "Of course it's not. This is what we are all about – taking direct action, forcing change."

I fear that I'm about to be subjected to one of his interminable rants, but the sound of a key in the front door signals that Ruthie has returned, and distracts him. I take the opportunity to make a show of checking my watch. "I've got a lot that I need to be getting on with. I can do some research online, but I have to physically recce each of the targets thoroughly to really understand them." I get to my feet. "Is it okay if I head off and make a start? And is it okay to contact you to update you and discuss what might work?"

"Of course it is, Josh. You're my main man on this now. You've got my number. Give me a bell any time. And keep me posted." He's not been caught up inside his own head at all. He's been manipulating me. He places his hand on my shoulder, almost as some sort of benediction, and I smile my gratitude. I shout my goodbyes to Ruthie, who has gone through to the kitchen, and make my exit.

Chapter 14

I hate being late for any appointment. An unexpected call from Vi to check how I feel about her inviting Meelie to dinner slowed me down, which meant I missed my connection after scouting Drayton Park station. Now I'm five minutes late for the meeting with Molly. Not a good start, given that I'm already on the back foot with her.

I can just see her through the window of *The Milton Street Bistro*, in the far back corner, side on to the street sipping a coffee, with another large mug – presumably for me – opposite her. It's part of one of the oldest buildings in this bit of the city. The internal acoustics are poor, which makes it hard for our conversations to be overheard, and the construction materials interfere with most listening technologies that a would-be eavesdropper might deploy. I push the glass door open, walk around to her table and take my seat on the wooden chair in front of the second coffee. She looks at me over the top of her mug, saying nothing.

"Thanks for getting me this." I lift my mug and toast her with it.

"You're late."

"Sorry about that. I got an unexpected call and I missed my train."

"I'm not happy, Josh."

"Okay then, which of the dwarves are you?" Big mistake. For a split second I think she might be going to throw her coffee over me.

She takes a deep breath and holds it. "Don't screw around. You are on thin enough ice as it is. No bullshit or pathetic attempts at wisecracks – just give me your report."

So, I do. I talk her through this morning's meeting with Ryan, the four prospective targets, Ryan's suggestion that he should be able to control the detonations remotely. I explain my suspicion that he is perfectly willing, perhaps even keen, to sacrifice team members.

She listens intently, interrupting only occasionally to get me to clarify or expand on something. When I finish there's a silence between us, hanging in the air like a cloud on a windless day. Just as the quiet is on the point of becoming uncomfortable, Molly breaks it. "What makes you think he's willing to sacrifice the team?"

"I don't know exactly. It's just instinct. He actually denied it, but there was a look in his eye that he couldn't disguise. I'm certain that, if he believes sacrificing group members will make the operation more successful, he wouldn't think twice about it."

"But why? *Why* spend time growing and developing a team, then...pfffft!" She simulates an explosion using her hands and fingers.

"As I say, if he thinks it would make the mission more successful, maybe? Or, in his crazy mind, he might think that massive terrorist disruption on the 22nd is job done, and that he doesn't need a team after that?"

"There might be something in that, but we're just speculating now. What isn't speculation is that this maniac is planning the greatest terrorist carnage in this country's history." She's put her half-drunk coffee on the table and is looking directly at me. "What are your next steps?"

"I need to scout the targets properly – identify locations for the bombs, determine the best kind of devices, take photographs and the like. The more credible collateral I've got to share with Ryan, the more time I can spend with him and perhaps learn more about whoever it is he's liaising with."

"Is that what you were doing yesterday and earlier today?"

"I checked out Drayton Park station earlier. Yesterday I had to attend a funeral."

Her eyes haven't left mine. She arches one eyebrow quizzically. "A funeral?"

"Yes. Vi's mother died of cancer. The funeral was yesterday and Vi asked me if I would accompany her."

"And you agreed? With all of this going on, you took a day out to go to her mother's funeral? Haven't you got your priorities a bit wrong here, Josh?"

"You don't understand. Vi was abused by her father when she was a child. She was terrified about seeing him again and needed somebody with her."

The coffee shop has got much busier while we have been talking. A couple of school-age teens are making eyes and holding hands at one table. At another there's a guy who can't seem to decide between reading his broadsheet newspaper and fiddling with his mobile phone. Three mothers with toddlers in pushchairs are engaged in animated *thank God I'm talking to another adult* conversations while their offspring sleep in their buggies. The background hubbub forces Molly to lean forward so that she can still be heard without having to speak louder. "She needed *somebody*. Did that somebody need to be you?" She pauses, leans even closer and places a hand on top of mine. "Josh, tell me you're not getting involved. Not overstepping the mark. Tell me you're not sleeping with her."

I lean in to match her. "And would it bother you if I was?"

"Don't flatter yourself, Officer Gray." Her frown underscores the depth of her anger.

Suddenly my mental radar pings. "Don't make any sudden movements, or turn round."

"What?"

"We're being watched."

"What! You're going to have to do better than that! Answer the question. Are you sleeping with one of the suspects?"

"There's a man at a table over your shoulder, right up by the counter. Maybe mid-thirties, short brown hair, smart suit." There's the briefest flash of something in Moll's eyes – recognition, maybe? "He's been fiddling with his phone and reading a broadsheet newspaper. Nobody under the age of fifty or sixty buys a newspaper anymore – especially not if they have a mobile phone. He's not reading the paper, he's using it to hide behind while he tries to watch us. I think he's realised I've clocked him."

The guy gets to his feet, manoeuvres his way through tables and chairs to the door and exits, all while managing to avert his face from me, other than when he casts the briefest of glances towards us as he reaches the door.

"It's okay, he's gone now."

"You can try the *Oh look – there's a squirrel* routine all you like, Josh, but I'm not buying it. Stop avoiding the question. Are you sleeping with a member of the group that you are engaged in surveillance of? It's a simple enough question."

Her eyes are boring into mine. I used to think they were the most beautiful eyes in the world. That she was the most beautiful woman in the world. But that was when I loved her and was stupid enough to believe she loved me. Before she showed that the only thing she really loved was her career.

"No, I am not sleeping with Vi. My cover is that I'm a gay ex-soldier, for God's sake. Why would I jeopardise that?"

"Okay, Josh – I had to ask. This operation is too huge to run any unnecessary risks. I believe you." I can see that she does. "What did you learn at Drayton Park?"

"It's a national rail station. Conventional two-platform suburban set up. They shut it prior to weekend matches and after all other matches because of safety concerns, in case the narrow island platform becomes overcrowded. A device positioned inside the station building or on the staircase to the platform would have the greatest impact." Moll visibly shudders as she considers the implications of my words.

We discuss next steps. I outline my provisional timescales for scouting the targets in more detail and then meeting up with Ryan again. She explains that she is required to phone the AC to update her on our meeting immediately after we finish. She also has a face-to-face meeting scheduled with the AC tomorrow. Since the danger posed by the group was highlighted, a massive anti-terrorist operation has been mobilised, and we are now just a subset of that. The AC is our link to the wider operation and, if there's any intel from her meeting with Moll that could help me, I'll get a text to my safe phone.

I'm ready and waiting for Molly to dig me up about the attack on the woman last week when I beat up the two goons, but she doesn't mention it. She's smart enough to have decided that we have much bigger fish to fry, and time raking over those events would be wasted. We agree that things are happening so fast now that we can't leave it another week for our next meeting. We set the default as this same venue, at 11 am in three days' time. If something urgent comes to light before then on either side, we will communicate by text. I need to adapt my schedule to check my safe phone each day.

"If I head off now, I should be able to scout North Greenwich tube station. Elton John has sold out the O2 tonight on his latest farewell tour, so I'll get a good feel for how crowded the station is when it's coping with a big event at the arena."

"Makes sense. I'm going to hang on here and phone the AC."

"No problem." I get to my feet, preparing to leave.

"Josh."

"Yes?"

"You will be careful, won't you?"

"Always." I give her an empty smile and head out.

The streets are getting busier with both traffic and pedestrians as rush hour draws near. I'm familiar enough with this area to know that, apart from shop security cams, there's no other CCTV to have to take into consideration. I've got plenty of time to get to North Greenwich and I'm playing over what I saw at Drayton Park earlier when the hairs on the back of my neck stand to attention.

Every sense switches to overdrive as I enter full alert mode, while making sure I don't break stride or give any other signal that betrays the fact I know I'm either being watched or followed. There's a Tesco Metro fifty metres ahead on the other side of the road that's got a stand outside the front dispensing free copies of the Evening Standard. I stop on the edge of the pavement, wait for a break in the traffic, then cross. My peripheral vision is excellent and the man who was watching me in the bistro almost certainly won't realise that I've sussed him.

I pick up a copy of the paper and make a show of checking the headlines, which lets me clock the fact that he's following me across the road. I fold the paper under my arm and take a sharp right turn down an alleyway between the Tesco store and the next shop. The building on the left is shallower, running only half the length of the supermarket on my right. I duck left into an empty loading bay which runs down to a quiet service road at the rear, and press my back against the wall.

I don't have long to wait until my pursuer rounds the corner and finds himself face-to-face with me. Despite the fact that he's been following me, he seems confused to have found me. I grab him by the shoulder and pull him roughly into the loading bay. "Okay then! Who are you?"

"More like who are you?" He has a particularly plummy voice which somehow accentuates the tone of indignation that accompanies his words. He raises both fists and begins bobbing on the balls of his feet. There's something faintly ridiculous about him. Serious players don't allow themselves to be spotted as easily as him, and they certainly don't adopt Marquis of Queensberry rules when it comes to a confrontation.

"I'll ask you one more time. Who the hell are you?"

"I'm Freddie Forsyth." He seems surprised that I don't immediately recognise him. "I'm Molly Leishman's boyfriend." He comes towards me, swinging both fists. I'm able to sidestep him easily.

"Look, Freddie, I've no idea what your problem is, but…"

He lunges at me again, and one of his swings connects full-square with my jaw. "***You're*** my problem, matey-boy." He's breathing heavily as he turns and throws another punch.

I parry the attempted blow with my wrist. "Freddie, I have no idea what you think you're doing – but if you keep trying to attack me, you'll regret it."

"I doubt that very much." He's shouting now, as he comes at me again. He's quicker than I anticipate this time, and his fist glances off my temple. The weight he's put into the punch carries his whole body past me, and I spin through a hundred and eighty degrees and crouch right down to waist height behind him. As he turns back to have another go at me, I spring up to my full height and smash the heel of my left hand into his face. The feel of his nose breaking is as satisfying as the gloopy crunching noise, before he staggers backwards, both palms over his face in a vain attempt to stem the flow of red.

He is eventually backed up against the air conditioning

condenser abutting the rear of the building, water-filled eyes peering back at me from above his mitts. Blood is oozing out below his hands, and a large bead forms on his chin before dropping with a splat on to his left black Oxford brogue and splashing back on to his trouser leg.

He flinches as I step towards him, before accepting the handkerchief I'm proffering. He touches the cloth to his nose and winces with pain, before positioning it to staunch the flow of blood. His resentful eyes never leave mine for a second.

"I'm not sorry I hit you, Freddie. You left me no choice. And I'm not sorry I bust your nose either. I'm sure it hurts like hell, and I'm glad about that. Perhaps in future you'll be more minded to engage in jaw-jaw rather than war-war. I've no idea who this Leishman woman is that you're talking about. If you've got girlfriend problems, I suggest you sort them out, rather than attacking total strangers. You were lucky that I'm in a seriously forgiving mood."

I take a pace closer to him and lean in towards him. "But if I ever – ever – see you again, you will be a hospital in-patient for a very long time. Do I make myself clear?" He appears frozen. I lean in closer and shout, "Kapiche?"

His eyes widen even further and he nods his head just sufficiently for it to be perceptible. I step away, turn and make my way back up the alley. What a waste of a good linen handkerchief.

As I step out of the alley into the street, my cartoon double-take is mirrored by Molly, twenty metres away, walking towards me in the same direction as I intend to go. She approaches with an exaggerated expression of confusion. "I thought you'd be well on your way to North Greenwich."

"I would have been, if your boyfriend hadn't decided to provide a diversion."

"What? What on earth are you talking about?" Her expression has morphed into one of genuine puzzlement.

"The man watching us in the bistro – you remember? Well, he was waiting outside and tailed me. He followed me down that alley," I nod back over my shoulder, "and then announced he was Freddie Forsyth, your boyfriend, and that I was a problem. Then he attacked me."

Moll's face is a study in horror. She grabs my arm and pulls me into a shop doorway. "What do you mean, he attacked you?"

"What the fuck do you think I mean, Moll? He came at me, swinging. He wouldn't talk or even try to see reason."

"Shit! Did he hurt you?"

"No. I'm bigger, stronger and faster than him."

"Good." There's a pause as she continues to look up at me. "Did you hurt him?"

"I left him with a face like a stuntman's knee, but there's no long term damage. He'll mend okay, although maybe just not as pretty as before. But seriously, Moll, you need to have a word with him. The guy was acting like he's deranged." I can feel my anger rising. "And you need to take a fucking good look at yourself. You allowed yourself to be followed to the bistro, and compromised the meeting. A meeting where you were quizzing me on whether my personal relationships were jeopardising the operation. How fucking ironic is that?"

"He's not my boyfriend, Josh." She's looking right at me. "I went out with him twice – last time on Saturday night. He was a nice enough guy, but I knew it wasn't going to go anywhere, so I ended it with him on Monday. By phone." She looks slightly sheepish. "He didn't take it well. He phoned back three times and kept asking me to reconsider. He wouldn't put the phone down, so I ended up having to hang up on him. He kept calling, texting and leaving voice messages. Eventually, I just blocked his number. To be honest, I never gave him a second thought after that. I certainly didn't think he would follow me, although I accept that I should have taken precautions."

"And now he's gone full-on stalker. Do you want me to go back and warn him off properly?" Her explanation has taken the wind out of my sails.

She looks up at me, eyes ablaze. "Freddie Forsyth doesn't intimidate me one single iota. You can leave me to deal with him by myself. He's not the brightest – in fact he's about as sharp as a bowling ball. Once I've finished with him, you can be absolutely sure that he will not be interfering in my business or in any police business again." I have no idea what plan she has to sort Freddie Forsyth out, but I'm very pleased that I'm not him.

"Okay – if you're sure." She nods. "Right then, I'd better be on my way to North Greenwich." I give her a mini-wave, which she returns, before I turn and take a break in traffic as my opportunity to cross the road.

Once on the other side I up my pace and don't look back. I try to think ahead to what I need to recce when I get there, but I'm finding it hard to concentrate. I don't care about Moll any more. So why, when this Freddie character announced himself as her boyfriend, did it feel so satisfying to smash his face? Why, when I realised he was stalking her, did I genuinely want to go back down that alley and give him a proper doing?

Chapter 15

It's dark and raining lightly as I make the quarter-mile walk home from the bus stop. The sodium streetlights wear orange haloes as their light reflects back off the wet tarmac.

The trip to North Greenwich was worthwhile. Even though I'd been there several times before on my way to events at the O2, I'd never cased the place as a target to attack. My online research had shown that it only opened in 1999, so it's very much a modern station compared to most of the rest of the network. It was designed to cope with large numbers of visitors using the arena, and is capable of handling 20,000 passengers in an hour.

When I was there it was useful to be reminded of how the concourse is open and cavernous, under a high corrugated metal ceiling. The right kind of device going off there would likely cause more casualties than anywhere else in the station. PETN combined with either TNT or, more likely, RDX would deliver maximum impact if triggered when the place is thronged with concert-goers, as it was earlier this evening. Aside from triggering the device at the optimum time, the other challenge will be security. There were a number of stewards positioned around the station, and simply leaving the device in the middle of the concourse is going to see it identified immediately. Which means Ryan is likely to find the notion of using someone expendable as a delivery mule more attractive.

As I get closer to home, voices, both male and female – maybe four in total, interrupt my train of thought and alert me to the presence of others around the corner about seventy metres ahead. Although the words are indistinct, I'm pretty sure that the accents are from the north east. Two pairs of figures appear out of the gloom, four pinpricks of orange either in front of their faces or held by their sides signal that they are all smokers. The streetlight reflects off four shaven heads, and I can see each of them is in uniform – Harrington jacket, probably green but hard to be sure under the artificial light, rolled-up denim jeans or

Levi sta-prest trousers that reach just over halfway down their shins, above Doc Marten's Astronauts or AirWair.

Their voices drop lower, before disappearing into silence as they become aware of my presence. I continue forward, studiously avoiding eye contact. Moll's perennial advice about not getting involved in anything avoidable makes perfect sense. These young adults – I reckon late teens, maybe early twenties – haven't done anything to provoke me. I suspect they're looking for trouble, brazenly wandering around in full skinhead gear in such a multicultural, ethnically-mixed area. They probably get a kick out of intimidating people just through their appearance. It crosses my mind that they might be responsible for the swastikas and other right wing graffiti in the entrance to the flats. I step off the pavement in a sign of deference and, as we pass, I can smell that at least one of the cigarettes is a joint. I don't look behind me, and can soon hear their conversation pick up again before it fades as the distance between us grows.

I check my wristwatch as I pass below the streetlamp on the next corner, where I turn left towards our block of flats – twenty past nine. I wonder if Vi got hold of Meelie. I did say that I might have to work a few extra hours to cover at the hotel, so not to bother waiting for me to eat. The prospect that Meelie might be at the flat has me feeling ambivalent. There's something about her that makes me feel a bit unsettled, but there's also no denying that she is absolutely gorgeous. I realise that my pace has quickened without me thinking about it.

I turn the key and push the door open.

"That'll be Josh now." Vi's voice is conversational, before she raises it for my benefit, "Is that you, Josh?"

"Yes, just hanging up my jacket."

"Come through and join us. Meelie's here."

The hallway lightbulb needs replacing and I enter the living room blinking, as my eyes adjust to brightness. Vi and Meelie are sitting at a ninety degree angle to each other at the little square dining table, both looking up at me. I can see that, like for her mother's funeral, Vi has made a real effort with her appearance. She's wearing make-up, has straightened her hair and is wearing the lovely pink cashmere cardigan with pearlescent buttons that she only ever wears for special occasions. It's clear that she wants to create a favourable impression with Meelie, and I think that's a good thing.

But my focus is drawn to our visitor, whose huge, sparkly eyes capture my attention and hold it like a tractor beam. She has thick, shoulder-length straight raven hair so shiny that she could earn a living as a model for shampoo adverts on TV. Her flawless pale skin contrasts with Vi's darker complexion and accentuates her Ferrari red lipstick. Her lips are parted in a grin that showcases teeth which would make a dentist swoon. She looks like a star from the golden age of Hollywood, transported to a grotty flat in 21st century London.

"Aren't you going to say hello, and apologise for your rudeness in being so late?" Vi's teasing breaks the spell.

"Oh. What? Sorry – yes. Yes. Hello, Meelie – lovely to see you again." I flash her what I hope is my best smile and turn to Vi. "I did say I might have to work late and not to wait for me." I see used plates and cutlery on the table. "And I see that you've taken me at my word."

"I'm only joshing with you, Josh." She giggles at what I suspect wasn't intended as a pun. "Oops! Have you eaten? There's some lasagne left that I can re-heat in the microwave, if you're hungry."

"No, I'm fine, thanks. I was in the kitchens at the hotel this evening and managed to grab myself something there." I actually had a particularly foul burger from a van near the bus station.

"Okay. Fetch yourself a glass from the kitchen and join us."

I do as I am bid and return with a wine glass, before taking a place at the table with Vi on my left and Meelie opposite. There's an unopened bottle of red and a white that is just under half full.

"Is white all right for you, Josh?" Meelie beams a smile as she hovers the neck of the bottle above my glass.

"Yes, that'd be lovely. Thank you."

"Oh, thank goodness for that." She's still smiling as her eyes focus on pouring my drink. "I poured that…" she nods at Vi's half full glass, "…at the start of the meal, and she's nursed it ever since. I was beginning to feel like a lush, drinking by myself."

"You needn't worry about that any more. Cheers!" I clink my glass against hers.

"We were just talking about the funniest thing before you came in." Vi smiles and nods at Meelie. "Go on Meels, tell Josh about it."

"Oh, god. Really Veeva? I'm sure Josh doesn't want to be bored to death by stories from our schooldays." She rolls those beautiful eyes and feigns exasperation, before laughing.

"Yes he does. It's funny. You do want to hear, don't you, Josh?"

I nod to Meelie.

"Okay then, but I did warn you!" That beguiling smile again, and a bit of the devil flashing in her eyes. "Well, when Veeva and I were about fourteen, we both had the most enormous crush on a history teacher called Mr. Forrester. I think that it must have been his first ever teaching role, and…"

Meelie goes on to tell a genuinely funny story, largely at her own expense, that causes me to laugh out loud. It is the prelude to one of the most enjoyable evenings of conversation that I've had in as long a time as I can remember. Vi and Meelie spark off of, and clearly enjoy, each other's company enormously. They are both polite and take care to involve me enough so that I don't feel like I'm intruding. The bottle of red is soon open, with Meelie and me teasing Vi about being a lightweight for not having any. I have never seen Vi like this before – and it dawns on me that she is *happy*. Meelie's energy and *joie de vivre* seem to transmit and take root in Vi, and I can see a hint of the potential she must have had before she suffered so terribly at the hands of Mallingford.

However, it is Meelie who has me mesmerised. I sense that she really cares about Vi and that she is here to support her old friend following her bereavement. While she is sparkling and witty and fun, I can see how attentive she is to Vi's vulnerability. She is kind and compassionate, instinctively. And, my god, she is beautiful. She uses her hands a lot for emphasis, and throws her head back often when she laughs her throaty, sexy laugh. Her lips are perfect, and I find myself jealous of her glass, with its traces of lipstick left behind when she sips her wine. But it is those stunning, wonderful eyes, flashing and dancing and so full of life – her eyes are what hypnotise me.

"Isn't that right, Josh?" The tone of Vi's voice means this isn't the first time she's asked whatever she's asking.

"Sorry, I was miles away."

"Are we keeping you up?"

"Just a long shift at work, that's all. Now what were you saying?"

"Meelie was just saying how much she likes a man with a beard, and I said that you'd only shaved yours off less than a week ago." They're both looking right at me.

"Yes, that's right. I thought I should try to look smart for Vi's mum's funeral. And anyway, I'd been thinking about shaving it off for a while anyway."

"I bet it was a real hipster job." Meelie is tilting her head to the side, and arches an eyebrow.

Before I can answer, Vi cuts across me. "Good god, no! He had a full, thick hairy number. It was horrible – always full of breakfast, or whatever the last meal was that he'd eaten." She breaks into a giggle.

"Oi! Steady on, you! I'd grown quite attached to that beard. And anyway, you never said anything." I straighten my back and tilt my chin in mock indignation.

"I'm sure that it was a lovely beard." Meelie coos sympathetically. "And a very useful snack box as well." The two women dissolve into giggles.

"How dare you!" I play to the gallery by dialling up my false pique.

"Oh no! I've just realised the time." Meelie is looking at her phone and does seem genuinely surprised. "It's quarter to midnight, and I've got an early appointment in the morning."

I've got a shedload of things to do tomorrow, so a late, boozy night isn't ideal for me either. But I'd happily sit up drinking and chatting for hours yet, just to be in Meelie's company.

"Shall I call you a taxi?" Vi has got her phone out now too.

"Oh, yes – thanks."

"Where shall I tell them it's taking you?"

"Little Venice, please."

"Sounds like whatever job you've got pays pretty well," I venture, as Molly makes the call to the cab firm.

"It's just a bedsit, although the rent is eye-watering. To be honest – and this is a bit embarrassing – if my parents didn't help me out, I wouldn't be able to afford it. But it's a great place to live, and really handy for work." Her voice is lowered to just above a whisper, so as not to distract Vi on her phone.

I find myself automatically whispering my response. "You didn't actually say what your job is."

"I flatter myself by saying that I'm a journalist. I work for The Herald." She's unable to disguise the note of pride in her voice as she tells me.

"All booked. Your car will be here in two minutes." Vi's breezy interjection shatters the precious intimacy of our whispered conversation.

"Meelie was just explaining to me that she's a journalist with The Herald."

"Yes, we were talking about that before you got back. We need to make sure we buy The Herald, and look out for her byline – Amelia Harris."

SHIIIIT!

Shit, shit, shit! The woman who was attacked in the alleyway! Amelia! Oh shit!

Has she clocked me yet? I can't believe I didn't recognise her. She was a complete mess when I first saw her, but I should have recognised those eyes. And she's a journalist! How much worse could this be? I need my poker face. If she hasn't recognised me, I don't want to send any signal that might alert her.

"That sounds very impressive, Meelie. A journalist with The Herald! Well done you."

"I say journalist, but I'm really just a junior reporter. I'm sure they only keep me on because I'm willing to work for peanuts." She's looking right into my eyes, and I don't know whether she's assessing me, or whether I'm imagining it.

"I'm sure you're just being modest." We exchange smiles.

Vi's phone buzzes. "That's your cab already!"

The next few minutes pass in a blur of hugs, thankyous, goodbyes and I'll-call-you-tomorrows, and Meelie is gone. I say my goodnights to Vi, carry out my ablutions and go to my bedroom. I put out the light and lie down to contemplate how much more complicated life has just become.

Chapter 16

A particularly fitful night's sleep, but it's 5.50 am, so I'm awake. I reach across and switch off the bedside alarm, set to go off five minutes hence. Inventory time.

I need to get to my safe phone and check for any texts from Moll.

Probably need to bring my safe phone to the flat. I think the risk is minimal and I can't afford the time to travel to it daily.

Do I tell Moll about Meelie – Amelia Harris? My whole cover might be compromised.

Did Meelie recognise me? Was the beard discussion her signalling that she did?

I need to recce Stratton Primary School and Pilton Community Centre.

I need to set up another meeting with Ryan.

If I go south of the river to Pilton, then swing back east to the school, I can pick up my phone after that, and then decide on next steps.

It's ten to eight, and bright and chilly when I get to the community centre – a sprawling timber-clad single-storey structure set between a parade of shops and a small library. The area suffers from what commentators condescendingly call "deprivation", and is a favoured field trip destination for A-level human geography students doing case studies into urban poverty.

Surprisingly, given the area, there's no sign of CCTV anywhere other than above the convenience store a good eighty metres away from the community centre. An elderly man in overalls that have seen better days is struggling with the keys to the reinforced glass doors to the place. I introduce myself as Peter Watson, on my way home from nightshift and just wanting to make a quick enquiry about hiring the main hall for my wedding reception next year. He tells me to come back after nine, when the staff who deal with that sort of thing will be in.

I look disappointed, feign stifling a yawn and say something about needing to get to my bed. He takes pity on me, lets me in and gives me a quick guided tour.

The janitor shows me the large hall with its sizable stage and explains, proudly, that it can accommodate five hundred people seated in its main body. We discuss what kind of band I might want and whether I would want the centre to do catering for the reception, whilst I calculate the likely layout of the hall for the hustings, and where the optimum place would be to place the device. He's happy to let me take photos on my phone to share with my fiancé. Just after ten past eight I'm saying my goodbyes and thankyous, taking the leaflet with the centre's contact details, and reassuring him that my fiancé will be in touch with the staff sometime in the next week or so to arrange a booking.

Two tube trains and a short two minute walk deliver me to the end of Bosworth Road, in east London, just after ten o' clock. Stratton Primary School is at the far end of the road, a 1980s rebuild on the site of the original Victorian school. It's a single storey concrete edifice surrounded by a tarmac playground, enclosed on all sides by a seven foot high wire fence. Despite a set of swings and a see-saw, it looks like nothing so much as a prison - a notion heightened by the prevalence of security cameras in virtually every strategic position. From a distance of fifty metres, it's clear from the layout and surprisingly high levels of security that the school is simply not a viable target. I turn on my heel and head back towards the tube.

An underground ride and a bus journey deliver me to the warehouse at 11.00 am, and by quarter past I've retrieved my 'safe' phone and am seated in my favoured corner seat by the window in the virtually deserted coffee shop, with a cappuccino. I plug the phone into the charging socket and immediately see the red dot signifying that I have a text message. It's from Molly, timed just twenty minutes ago. *Had my meet with the AC. Imperative we talk ASAP.*

I press dial and she picks up on the first ring. *That was quicker than I thought you might be. I take it you're okay to talk?*

"I'm fine. I just saw the message to call ASAP. What's the

feedback from the AC?"

I had told her on the phone yesterday about the four targets that you had proposed to Ryan. At this morning's meeting she said that another agency had corroborated your intelligence.

"What? How can that be possible?"

*That was what she said – **corroborated**. So, who is this other agency's source?*

My brain clicks into top gear. "I told Ryan, as you know. Ruthie was there too. No-one else. That means it has to be one or other of them, or they've mentioned it to someone else who has fed it back." I pause briefly. "There's no chance that it's Ryan, and he is far too careful to have mentioned it to anyone else. Which means that it has to be Ruthie, or someone that she's told. Did the AC hint at which other agency had provided corroboration?"

No way – she's far too cute for that. It could be counter-terrorism – MI5, or it might be MI6 if there are foreign nationals involved. Maybe it's the NDEU or NETCU – who knows? It could be a spook from some outfit we've never heard of, or it could be from some foreign intelligence source. If there's someone else undercover on this case the protocols don't allow us to have an ID. The same protocols that protect you, Josh.

"Understood. I think it has to be Ruthie. Except…"

Except what?

"Except she is sleeping with Ryan, and doing so overtly. Such blatant contravention of APP section 7.5 makes me think it can't be her. Unless she's not governed by Authorised Professional Practice restrictions."

Well, someone's the source.

"Yes. I'll tread warily. There's something else, Moll."

Go on.

"Amelia Harris is an old friend of Vi's. She came to dinner at the flat last night."

The assault victim? Tell me you are kidding! Her voice sounds like broken glass.

"They hadn't seen each other in years, then met at the funeral. Vi invited her to dinner."

Jesus Christ Almighty! Did she recognise you? Are you blown?

"Honestly? I don't know." And I really don't. "I had long hair and a beard on the night she was attacked, so maybe not. She didn't give off any signals that she recognised me."

She's a fucking journalist, Josh! If she suspects there's something dodgy about you she's not going to blow her cover. She's going to dig around until she finds out more. And don't you think the whole thing's suspicious?

"What do you mean?"

She hasn't seen Vi for years, but then turns up at the funeral. Where you are in attendance, just days after you interrupted her attackers. That didn't set alarm bells ringing in that tiny fucking mind of yours?

Moll's right. It's one hell of a coincidence. I feel like a total plum for not even considering it until now. "No. Not until you mentioned it now."

You were explicitly told not to get involved in exactly the kind of shit that you did. And now you might have compromised the whole operation. I despair of you, Josh!

"What do you want me to say?"

Sorry might be a fucking good place to start. But let's not waste time on that now. I need to report this back to the AC and get her instructions. Is there anything else you've got for me?

"I've recce'd all four targets. Three are a go, but the school is a non-starter. I was hoping to get hold of Ryan to update him, and see what else I might be able to get from him."

Good – the AC says that your intel is vital to the wider investigation. We need as much info as possible, as quickly as possible. Anything else?

"I'm intending to take this phone back to the flat. I'm going to need to be in much more regular contact, and I can't afford the time to trail off to the safe location to get it every time."

Are you sure that's safe?

"As sure as I can be. Vi's never once been in my room and I can keep it on silent and hide it well out of sight."

Your call, Josh. If you get a meet set up with Ryan let me know immediately. Check for texts from me regularly. I'll let you know what the AC says. Goodbye.

"Goodbye." I need to get back to the flat ASAP and hide this phone. Then I must get a meet with Ryan. I *can't* let this whole op go belly up now.

As I round the corner of Holmesmeath Way, and the block containing the flat that is home comes into view, I can see immediately that something is wrong. Seriously wrong. There are two – no three – sets of blue flashing lights atop police squad cars positioned around the front of the flats. There are uniformed police officers looking busy, as well as a knot of perhaps half a dozen onlookers. There's a sizeable area in front of the flats cordoned off with yellow and black barricade tape, so something's really amiss.

I cover the two hundred metres quickly and make my way past the gaggle of rubberneckers towards the communal front door of the block. There is a narrow corridor between a low wall and the tape, presumably to allow access for residents. The taped off area includes the communal bin store and the wide expanse of paving slabs in front of them, and extends beyond out into the street and for several metres to the left. It's a big area – a few hundred square metres. But, more ominously, there's a second, much smaller area just in front of the bins with a rectangle of cones connected by red barrier tape. I know, just by looking, that the stain on the slabs is blood.

I'm approached by a serious looking constable. "Excuse me, sir. Can I ask if you are a resident of this block? Because if not I'll have to ask you to stand over there." He points in the direction of the rather bored looking bystanders.

"I do live here, officer. Flat 6, on the second floor." I nod in the direction of the front window of our flat.

"Flat 6?" His business-like expression immediately transforms to become pensive. "And can I ask your name, sir."

"Josh Gray." I feel frustration at the formalities, but I understand that he has to follow procedure.

"Would you mind waiting here, just for a minute, sir?" He waits for my nodded assent then turns and walks over to two other officers, an inspector and a sergeant, who are standing on the far side of the Red Zone. There's an exchange as he reports who I am, some glances in my direction, and a quick discussion between all three, before the constable strides back in my direction accompanied by the inspector.

"Mr. Gray, I am Inspector Lorraine Watt. I wonder whether I could speak to you inside the building, please?" It's a command phrased as a request, and she turns and starts walking briskly towards the door, followed by both the constable and me. Once we are inside she turns to face me. "It might be better if we talk inside your flat. This communal area is more private than outside, but only by a degree."

I am already making my way upstairs at pace, with the other two right behind. I search the key from my pocket on the way up, so that there is no delay when we arrive at the door. Once inside I lead them to the living room.

"May we sit down, Josh? May I call you Josh?" Her entire attention is on me now. I nod yes to both questions and follow her signal to also sit down. "Do you live in this flat with Vivienne Ambrose?" I nod yet again. "And can I ask what your relationship is to Miss Ambrose?"

"Oh, for God's sake! Just tell me what's happened! Is she dead?"

"Miss Ambrose is not dead." Inspector Watt is deploying the classic tactic of lowering her voice to promote calm. "Can I ask again what your relationship is with her?"

"We live together." It's an ambiguous answer that I hope will make the inspector feel legitimised to speak candidly to me. I follow up quickly to prevent her asking for more specifics about my relationship to Vi. "If she's not dead, then what's happened? It's obviously serious."

"I'm very sorry, Josh, but Miss Ambrose is the victim of a serious assault. She has been taken by ambulance to The Princess Royal Infirmary."

"Shit! What's happened to her? How serious are her injuries?" I'm already surmising that this has something to do with Mallingford.

"I can't comment on how serious the injuries are, although I do know that she was unconscious when the ambulance took her. We will arrange transport for you to the hospital, but I'd like to ask you a few questions first. Is that all right with you?"

She's doing her job, and doing it properly. "Yes."

"Thank you. Can you think of anyone who might want to harm Miss Ambrose? Anyone with a grudge or a grievance?"

I certainly can, but I'm not going to say anything. "Vi hasn't got any enemies that I can think of."

"Are you sure? She hasn't mentioned anyone or anything that might provide a clue?"

"No. Nothing. Please tell me what's happened. What do you know?"

Inspector Watt morphs seamlessly from professional inquisitor to compassionate messenger. She leans forward and softens her already lowered voice, speaking slowly and clearly. "We believe that Miss Ambrose is the victim of a sustained, brutal attack that was racially motivated."

My mind is reeling with all sorts of questions and emotions, but all I can manage to articulate is "What?"

"We have a witness who has been able to provide us with a very detailed account of what happened." She's looking at me, assessing how robust I am, and how to pitch it.

"I understand. Please tell me what happened. I need to know."

"The witness is Mrs. Petrescu, from Flat 1 on the ground floor. Mrs. Petrescu was leaving the block this morning at half past ten, with her babies in a pushchair. There were four people, two men and two women who she describes as what we would recognise as skinheads, loitering in front of the building near the bins."

She pauses to let me digest the information. I know who the witness is, and I'm certain the four individuals are the ones I passed yesterday evening. I nod encouragement for her to continue.

The four individuals were shouting abuse at Mrs. Petrescu. They called her a series of names including gipsy, refugee, scrounger and asylum seeker. The two women were taking the lead, egged on by the two men. They surrounded her and threatened to snatch a baby and put it in a bin."

"Bastards."

"Mrs. Petrescu was paralysed by fear. She didn't even think to try to get back inside to her own flat to get help from her husband. He is a nightshift worker and was asleep, oblivious to the attack on his wife. It was at this point that Miss Ambrose approached the scene from the street. She was carrying a bag of groceries so we believe she was returning form the local shopping parade."

There's another pause, before she continues. "Miss Ambrose moved to stand next to Mrs. Petrescu and started shouting at her tormentors, demanding that they leave her alone and go away. It appears that this led them to focus all of their attention and abuse on Miss Ambrose. The witness remembers one of them calling her 'a filthy fucking n-word'. It appears the exchange escalated quickly and the two females attacked Miss Ambrose, knocking her to the ground and kicking her repeatedly as she lay prone. The witness describes one woman jumping on her head while the other continued to kick viciously at her torso."

The description makes me feel sick.

"Josh, I'm terribly sorry. Can we get you anything? A cup of tea perhaps?"

"I'm fine, thanks." Of course, I'm not at all fine, and my voice is barely a whisper.

"All right. Just a couple more questions, then Constable Reilly will arrange transport for you to the Infirmary." I nod for her to go on. "This may seem insensitive, but I do need to ask. Based on the account of events from the witness, we are assuming that Miss Ambrose is black. Is that correct?"

"Vi is mixed race. Her late mother was black and her father is white."

"I see, thank you. Can I ask you again please, Josh, can you think of anyone with a motive to harm Miss Ambrose, to harm Vi?"

"No, I can't. But I think I saw group who attacked her when I was on my way home to the flat last night."

My revelation leads to a flurry of further questions and note taking, as they seek to gather every detail possible. I tell them everything I can remember, although I'm pretty sure that none of it adds anything, other than the belief that all four had northern accents.

Eventually that line of questioning is exhausted and Inspector Watt is in wrap-up mode. "Is there anyone else you would like us to contact? You mentioned Vi's father."

"No. She and her father are estranged."

"Okay, understood. There's a car waiting downstairs to get you to the hospital. We'll be in touch again. Meantime, I hope that Vi is all right."

"Thank you."

I've been waiting in the hospital for 45 minutes. I still have my safe phone with me and have texted Moll to advise her about the attack on Vi. I've not heard anything back. I'm trying to apply logic to the situation in an effort to suppress the feelings of anger and dread.

My maternal grandmother is a Tamil. Unless someone knew that, they would judge from my pigmentation that I'm completely white, with no hint of mixed race. My sister, Mel, one year my junior, has the same skin tone as me. My younger sister, Evie, who is three years younger has exactly the same skin colour as our grandmother. I watched how she was treated differently from Mel and me by strangers, kids at school and even some members of our extended family. Not everyone, by any stretch of the imagination, but way more than enough for it to matter. I have hated racism in all its forms ever since I saw Evie fall victim to it. The attack on Vi has stirred all that up again and it would not take much for my anger to explode.

I also know what the red barrier tape at the crime scene means. They think that this is likely to turn into a murder inquiry, presumably based on the injuries they observed to Vi. Getting SOCO in to capture the maximum amount of forensic evidence as early as possible, particularly with an outdoor crime scene, is just good policing. I almost wish I didn't understand all of that, as it simply fuels my sense of dread.

I need to focus, to think this through logically. I need to understand if the attack on Vi was just random, or whether there is any link between the skinheads and Mallingford. They were giving Mrs. Petrescu a hard time before Vi intervened, so maybe it was just random. Or maybe they'd seen her go out with her shopping bag and knew she'd soon back from the local shop, and were waiting? There's not enough evidence – yet – to know anything for certain. I'm sure that all four of them sounded northern. What does that mean, if anything? Does it matter? Whatever the doctors say, it's obvious that Vi is not going to be able to play any sort of active role in Ryan's group for a very long time, if ever. I need to contact Ryan to explain what's happened to Vi, as well as report my intel from recceing the targets. The potential size of what Ryan and others are planning is massive, and has to be my focus. I need to find out everything I can, otherwise god alone knows how many more innocent lives will be at risk. What has happened to Vi is terrible. Horrible. And it needs investigating and sorting, but it can't be my priority. I need to stay focused. To stay in control.

"Mr. Gray?" The voice shakes me out of my introspection and I turn to see a short, ginger-haired and bearded man in his forties, wearing green scrubs.

"Yes."

He takes his seat on the vacant plastic chair adjacent to the one I'm sitting on and leans forward towards me. "I understand that you are Vivienne Ambrose's partner?"

I nod rather than say the lie out loud.

"I am Mr. Colquhoun, Vivienne's consultant. We have managed to stabilise her, for now."

"That's good," is all I can manage, waiting for the inevitable but.

"But I need to advise you that her injuries are most severe."

"How severe?"

"It is still very early days, Mr Gray. There are a number of tests that we need to run, and how her body responds over the next 24, 48 and 72 hours will be crucial. We'll know more then."

"I understand, Mr. Colquhoun. But you must already have your initial prognosis. I understand it might change, but I'd like to know how bad things are." I pause. "Please?"

There's a hint of a sigh. "Vivienne has suffered severe head trauma and, although we will need scans and test results to assess the degree, I'm afraid you need to prepare yourself for the likelihood that she has suffered brain damage. Both her lungs have been punctured, her collar bone is broken and she has a total of nine broken ribs. She lost a considerable amount of blood from internal injuries, mainly from the abdomen." He pauses and I can sense that he is steeling himself.

"What else?"

"I'm afraid that we were unable to save the babies. Sorry."

"Babies?"

"Yes. Vivienne was, I'd estimate, somewhere between thirteen and fifteen weeks pregnant with twins." He pauses and looks at me quizzically. "You did know?"

"Not that it was twins. I didn't…" My voice tails off into nothingness and my head is swimming.

"Would you like to see her? I need to warn you that she is attached to various pieces of equipment, including a ventilator, and that her face is badly disfigured as a result of the assault that she has suffered." He pauses to let this sink in. "So, would you like to see her?"

"No. No, I'm not ready for that. I need to go outside and get some air. Can I visit later?"

"Yes. Yes, of course. You can visit whenever you like. Please can I ask that you leave your contact details, particularly your mobile phone number, at reception on the way out. It would be good if we have the means to contact you quickly if needed."

"Yes. Thank you." I turn away from him and head along the corridor, through the doors at the end, turn right following the exit signs, and make my way out past reception through the main door. Once outside I cross the expanse of paving and tarmac and go into a thicket of bushes. I bend double and puke and puke again until there is only bile.

Chapter 17

I feel the safe phone vibrate in my pocket. Moll.

"Hello, Moll?"

Can you talk?

"Yes. I'm outside and I'm alone."

I got your text about Vi. Is everything okay?

"She's in the ICU in the Princess Royal Infirmary. She's been the victim of a racist attack. I think it's touch and go whether she'll make it."

Jesus! I'm sorry to hear that.

"An unwelcome distraction to say the least. The case is being handled by an Inspector Lorraine Watt. If you could keep your ear to the ground and let me know of any developments I'd appreciate it."

No problem. What does this mean for the case?

"It's not quite the excuse I had planned for contacting Ryan, but it'll do. I'll touch base with him after this call. Is there anything from your end?" I adjust my position on the bench and press my forefinger to my other ear to deaden the sound of the siren announcing the approach of another ambulance to the hospital.

Lots. As expected, the AC is giving nothing away regarding who provided the corroboration of your proposed targets. But she has shared something big.

"Go on."

The intelligence services have identified the contact that they believe supplied the explosives to Ryan for the Brightwater View raid. They've ascertained that same individual is also liaising with another group that is suspected to be planning attacks along similar lines to Ryan's.

"That *is* big."

And that's not all. It appears that there might be another group in addition to that one.

"Bloody hell, Moll. If there are three separate groups all being co-ordinated to strike simultaneously then this is massive.

Whoever is behind all of this must have incredible resources available to them."

No doubt about it. I asked if some foreign government was suspected, but the AC wouldn't be drawn. The less we know – specifically, the less you know – then the less there is to give away if you get blown.

"Understood. Whoever is behind all of this might also be hedging their bets. The more attacks they have planned, the more likely it is that some of them will come off."

We need to... Moll's words are obliterated by the two-tone siren of the ambulance as it screeches past less than five metres away. *Where are you? Are you at the hospital?*

"Yes, I'm just outside the Princess Royal Infirmary. Sorry about that."

It's okay. I was just going to say that we need to keep playing this through as though we intend to carry out the attacks for real.

"Definitely. Everything has to be completely authentic. Any tiny inconsistency could easily see us blown – if not by Ryan, then by whoever is running him. Once I've confirmed the targets with him I need to specify devices that are entirely appropriate to the objective, otherwise the supplier is likely to twig something's not right."

So, you're going to arrange a meet with Ryan next?

"Pretty much. There are a couple of things I need to sort out first. For example, I've obviously still got this phone on me. I need to drop that back at the flat before I meet him."

Sure. Let me know when you've got something arranged.

"Will do. 'Bye."

'Bye.

I switch phones and start texting.

Me: *Need to see you. Urgent.*
Ryan: *Okay. Come now.*
Me: *With you ASAP.*

I switch back to the safe phone and drop a line to Moll, letting her know that I've arranged to meet Ryan, and that I'll update her later. Then I head back into the main building and leave my contact details with a man behind the reception desk. The thought crosses my mind that perhaps I ought to go back and see Vi, but I dismiss the notion as quickly as it surfaces. I've got to stay focused and avoid any unnecessary distractions.

Back outside I catch a cab and on the journey back to the flat I try to rehearse the update I need to provide Ryan, but I keep being interrupted by the doctor's words: *somewhere between thirteen and fifteen weeks pregnant with twins.* My mind wanders further and I recollect Moll telling me she'd had a termination, when I hadn't even known she was pregnant. I remember the shock, disbelief and anger. I don't feel that anger this time. Shock – yes. Disbelief – not sure. Anger – no. But I do realise that this has the potential to distract me if I let my emotions take hold, if I speculate that I might be the father. I need to compartmentalise it – put it away somewhere to be dealt with later. I have to focus.

When the cab gets to the flats I ask the driver to wait. There's still one squad car there and a couple of bored looking uniforms, including the officer who'd first intercepted me when I returned home earlier. He recognises me and acknowledges me with a nod as I make my way between the wall and barricade tape. I notice that the Red Zone has gone – presumably SOCO got everything they wanted. I race upstairs and place the safe phone and charging lead in the shoebox in my wardrobe, then immediately head back down. Once back in the cab I give the driver Ryan's address and rehearse myself to prepare for our meeting.

"You took longer than I thought." Ryan's clearly unhappy.

"Sorry. I had to come via the hospital. I took a cab to make up time."

"Why did you have to go to the hospital?"

I talk him through the attack on Vi. What the witness reported. The skinheads, and the fact I'd seen them around the night before. I tell him that the doctor thinks that there might be brain damage. I explain that her injuries are severe and that the next hours and days will be crucial.

Ryan is quiet for a moment, with an expression I'd describe as contemplative. Then he focuses on me. "What about the baby?"

"What?"

"The baby. Vi was pregnant, Josh. Didn't the doctor say anything?"

"Well, yes. He said that she'd lost twins."

"Twins. Wow." He makes a *would you believe it* face, as if I've just told him there's a daffodil blooming in the garden in Autumn. Surprised, but not upset or concerned.

"I didn't know she was pregnant."

"No reason you should, Josh." He sees my confusion. "No offence, but a bender like you isn't going to be the father, so why tell you?"

"So, you're the father? I thought you and Vi had finished ages back."

"Yeah, we had finished. But, you know how it is – occasionally you like a bit of variety. Sometimes it's nice to have a bit of darker meat. I called round a couple of times – actually, probably round about the time you first moved in."

He leers at me, and throws me a wink. I feel my stomach somersault and every muscle in my body straining. I want to grab his head in both hands and twist so that his neck snaps. But I mustn't. I let him continue.

"I'm sure it's the same with you bum bandits – bedding different people just adds some spice." He's actually fucking smiling at me now. "Anyway, to answer your question, no idea if I was the father. Not that it matters anyway."

"You've no idea if you're the father?"

"She could have slept with anyone. She mentioned she'd had a one night stand with some random bloke." He shrugs. "Anyway, as I say, it doesn't actually matter now anyway – does it?"

"I guess not."

"More to the point, what's happened to Vi is obviously tragic, but it makes allocating the targets more straightforward."

I'm looking and listening closely, while trying not to make it too obvious, to see if there's emotion there – but, if there is, I can't see it. "Sorry, but you've lost me."

He smiles almost benignly. "There's four targets, Josh. With

Jonno out of the way that left you, Vi, Ruthie, Nate and Merv. Now, with Vi – what would you call it…" He hesitates as he searches for the right word, "…incapacitated – then there's no longer a selection issue. Pretty neat actually."

There's no artifice about Ryan right now. This is him being authentic. Jonno and Vi are no longer part of the equation – no big deal. Just move on. Well, it's time for me to complicate things for the smug bastard. "I'm afraid it's not actually that neat."

His scowl confirms his displeasure. "What?"

I explain the recce of Stratton Primary School and why it's entirely unsuitable as a target. He's not happy and challenges me a couple of times before he seems satisfied that it really isn't viable. He presses me for an alternative target and we spend a tense few minutes before he finally accepts my argument that even targeting three locations is hugely ambitious and will be incredibly challenging.

"Fair enough, Josh. You're the expert when it comes to this. How are you fixed for the next couple of hours?"

"I'd like to get back to the hospital at some point to check on Vi, but other than that I'm pretty flexible. Why?"

"Nate and Merv are due here…" He pauses to check the time on his phone, "…actually, they're due here in twenty minutes. And Ruthie will be back any minute. It would be good for everyone to hear your feedback."

"You're happy to bring everyone inside the tent?" I try to pitch the question with the appropriate mix of scepticism and respect.

He throws me a quizzical glance. "Ruthie was here when we discussed the potential targets in the first place, remember? And I updated Nate and Merv later that evening."

So now there are three possible sources for the corroboration, rather than just Ruthie. "Ah, okay. I wasn't going to say anything to anyone, including Vi, until you said it was all right to do so." I see the satisfaction in his eyes at my acquiescence to his authority.

I'm framing my next question when the sound of Ruthie returning through the front door changes the dynamic. She joins us in the living room and seems visibly upset as I explain what has happened to Vi. Ryan remains unconcerned and suggests that he fetch his laptop so that I can upload my photos on to it for sharing on the bigger screen, and for looking at the targets online.

Nate and Merv arrive sooner than expected and join Ruthie and me on seats in the living room, while Ryan boots up his machine. Merv is a caricature of everyone's image of a right-on, too-much-denim student type from the 1970's, except that he's in his forties and his already ridiculous ponytail looks all the more stupid given his aggressively receding hairline. A gaunt, angular man, so skinny that his ribs can be discerned through his tee-shirt, he has dark, darting eyes that flit about almost as much as his conspiracy-theorist mind. He's even more full of bullshit than Ryan, and is spouting about the Internet of Things and how governments have developed technology that enables spinach to detect certain substances, like explosives. He tells us chemical signals from the spinach enable the plant to transmit an email alert about the presence of explosives, and that we need to be careful.

I'm genuinely grateful when Nate says, "Just shut up, Merv, for god's sake." Nate doesn't usually speak much. I believe that he's embarrassed by his quite pronounced stammer and a set of teeth that look like a burnt fence. Nate's the only member of the group I'd describe as genuinely frightening, apart from Ryan. He has a pallor that might make you think he is already dead. Muscular, with a bullet-shaped head and a penchant for violence, he supplements his unemployment money by breeding and selling dogs. He crosses Staffordshire bull terriers with Labradors and markets them online as Stabrador puppies – and turns a tidy sum, according to him. As often as not he has either a plaster or bandage where a dog has nipped his hand. His default expression is a scowl, although he laughs readily at any misfortune that befalls others.

I'm having a hard time believing that either Nate or Merv are working on behalf of some other agency – unless one of them is a RADA-trained actor. I suppose it's possible that Merv has said something to somebody and that's the source of corroboration that the AC mentioned to Moll. My musing is interrupted by Ryan, asking me to forward the photos I've taken of the targets so he can show them to everyone on the laptop screen. I send them while Ryan switches on his VPN so that we can also browse relevant sites without any possibility of being traced.

We spend almost two hours reviewing my photos alongside other online images and articles about each of the three targets. The other four are completely engaged in the process, and there is excited debate about exactly where the devices should be placed for maximum impact.

At Drayton Park we settle upon a location on the concourse that isn't covered by CCTV. The consensus view is that, by resting the bag or rucksack containing the device against the barrier at that particular point, the carrier can make a swift exit out of the main front door in just three of four seconds, detonating it remotely behind him or her. If the timing is right, maximum carnage should be achieved on the concourse. There is the possibility of an added "bonus" if the confusion and panic spreads back down the stairs to the platforms below. People could spill onto the rail tracks, increasing the potential for further casualties, and possibly even a derailment.

North Greenwich Station causes much more debate, with differing cases being argued for detonating on the concourse, or the area at the foot of the four escalators, or even on the escalators themselves. Eventually, the location of CCTV cameras, plus my advice on where security personnel will probably be located, leads to the decision that the concourse is the prime location for this target. A similar strategy as for Drayton Park is agreed, with an acknowledgement that the CCTV coverage means the carrier should be particularly well disguised.

There's virtually nothing useful available online with regard to Pilton Community Centre, so the others are heavily reliant on my photos and commentary. It's quickly obvious that maximum impact will be achieved by having the device detonate as near the centre of the seated audience as possible. We agree that the carrier will need to be in early enough to choose a centrally located seat. They will need to engage with someone in a neighbouring seat and ask them to "look after my bag, please" while they pop out to the toilet. Whoever is designated as this carrier needs to accept that, with the addition of broadcast quality TV cameras on site, they are more likely than not to be identified afterwards.

Nate volunteers that he'd like to be the carrier for the North Greenwich device. When asked why, he answers – in all sincerity – that he believes it is the target where we have the chance of killing the most people. Ryan laughs, taps him on the shoulder almost affectionately, and says that he'll need to sleep on it before deciding who is allocated to each target. Absolutely nothing is said, but there's something about Ryan's demeanour throughout the entire two hours that reinforces my belief that he views the carriers as expendable. I wonder whether the idea that he can send people to their death unknowingly gives him some kind of a buzz. I explain that the next stage is for me to do some maths and work up the specification for each device and get it back to Ryan as soon as possible.

Nate and Merv both seem genuinely concerned when I tell them about Vi. Merv volunteers to visit her in hospital and Nate suggests that he might visit our estate and have a hunt round for the skinheads. We agree that no-one should do anything until Vi's situation becomes a bit clearer. I explain my intention to visit her this evening and promise to update Ryan, so that he can relay any news on to the others. I use the desire to visit Vi as my excuse to leave the meeting before the others are completely ready for it to break up. I pretend to believe that Ryan is sincere when he tells me to, as far as is possible, let Vi know that everyone is rooting for her.

Chapter 18

By the time I get back to the flat it's already ten to six. I go to my room and retrieve the safe phone. Although I'm alone in the flat, I decide to make the call from my room – establishing the principle that the safe phone mustn't ever leave there. Now that I realise Ryan has visited Vi here since I moved in, I need to scan the room again – something I haven't done since my first week here. I retrieve the RF detector from the shoebox inside the wardrobe and systematically sweep the room in a clockwise direction. All clear.

I dial Moll, and I'm surprised that it rings out three times before she answers. *Yes, Josh?*

"Is now a good time?"

Yes, it's fine. How did the meeting with Ryan go?

"It turned into a bigger gathering than I'd anticipated. Ruthie, Nate and Merv joined us for me to brief them on what I'd recce'd on each target. It turns out that Nate and Merv knew about the targets as well as Ruthie."

So, either of them could be the source of corroboration – not just Ruthie?

"Yes. Although I find it hard to imagine any of the three of them as being undercover. Maybe one of them has let something slip to a third party."

We're only speculating now, Josh. Did anything else concrete come out of the meeting?

"Nothing that was said. We spent a couple of hours doing a deep dive on each target – identifying the best place to trigger the devices for maximum impact, understanding the layout, optimum routes for carriers to exit the targets before detonation – that sort of thing."

And what about what wasn't said?

"I just know in my bones that Ryan is playing to a slightly different agenda. I really believe that he has no qualms about blowing up the carriers." I roll back on my bed and rest my head on the pillow as I articulate what's been simmering away at the back of my mind during the journey home. "He's been really careful about who he has recruited. Every one of us is some sort of damaged loner, with a grudge against society and no domestic or family support to provide balance. Merv is a conspiracy theorist who lives in a static caravan, Nate is a major psycho who gets off on violence big time, Jonno was a sad loser who would do anything for approval from Ryan…"

…You are a gay ex-squaddie sickened by the cynicism of the political classes, Vi is a sexually exploited poor-little-rich-girl, and Ruthie is a fruit-loop who believes that causing mayhem will lead to some Disneyland utopia. We know all this, Josh. What's your point? Moll's interruption stings, but helps me focus.

"The point is that none of us has anyone that cares for us. We are totally expendable. No-one would notice if we weren't around anymore. Think about it – nobody has flagged up any concern about Jonno. If it weren't for me, and maybe some others in the group, no-one would notice or give a shit about Vi."

And your point is?

"Ryan obviously briefed Jonno differently from the rest of us. They were planning a spectacular additional explosion from the extra charge that I hadn't been told about. When that all went south and Jonno was killed, Ryan didn't bat an eyelid. He was completely thrilled that we'd managed to bring the crane down. Today I told him about the attack on Vi and that her life was in the balance. He was no more interested than if I'd told him one of my radiators wasn't working. Listen, Moll, this group is the very definition of 'useful idiots' – I really think he's intending to blow the carriers up along with the devices."

There's a pause. *Shit. We have to operate on the basis that you're right. Do you think that the other two groups might be planning along similar lines?*

"That's way above our pay grade, Moll. We can let the AC and the big boys at CTOC worry about the other groups. We can only concentrate on Ryan."

I understand that, Josh. But if the attack model that Ryan is working to looks convincing, it might persuade whoever he is liaising with to have it adopted by the other two groups. We could have three separate groups all with the equivalent of suicide bombers attacking targets all over the country.

"I suppose so. All you can do is feed back and let the top brass decide what to do with the intel."

Agreed. What are the next steps for you?

"Tonight I'm going to visit the hospital to check on Vi. I've agreed with Ryan that I'll work on spec'ing what kind of devices we will require. The actual devices themselves will be quite straightforward – it's the trigger mechanism that will need some real thought. I made out to Ryan that it was more complicated than it really is, so he's not expecting me to get back to him until the day after tomorrow."

Okay. Anything else I should know?

"Nothing. Did you manage to check on Inspector Watt's investigation into the attack on Vi?"

I put in a call, but the investigation is very early stage. Plenty of resources being applied, though – so fingers crossed for a quick breakthrough. If there's nothing else…

"There isn't."

…then I'll let you get off to the hospital. Keep me posted on any further contact with Ryan, or anyone else in the group. 'Bye.

"'Bye, Moll." I return the safe phone to the shoebox in the wardrobe and use my everyday device to book a cab to take me to the hospital.

I step out of the ICU, accompanied by one of the nurses who has been attending to Vi. "Are you all right?" she asks.

"Yes, thank you. I'm fine."

She's experienced enough to distinguish between an honest answer and an autopilot response. "Mr. Colquhoun said that you didn't actually see her earlier. It can be something of a shock. Are there any questions you'd like to ask me?"

"No. Thank you, no."

"It might be wise for you to take a seat in the relatives room." Her fingertips steer me in the right direction with a butterfly kiss on my shoulder. "I'll bring you in a cup of tea. A proper brew from the nurse's station – none of that machine rubbish. How do you take it?"

"White, no sugar – please." I step over the threshold into a rectangular room, eight metres by four. There's no-one else there, and I select the cushioned wooden chair facing the door. I count eleven other matching chairs and two benches that should seat three or four people each all around the edges of the room against the walls. There's a flat screen TV high on the wall to the right, showing the news on silent with subtitles. There are two low tables piled with magazines in the middle of the room, and a box in the far corner piled high with toys.

I didn't expect that seeing Vi would faze me to the extent it has. I have seen men, women and children literally in pieces in a gruesome scene after a bomb exploded at a wedding. I've seen colleagues killed, maimed and lose limbs in combat. But I wasn't prepared for seeing Vi in that room. The only part of *her* I could see was her hair, her forehead and her closed eyes – hideously swollen and discoloured. Every other part of her was hidden by machines, connections to machines, bandages, a plaster cast or bedsheets. The repetitive hiss-tap-tap, hiss-tap-tap of the ventilator provided a rhythmic bass line to the intermittent pings of the vital signs monitor and the soft, whispered chorus of the two nurses assigned to watch over her.

But it wasn't anything tangible that's triggered an unwelcome but familiar sensation that death is nearby. It's not the done thing for squaddies to discuss it when still serving – such conversations usually only take place between ex-servicemen. Then they will talk about the almost-taste and the nearly-smell which are part of the heightened sense that death is nearby, just before you deploy on some operations. I felt it in that room with Vi, and now I'm grieving for the loss that I believe is inevitable.

The nurse returns and hands me a mug of steaming tea with a silent nod and a smile, and I wonder whether she and her colleagues have developed that same, unwelcome sense. I'm certain that they must have. As she exits I'm surprised to see Ruthie come in the opposite direction, blinking back tears. I rise to my feet instinctively and she pulls me into a tight embrace. Her body shudders against mine twice, before she sighs mightily, relaxes her hold and takes a step backwards. "Sorry, Josh. I've just been into see Vi and I simply wasn't prepared…"

"I know, Ruthie. It threw me too. Here…" I gesture with my arm, "…why don't you take a seat?" She follows the suggestion and I take my place in the chair beside her. She explains that, although I had promised to provide Ryan with an update on Vi's condition, she had felt compelled to visit personally. We talk about Vi, her background, the fact that her mother has only just died and, of course, we talk about the attack and the state it has left her in. The conversation is punctuated by both long and short silences, but nonetheless feels natural and comfortable.

This is the only time I have ever spoken one-to-one with Ruthie. Indeed, it's the only time I can remember being alone in her presence. Her sincerity and compassion for Vi make me warm to her. She leans towards me and drops her voice to a whisper. "This is the kind of thing that proves what we are doing is right."

"What do you mean, Ruthie?" No artifice from me – I haven't any idea what she is talking about.

"What happened to Vi. Any society where that kind of thing can occur is rotten to its very core. The whole thing needs torn down so we can start all over again. What we are going to do in the next couple of weeks will help speed that day." She makes big *I'm right aren't I* eyes.

"Absolutely." I nod to underscore my affirmation. A useful reminder that she is a total fruit loop.

Our conversation has reached its natural break point and we agree it is time to be going our separate ways. We say our goodbyes and confirm that we will see each other again soon.

I get out of the taxi in front of our block of flats and realise that every sign of the attack on Vi, and the subsequent investigation, has gone – as if it never happened. I make my way past the scene, up the stairs and into the flat. As I press the door closed behind me, I realise that I am famished. I flick the light on as I pass the living room, and do the same as I enter the kitchen. A quick check of the larder reveals some dry penne and a jar of arabiata sauce, which I can knock up in ten minutes or so. I fill the kettle and put it on to save time waiting for a pot of water to boil. Just as I return to the larder to fetch the ingredients the front doorbell chimes.

Although the hallway is dark as I open the door, I can see immediately that Amelia is the visitor. "Hi, Josh. Sorry to bother you. I just wanted to catch up with Vi."

"Oh."

"Is something wrong?"

"You better come in." I pull the door wider open with one hand and extend my other arm to invite her inside. She heads towards the living room as I shut the door and follow on behind.

When I reach the threshold she's in the middle of the room, facing me. She's wearing a mid-grey knee-length coat, belted at the waist, that meets mustard leather boots at her knees, and a cloche hat that matches her boots. Her make up is immaculate and the whole impression is of someone who has stepped out of the pages of Vogue. "Okay, Josh – what have you done with Vi? Where is she? We were meant to be meeting for coffee this afternoon, but she didn't show up. She's not returning my calls." There's no attempt to disguise the anxiety in her voice.

"You might want to sit down for this."

"Just tell me."

So, I tell her. I tell her pretty much verbatim what Inspector Watt told me about the attack, and what Mr. Colquhoun said at the hospital. Amelia listens intently and seems completely focused on every word I have to say. She asks questions throughout, occasionally refining them until she elicits a level of precision in my answers that she finds satisfactory. I realise that she's switched into journalist mode, and wonder whether that's a coping mechanism for dealing with the shock she must be feeling.

Her questioning is forensic. She is particularly painstaking when quizzing me about what I saw the evening before – as thorough as the police officers who interviewed me. What about the height and build of the four individuals? Surely I must have seen at least one of their faces? Were the north east accents Geordie or Mackem or Northumbrian? Despite the persistence of her questioning, it doesn't feel intrusive or inappropriate. I sense her need to know and her desire to understand.

The veneer doesn't so much crack as shatter, however, when I mention that Vi had been pregnant with twins and has lost them. Amelia has no more questions; indeed, she has

no more words. Her luminous eyes shine even brighter as they fill with tears that pause briefly before tumbling down her cheeks. She pulls off her hat with one hand and twists it out of shape with the other. Her eyes catch mine and she steps forward, dropping the hat as she does so, and throws her arms around me.

For the second time in less than two hours I find myself trying to provide comfort to someone distressed by what has happened to Vi. Amelia is enclosed in my arms, head on my chest, holding me tight. I feel the rhythm of her breathing gradually slowing as she regains her composure. Having her pressed against me feels good. Her perfume is subtle and delicious, and it's a struggle to resist the temptation to nuzzle her and inhale deeply. I don't know what it is about this woman, but even when she's neither looking at me nor speaking to me she still has the ability to completely entrance me.

I feel her hold loosen and we each take a step backwards. "I'm sorry. When you mentioned the babies, it just tipped me over the edge."

"I understand. When the consultant told me at the hospital, I was completely wrong-footed. I had no idea she was pregnant."

"May I?" Amelia gestures that she'd like to take off her coat. "That's if you don't mind. It's just that it's so warm in here."

"By all means." I take her coat, bend to pick up her hat and then place both at one end of the sofa. She follows my indication that she should take a seat beside them, and I place myself in the armchair opposite her.

"Have you been to see her?"

"Yes. In fact, I only got back from the hospital around twenty minutes ago."

"And how is she?"

"Not good. She's hooked up to all sorts of equipment and has a machine to help her breathe. As I said before, the consultant mentioned that the next hours and days will be critical. But…"

"But what?"

"I don't think it looks good. Just a feeling."

My words trail off and a silence hangs in the air between us. Neither of us know what to say next. Eventually it's Amelia who speaks. Her voice is soft, steady and measured. "I can't believe that this has happened. I just reconnected with her after all these years and then this happens."

"At least you did manage to reconnect with her."

"Yes. But…" she tilts her head slightly to one side and looks straight at me. "I wasn't even completely honest about that."

"I don't understand."

"I told Vi that I was at her mother's funeral in the hope that she might be there and that I would get the chance to catch up with her."

"I remember."

"That was true, but it wasn't the main reason I was there – more like a bonus. I was at the funeral because I was working." She gauges my reaction before continuing. "I've been involved with a project for over a year now. Kind of a below the radar investigation into a man called Lord Waterson. He's incredibly secretive and difficult to track down. But he's a close friend and associate of Vi's father, so I suspected he might be at the funeral. My plan was to show up and see, if he was there, whether or not he seemed particularly familiar with anyone else in attendance."

I'm on full alert now. Amelia is as smart as she is beautiful. She's also clearly skilled in the art of deception. She's not choosing to share this with me for no reason. At least I don't think so. I throw her a titbit. "Vi and I shared a cab to the funeral with an older couple. The man introduced himself as Martin Waterson Jones."

"That's him!" I can see I've surprised her. "Lord Waterson was just plain old Martin Jones before he was ennobled. You say that he travelled in a taxi?" There's a note of incredulity in her voice.

"Yes. There was a mix up at the station and the taxi I had booked for Vi and me didn't wait when the train was delayed. Martin and his wife Sara had another taxi booked that they volunteered to share with us."

"So, how long was the cab journey?" I can almost feel the intensity of her excitement. "Was there much conversation? What was said?"

"Sorry to disappoint, Amelia, but it was pretty mundane stuff. The journey lasted about ten minutes and we discussed the weather and the fact that we had all been worried we might miss the funeral when the train was delayed. Now, I know you're the journalist, but can I ask you a question?"

She smiles. "Depends what you want to ask." She's cool, playing at being coy.

"Was all this interest in Vi just a pretence? Were you pretending to rekindle an old friendship just because you felt that you might be able to get more on Lord Waterson via Vi and her father?"

"No!" The look of denial on her face is even more forceful than her exclamation. She's either sincere or putting on an Oscar-winning performance. "I had hoped Vi would be at the funeral, but hadn't really expected her to be. I didn't want to get my hopes up. I was overjoyed to see her, and then to catch up again last night."

"Why didn't you think she'd be at her own mother's funeral?"

Amelia has regained her composure. "She disappeared off the face of the earth when we were sixteen. I didn't even know if she was still alive. Also, although she never said so explicitly, I was suspicious that she suffered abuse at home – probably from her father. Put both of those things together and it seemed unlikely she'd be at the funeral." She's boring into me with those eyes, evaluating my reaction.

I think that I believe her. Vi said she's never told anyone about the abuse from her father. But if Amelia was as close a friend as she seems to have been, she probably would have developed suspicions. "So how did you feel when she was at the funeral?"

"All sorts – surprised, distracted, elated. And you, Josh? How did you feel at the funeral?"

My alert level has just risen to a notch I didn't know existed. "What do you mean?"

"For god's sake, Josh. We're in full disclosure mode now. When we met at the funeral, how did you feel?"

I see what's coming. "What exactly do you mean?"

"Each of us knows who the other is, Josh. Seeing Vi at the funeral wasn't as big a surprise as seeing you. I wasn't 100% sure until last night – but when Vi confirmed you'd had that beard, I knew for certain. So, when did you know? I could see when Vi mentioned my by-line in the newspaper that you knew – did you realise before that?"

"No. There was something familiar about you at the funeral, but it didn't all click into place until last night." Shit! Why did I say that?

"Who am I talking to? I don't believe that you're Jamie Mackie, heroic Scotsman who rescues people being attacked on the street. I don't believe that you're Josh Gray, an ex-squaddie working cash-in-hand at a hotel." Her eyes are locked on mine. Her voice is calm, clear and utterly fearless. "I'm Amelia Harris, a journalist and old school friend of Vi. Who the hell are you?"

Shit! "I'm sorry, Amelia, I don't know what you're talking about." We hold each other's gaze, without words.

"All right, if that's how you want it." Amelia gets to her feet and starts to gather her coat and hat. She fishes a card from her coat pocket and hands it to me. "My contact details. I want you to ring me with any updates on Vi."

"I'll ring the hospital before bed time and drop you a text."

"Thank you." She finishes buttoning her coat and tightens the belt, but holds her hat in her hand. I get to my feet as she takes a step towards the door. "Don't worry, I can let myself out." She pauses and turns her head to look me full in the face. "And thank you too, for what you did that night in the alley."

"Good night, Amelia."

"Good night." She turns and makes her way along the hall. I hear the door close behind her. I don't feel hungry any more.

Chapter 19

Another night of badly fractured sleep.

Images of Vi in the ICU, Ryan's callous disregard for anything other than his own agenda, and particularly Amelia's revelation all conspired to fuel wakefulness. I spent the night struggling to get to sleep, thinking about Amelia and trying not to think about Amelia. Why was she in the alleyway that night? Why were those two thugs attacking her? Could it have been some sort of set up? No – that's ridiculous. She was genuinely terrified. Or was she? How good an actress is she? Was she really surprised that I'd shared a taxi with Lord Waterson? Or was that just another act? Was the performance at dinner the other evening with Vi and me just a pretence? Surely not? She said she'd been surprised to see me at the funeral, but was only sure that it was me when Vi had told her I'd had a beard. That doesn't quite add up.

And so on, over and over, throughout the night. Snatches of sleep, punctuated by thoughts of Vi and Ryan, but mostly Amelia. Trying to puzzle her out exercised my brain. Thinking about her lips, her eyes, her hair, her smell and how it felt when she was holding me helped me to drift off, before the next interruption jolted me back awake.

I switch off the alarm clock and turn on the bedside lamp before throwing the duvet back, then swing out of bed and cross to the wardrobe to fetch the safe phone. I text Moll. *Amelia Harris called by last night. We need to talk.* It's 5.35 am, so I don't expect an immediate response. Moll is a six o' clock riser.

I grab my dressing gown from the hook on the door, tie the belt tight at the waist, and put the safe phone in one pocket and the everyday phone on the other. I make my way to the kitchen, flick the light switch and put the kettle on. I take the everyday phone and call the Princess Royal Infirmary. The switchboard operator puts me through to the ICU immediately, and my call is answered within two rings. Once the nurse has confirmed my identity and relationship to Vi, she advises me that there has been no change in her condition overnight. I ask whether anyone else has called and the answer is no. I thank her and end the call. I start to text Amelia with the update, just as I did yesterday evening. I wonder how I am listed on her phone. What comes up as my caller ID? Does she list me as Josh, or something else?

The safe phone vibrates in my pocket. Moll.

"Five forty-five. An early start for you, Moll."

She completely ignores my comment. *So, what happened last night?*

"After I got back from the hospital, I was about to make something to eat when the doorbell rang. It was Amelia Harris."

And you let her in?

"Of course I bloody let her in. What else could I do?"

What happened?

"Vi was meant to meet her but hadn't shown up, obviously. Amelia got no response when she tried Vi's phone, so she called round to see her."

And?

"I had to tell her what had happened to Vi. She seemed really upset. I was…"

*Seemed? You say she **seemed** upset. Do you think she wasn't really upset? Was she putting on an act?*

"I don't know, Moll. Don't read too much into one word. If I had to make a call, I'd say she was being genuine. But ever since you pointed out how many coincidences there were associated with her, I've been on my guard."

Good. Now get to the point. What do you need to tell me?

So, I get to the point. As I make myself a coffee one-handed, I report the revelations from the previous evening. How Amelia Harris was actually working on a story when she attended the funeral, that she is investigating Lord Waterson – Martin Jones, that she knows I am the man who interrupted the attack on her, and that she doesn't buy my cover story at all. Moll hears all of this out without interruption, although I know she'll be scribbling notes as I'm speaking.

Shit! This Lord Waterson character – you never mentioned him in previous reports.

"I had no reason to think that there was any relevance. He was just someone we shared a short cab journey with."

You're not being paid to think, Josh. You're being paid to report back to me – and that means you report every-fucking-thing. There's an awkward pause as she waits for a response. I take a mouthful of coffee and say nothing, until the silence strongarms Moll into continuing. *And this Amelia Harris, there's no doubt that she's on to you?*

"She absolutely knows that I was the man who interrupted the attack on her. And she explicitly said that she didn't believe my cover story."

That's not good. Not good at all. Did she say anything else?

"No, nothing else."

Okay. What are you plans for the rest of today?

"I intend to stay here and do some online research, mainly into alternative triggering systems for the devices." I pause briefly. "What happens next?"

I don't know, Josh. I'll pass your report up the line and see what happens. I presume that, if you're staying in the flat, you'll have this phone with you and can be contacted.

"Yes, that's fine. When should I expect to hear from you?"

I don't know that either, Josh. You'll hear from me when I've got something to communicate. Meantime, try not to do anything else that could jeopardise the operation.

"Okay, Moll. 'Bye."

'Bye, Josh.

I return the phone to my pocket and put the empty coffee mug in the dishwasher.

It's 3.40 pm when the safe phone buzzes. A text from Moll: *Are you free to speak?*

I text 'Yes', and the phone rings immediately.

Josh, we want you to come in.

"What?" This is very, very bad. "What do you mean?" It's incredibly rare for someone on a clandestine op to be called in. Really incredibly rare – more so when the op is reaching a critical stage, like this one is.

You heard me, Josh. We want you to come in.

"Who is we?" The risks of going in are enormous. Every cop shop has its moles. If I get recognised my cover could be blown and the whole operation with it. Moll knows that.
Are you alone now?
"Yes. I need you to…"
Are you expected anywhere later?
"No. Moll, I need you to…"
A car will collect you outside your building in ten minutes. Be ready. The call ends and she's gone.

Every fibre of my being is supercharged. I can't stay still. I fetch my shoes and put them on. Who is it that has decided I should be called in? I go to the window to check whether the car has arrived. Of course it hasn't – it's barely a minute since the call ended. Are they calling me in for some sort of briefing, or are they calling me in for good? I go to the hallway to get my jacket and carry it back into the living room. What did Moll mean when she said *be ready*? Ready for the car to collect me, or ready for whatever awaits me? I slip the jacket on and three-quarters zip it up. Moll's tone was unreadable. There was minimal engagement on the call. Was she alone? Did she want to say more but couldn't? I check the window again – still nothing. If I'm in the shit, will Moll have my back? Or will she just be looking out for number one, as usual? I'm pacing in a circle like a ham actor in a bad movie – I might as well go down and wait outside.

Less than two minutes later a navy blue Jaguar I-Pace pulls up and a horse-faced man in the passenger seat rolls down the window to check my identity before signalling I should get in the back. I take a seat and the car moves off as I'm still putting my seatbelt on. There's a click, as the doors all lock – I'm not familiar with the vehicle, so don't know if that happens automatically, or requires manual intervention. There is absolutely no dialogue between the driver and the fellow in the passenger seat, and I sense that any attempt by me to engage with either of them would be futile. The car radio isn't on, which helps amplify the near silence of the electric engine as we zip through the suburbs in an easterly direction.

After twenty-five minutes we are travelling along a

carriageway through the Badlands between the A12 and A13 when the car takes a sharp left into a modern looking commercial estate. A three metre high wire fence separates the estate from the road, and we enter via a gate and barrier manned by a couple of uniformed security guards. The driver flashes a pass at the guards and we are waved through without the need for anyone to speak. The site is a collection of single-storey industrial units, interspersed with four-storey office buildings in a ratio of about eight to one. A few of the warehouse-type units have the odd pantechnicon parked outside and one of the office blocks has lights on and several cars in the car park, but otherwise most of the properties appear vacant.

We round a corner then turn into a second office block, where the lights indicate that it is occupied, and pull into an undercroft car park in which I count eleven other vehicles already parked. The fellow in the passenger seat in front gets out, opens my door and beckons me to follow him. I slam the door behind me and follow the charcoal-suited Mr. Chatty to a door, which he opens after flashing a card at a reader. Inside we ascend one level up a well-lit staircase, through a door and along a bright, characterless corridor. My companion stops outside an open door and uses his arm to indicate that I should enter. The room is entirely bare, save for a rectangular grey melamine table and four matching chairs.

"Take a seat and wait here." The conversationalist of the year waits to ensure I sit down then disappears.

No more than twenty seconds later I hear footsteps – more than one person – approaching. Moll enters the room accompanied by another woman I know must be the AC, the reason for her "Hawk" nickname self-evident. "Josh, this is Assistant Commissioner Carswell."

"Ma'am." I nod. She indicates that I should remain seated.

AC Carswell does not sit down, but pushes the door closed behind her and takes a step to the side, so that we are square on to each other. She looks down at me. "You are an intelligent person, DC Gray, so you will know that something serious is afoot, given that we have called you in. Putting it simply, you are here to help us decide whether you remain an asset, or whether you have become a liability." Her piercing dark brown eyes are fixed on mine with an intensity that is unsettling, but I hold her gaze. "You are aware that a number of agencies are co-operating on this case, and concerns about your reliability have been raised that require immediate answers." Moll hasn't said anything and is looking at the floor.

"Yes, Ma'am. But I would like to…"

"Quiet!" The AC blocks me sharply without raising her voice, although I can see irritation flare in her eyes. "You will follow DI Leishman and me. We are going to another room where you will be required to answer a number of questions, including some from me. Now please get to your feet."

Chapter 20

I follow Moll and the AC back along the same corridor and out on to the stairwell. We climb two flights of stairs to the next floor and make our way along another corridor identical to the one below. Twenty metres along the pair stop outside a door to the right and turn to face me. The tilt of the AC's head indicates that I should follow her, before she precedes me through the door, with Moll escorting from the rear.

The room is surprisingly dimly lit and I blink a couple of times as my eyes adjust to the contrast with the brightness of the corridor. It's a sizeable space, roughly ten metres by eight, and the entire far wall is a window hidden behind a series of blinds. A table, two and a half metres square, sits in the centre of the room and the AC points me in the direction of an empty chair at the end nearest the door we have just come through. She takes a seat on the side of the table to my left, about one metre along. Moll sits at the far right corner from me and looks to make herself small.

There's a woman to the left of the AC who I would estimate is mid-forties. Despite the gloom, the cut of both her jacket and her bobbed blonde hair indicate someone who takes pride in her appearance and spends money accordingly. Beyond her, on the opposite corner to Moll, is another woman I'd put at around mid-twenties, her sharp features illuminated by the laptop screen that she is leaning in closely to. The reflection of the screen in her glasses shows that she is looking at text rather than numbers. Between her and Moll, directly opposite me, is a lean, angular man with buzz cut grey hair. He is in full army uniform and the crown over crossed baton and sword on his epaulette identifies him as a Lieutenant General. This is serious.

Evenly spaced on the right between Moll and me are two men, fiftyish, both in dark suits, collar and tie. The fellow nearer me has advanced male pattern baldness, with a shiny pate above on owl-like face, where rimless glasses perched atop a tiny hooked nose magnify his eyes to an extent that borders on alarming.

Almost as if to taunt him, the man to his right has a great mane of thick blonde hair swept back to give his high cheekbones, broad nose and heavy brows a vaguely leonine appearance. He has a small pad on the desk in front of him and is toying with a pencil.

My judgement is that Moll will speak only if spoken to and that the woman with the laptop is here to record what transpires in the meeting, rather than to have any other active participation. The AC, the Lieutenant General and the three civilians are clearly serious players, so I need to be on my mettle.

"DC Gray." The AC takes the lead. "As I advised you a few moments ago, there is uncertainty over whether you remain an asset, or have now become a liability to the operation that you are assigned to." Her eyes are fixed on mine. I quickly glance round the table and realise that everyone's eyes are on me. "We have a number of questions that we require you to answer, Detective Constable. Although this is not a court of law, you would be well-advised to answer truthfully and completely. Do you understand?"

"Yes, Ma'am."

"One week ago yesterday, you had a routine meeting with your handler, DI Leishman. At that meeting you gave no indication of the terrorist attack that you were to take part in two days later – an attack that caused loss of life and damage costing millions of pounds. Please explain yourself."

I clear my throat. "I believed that, if the attack went ahead successfully, those sponsoring the group I have infiltrated would show more of their hand. If I had reported on the planned attack it might not have been allowed to go ahead. I did not anticipate loss of life."

"So, DC Gray, you believed that you were qualified to make such a decision – to break the law – without reference to any senior officer? You decided alone that millions of pounds worth of destruction was a price worth paying in the hope that it would shed more light on those sponsoring the group? And you believe that failure to anticipate loss of life exonerates you from responsibility for such loss?

"Ma'am, the Covert Human Intelligence Sources Act of 2021

makes provision for undercover law enforcement agents to commit crime in the undertaking of their duty. It is widely acknowledged that undercover officers, due to the isolated nature of their roles, sometimes have to act on their own initiative in order to maintain their cover. My duty was to determine how dangerous this group was, and what it might get involved in. My judgement was that, as well as enhancing my credibility, going ahead with the attack would lead to much more valuable intelligence. I believe that judgement has been vindicated. The loss of life was unplanned as far as I was concerned, and was occasioned by other members of the group embarking on a sub-plot that I had not been privy to."

The AC has not broken eye contact with me, making it impossible for me to gauge the reactions of others around the table. She continues eyeballing me. "Quite the speech, DC Gray. And after you left the meeting with DI Leishman you became involved in an incident, occasioning the hospitalisation of two men. This was immediately after the meeting in which you were instructed to focus on your mission to exclusion of all else and to avoid involvement in anything that you did not have to."

"Yes, Ma'am."

The dialogue between the AC and me is interrupted by the Lieutenant-General. "So, effectively you disobeyed a direct order." All eyes in the room, including mine, are on him. His voice is low and well-modulated, with the faintest hint of a Bristolian accent. He has placed his hands in front of him, resting on the table, and is looking directly at me. I don't respond because he hasn't actually asked me a question, and because I sense he is going to say something else – which he does. "Is it acceptable to disobey a direct order?"

My gut tells me he's on my side. He's trying to help. "Sir, we both know that in the military you are responsible for your actions. If you are given an illegal order, for example, it is your duty to refuse to obey it. As a police officer I am required to obey all lawful orders and abide by the provisions of Police Regulations…" I pause for both breath and effect, "…unless there is good and sufficient cause to do otherwise. In the incident in question I encountered a member of the public under attack and in obvious danger. I believe that failure by me to intervene would have been a dereliction of my duty, Sir."

"Thank you DC Gray." The Lieutenant General's eyes briefly flicker approval as he nods to the AC to indicate that he is happy for her to continue. I use the brief pause as an opportunity to scan the room. Moll is focused on her lap, the woman on the other corner is reading something on her screen and owl-face is filling a glass from a carafe of water that he has collected from the centre of the table. The other two are looking towards the AC, waiting for her to resume the lead.

As she continues her focus on me I find it impossible to gauge whether she is an ally or a foe in this piece of theatre. "DC Gray, you have expertise in explosives that enabled the attack on Brightwater View. You have identified three further targets for the terrorists and are collaborating with them to identify the most appropriate devices that can be deployed to cause maximum loss of life. It could be inferred that you are actually an asset to this group and that you pose a genuine threat to the British public."

She raises her eyebrows to signal that I need to respond, which I do. I explain the strategy is to become an asset to the group *as far as they are concerned*, and to then use that position of trust to gather intelligence to report back. When I speak I do so in a calm, evenly paced voice, and I'm careful to answer fully and courteously. There are further questions posed by the AC focused on Amelia, the different individuals in the group, my views on Ryan, the attack on Vi, and my failure to report my meeting with Lord Waterson. Plenty of ancillary questions come from the Lieutenant General and from owl-face. The fellow beyond owl-face hasn't spoken, and has made no attempt to disguise the fact that he is doodling on his pad. The blonde haired woman has also been completely silent, and her face has been the very definition of inscrutable.

After just over an hour I'm feeling relatively comfortable. I've answered every question fully and honestly, and I'm confident that both the AC and the Lieutenant General are in my corner. Owl-face doesn't appear to have an agenda and has mainly asked questions of clarification.

"DC Gray." The unexpected intervention from the man between Moll and owl-face comes as a surprise. "Your cover is that you are a disillusioned gay former soldier. Isn't that correct?"

"Yes it is." I'm trying to work out where this is going, and I'm slightly disconcerted because he seems completely focused on the abstract pattern he's drawing on his pad. He hasn't lifted his eyes to look at me, even when speaking to me.

"But you are, in fact, heterosexual?"

"Yes, I am."

"So, have you remained celibate throughout this undercover assignment?"

"No, I have not."

"Please enlighten us further, DC Gray."

I explain that I still have my flat, and that my cover of working shifts in a hotel provides plenty of opportunity for me use a hook-up app to meet women and either go to their place or my flat. I stress how careful I am to make sure that I am never observed or followed when conducting these liaisons. I still can't anticipate where this is going, and I'm becoming increasingly angry that my interrogator continues to avoid eye contact as he seems to concentrate on his stupid doodle.

"And how often would you say that you are involved in these liaisons?"

For some reason my eyes flick towards Moll, who has stopped looking at her lap and is totally focused on me. "Fairly regularly. Not every week, probably somewhere between once a week and once a fortnight."

"A different partner each time, or is there someone regular?"

"A different partner each time."

"So, you are a young male, with what might be described as a healthy libido." He pauses his pencil and looks up directly as me.

I resent this line of interrogation, partly because it is intrusive, but mainly because I can't predict where it's going. I know that I can't challenge or question him, so I just have to suck it up. He hasn't asked a question, so I don't answer.

Instead, I give him my most disdainful look.

"Some of the group members are female. Have you engaged in sexual activity with any of them?" He's looking me right in the eye now. I still can't see where this is going.

"No. Doing so would contravene Authorised Professional Practice guidelines, as well as undermining my cover."

He looks down at his pad and places his pencil on top of it, before looking back at me. He tilts his chin forward almost imperceptibly, and I can sense he is ready to play his hand. "We have heard earlier about the regrettable attack on Vivienne, and the fact that she miscarried her twin babies. Analysis of DNA from the foetuses indicate that you are the father, DC Gray. Do you care to explain yourself?"

Shit! I'm struggling to contain my reaction. My head is swimming and I suspect that, if I weren't sitting down, I'd lose my balance. My stomach feels like a washing machine in spin mode and I'm worried I might actually be sick.

"Would you like a glass of water, DC Gray?" asks the AC. Owl-face passes me a glass from the stack in the middle of the table, and pushes the three-quarters full carafe in my direction. I'm grateful that he then pours the water for me. I pick up the glass and half drain it in just two slugs. I need to clear my mind.

"Well, DC Gray?" My interrogator closes in.

"Three weeks after I moved in with Vi, we both got quite drunk one evening. I don't clearly remember precisely what triggered things, but somehow we found ourselves in bed together. I do remember that the encounter was deeply unsatisfying for both of us, to the extent that Vi joked the next day that it was the last time she would try to turn a gay man straight. After that I resolved to be very careful about my alcohol consumption, and to arrange regular encounters with strangers to act as a release valve for pent up sexual tension."

A hush descends as everyone looks right at me. Moll is staring at me with an expression that I can't quite place, and even the woman recording proceedings on the laptop has paused to gaze at me. The silence is broken as my questioner presses me again, "And we are expected to believe this, DC Gray? Why on earth should we?"

"Because it's the truth." Four words. It's all I have. An even deeper quietness than previously falls over the room, like an early morning after a heavy snowfall.

After a moment, the AC resumes command. "Does anyone else have any further questions for DC Gray?" Each of the key players shake their head. "In that case, DI Leishman, can you escort DC Gray back to the other room, please?" Moll gets to her feet and heads past me towards the door. I get up and follow her, my body on autopilot.

Chapter 21

Back in the small room again, I'm seated in the same chair as before, with Moll opposite me. We've been here, completely quiet, for over quarter of an hour and I'm perfectly happy with that. But evidently Moll isn't.

"Why the fuck did you lie about sleeping with Vi?" Her voice is low and barbed.

"I wasn't sleeping with her. There was a one night drunken encounter that we both regretted. I had mentally written it off."

"A one night drunken encounter! Save that bullshit for the bigwigs in the other room. Do you really think anyone believes it? One single encounter and suddenly she's pregnant. That's a hell of a fucking coincidence, Josh. Why didn't you just come clean and say you were sleeping with her?" She's slightly out of her chair and leaning forward across the table towards me, hissing her words.

She's struggling to keep it together. I've seen her lose it before when we lived together. She's got a temper that could tame a lion. "My explanation in that room was the truth, the same as I just repeated to you." I keep my own voice low and steady, and look her in the eye as I speak. Moll sinks back on to her chair and into silence.

It doesn't last long. Although I'm not looking directly at her, I can sense from very slight adjustments in her positioning and subtle changes in her breathing that another eruption is imminent. I don't have to wait long.

"It's all about you, Josh, isn't it?" She leans across and stabs her forefinger into my chest. "You just piss around doing what you want, and hell mend the rest of us. You tell me what you want to tell me, rather than what you're meant to tell me. You make decisions way above your pay grade and leave me to pick up the pieces. You selfish bastard!"

"I'm sorry for placing you in an awkward position, Moll – but it's my career that's on the line here."

Her eyes and nostrils flare. "See! That's typical! You…" she leans forward and prods her finger into me more forcefully than before, "…only think about you!" She repeats the prodding on the beat of the last word, staring at me with naked fury. "My career is on the fucking line here too, you self-centred shit. Do you think if that fucking kangaroo court in there sees you for the liability you are, that you'll be the only casualty?" There's a pause as she studies my expression. "Yes, that's right, Josh. I backed you. I trusted you and I vouched for you when questions were asked."

I'm not sure if she's going to shout or reach out to strike me, but the question is rendered redundant as the door to the room opens. The AC's hand signals for me to remain seated as she addresses Moll. "DI Leishman, follow me please." Moll casts me a malevolent glare as she rises and follows the AC, closing the door behind them.

The interruption and Moll's departure afford me an opportunity for reflection. I do believe Moll when she says that she had my back and that she covered for me. I also believe she feels I've let her down – something I might almost take some satisfaction from, given how she let me down in the past. But that's all water under the bridge.

It's the thought of the two dead babies – that's how I think of them – that is front and centre of my mind. I've no idea which agency was able to get access to the foetal remains and arrange DNA testing at such short notice, but I have no doubt that I am indeed the father. There's an unexpected gnawing emptiness that I can actually feel physically in my gut, similar to the sensation when Moll told me about her termination. I've never consciously thought about parenthood, nor harboured ambitions to be a father, but perhaps there's some latent primal desire that's been triggered – I don't know. What I do know is that this kind of introspection isn't the best preparation for facing whatever fate is decreed for me.

The next forty minutes are spent alternately pacing round the room and sitting back down at the table, trying to anticipate what the decision is going to be. The possible outcomes range from me being pulled off the case and sacked at one extreme, to being given a green light and told to continue as before. Neither scenario seems very likely, particularly the latter. I'm not getting off with this Scot-free, but I can't imagine they would be crazy enough to jeopardise the entire project by pulling me out.

The sound of the door handle turning signals an end to speculation as AC Carswell re-enters the room and takes a seat opposite me. She is followed by Moll, who sits at the end of the table at right angles to us, and studiously avoids making eye contact with me.

"DC Gray, let me start by saying that I am very unhappy with you – *very* unhappy indeed. Your decision not to advise DI Leishman of the planned assault on Brightwater View, and your part in it, has created significant problems. You have caused considerable embarrassment to her, to me, to the Commissioner, the Home Secretary and the government. Your failure to follow protocol has caused the entire force to be on the back foot over the incident."

"I'm sorry, Ma'am, but as I tried to explain…"

"Be quiet, officer! I will tell you when you can speak." She has the demeanour of a crypt keeper, and the iciness in her voice chills me to the core. "Quoting the Covert Human Intelligence Sources Act of 2021 earlier was very slick, DC Gray, but it doesn't cut the mustard with me. We all understand that a UCO has to think on his or her feet and sometimes has to act in ways that would not otherwise be acceptable, but for the circumstances they find themselves in. That is most emphatically *not* the case in this instance. You were involved in a premeditated criminal act that you had ample opportunity to report to your senior officer in advance. You chose not to do so."

There's a pause as she fixes me with glacial eyes, spearing my disintegrating confidence that somehow I might see this out. This is not going well – not going well at all. I flick a glance towards Moll, but her head is bowed. The pause has lasted an uncomfortable number of seconds and I'm beginning to wonder whether I'm meant to respond. But that question is dismissed as the AC continues.

"You disobeyed an order from your direct superior less than

an hour after being given that order. Instead of providing comprehensive feedback on your activities you were selective and omitted to report on encounters that might be significant. You compromised your cover as a gay man by having sexual relations with a member of the group you were tasked with infiltrating. Your behaviour directly contravened Authorised Professional Practice guidelines that quite explicitly state that officers must never have intimate sexual activity during deployment. You further contravened APP guidelines by failing to report your breach to your senior officer."

She's effectively restated the charge sheet against me and it's pretty obvious the decision is that I'm guilty. My mouth is more arid than the Sahara as I wait for her to pronounce sentence.

The AC hasn't broken eye contact since she started to address me. I'm not sure that I've even registered her blinking. She's as impressive as she is terrifying. "So, DC Gray, given your list of misdemeanours, it will come as no surprise to you that I have decided to suspend you on full pay pending a thorough investigation into your behaviour. During the investigation you will be entitled to the full support of your Police Federation representative. It is not possible at this stage to be certain of how long the investigation process will last, but you should expect it to take a matter of weeks as a minimum."

So that's it! I'm screwed. It's over. I can't believe they've been so fucking stupid. So vindictive. Don't they understand I'm their best hope of avoiding a mass slaughter of innocent people? "Ma'am, I feel I must appeal to…"

"QUIET!" The previously arctic eyes flare like an erupting volcano. "I HAVE NOT GIVEN YOU PERMISSION TO SPEAK." She continues to look right at me for several seconds, before finally blinking and then bowing her head a few degrees to break eye contact. She holds that position for a few seconds as she takes a couple of deep breaths. When she looks back up at me her eyes are different – still angry, but somehow not the same. She resumes, in a calm, quiet voice. "DC Gray, given the timing and highly sensitive nature of the circumstances that we find ourselves in, I have decided that your suspension and the accompanying investigation should be delayed for three weeks.

This delay will enable you to continue in your current UCO role through to and beyond the anticipated date of the planned attacks. During this period of delay, I hardly need mention that you will be expected to conduct yourself in an exemplary manner."

She's a smart cookie, and has tailored a solution that allows her to have her cake and eat it. She gets to retain me as an asset during the critical phase of the operation, but also holds me to account for my perceived misconduct. "Yes, Ma'am – understood. Thank you."

She rises to her feet. "I need to make a phone call to the Commissioner. I will be back in ten minutes or so." I can tell from the body language and the millisecond-long glance between the AC and Moll that this interval is pre-arranged.

As AC Carswell closes the door behind her, Moll turns to look at me. "So, Josh, are you pleased with yourself?"

"What kind of a question is that, Moll? Of course I'm not pleased. I'm relieved they've seen enough sense to let me follow through on the operation, but I'm pissed off about the disciplinary action. Do those people not understand what's at stake?"

"I think they have a clearer idea than you do."

"Very cryptic, Moll. Who the hell are those people, and what exactly is going on?"

"The AC will be back shortly and she'll be able to fill you in about what's going on. Her diplomatic exit 'to make a phone call' is to give me a few minutes to brief you on the fuller context of that meeting – which is something that protocol dictates she can't discuss."

She's piqued my interest. "Go on."

"You're aware of the Counter-Terrorism Ops Centre where policing, the intelligence services and other elements of the criminal justice system are co-located to provide an integrated response to terrorist threats."

"For God's sake, Moll, I know what CTOC is – just cut to the chase." My exasperation is genuine, and I'm making no attempt to disguise it.

There's irritation in her eyes, and her breathing quickens a beat as she resists the urge to get into a slanging match. "Everyone agrees that the premise behind it is good. However, since its inception it has been riven by inter-agency rivalries and a lack of trust. It seems that your behaviour has identified you as a maverick and raised serious concerns about whether you were a liability to this and wider operations. A decision was taken that you would be interrogated in front of, and by, representatives from all the interested agencies."

"Shit." I shift uncomfortably in my chair, and an involuntary shiver surprises me. She's got my full attention now.

"Quite. Despite what you might have thought, the AC was on your side. I think it's obvious that the soldier was too."

"Hardly just 'a soldier', Moll – a full Lieutenant General. But why was he there? The military are nothing to do with CTOC."

"That's a question for the AC, Josh. I honestly don't know. The woman on the other side of him from me was some kind of legal eagle."

"I thought she was just there to record things."

"She did look young, but apparently she's a high-flier at the Ministry of Justice."

"Wow, okay. And what about the two guys on my right – the bald guy and the other one who gave me the hardest time."

"Spooks, both of them."

"Why would MI5 send two of them? Were they doing a good cop, bad cop routine?"

"The AC says that one of them was from Six."

"Why would Six be represented? This is domestic terrorism. Which of the two of them was from Five, and which from Six?"90

"The answer to both of your questions is that I don't know. What I do know is that the guy with the hair wasn't happy with your continuing involvement and was pressing very hard for your removal. It turns out the blonde woman seated beside the AC was the most senior person in the room. It was her that proposed you should be subject to a formal investigation, but suspended for three weeks. When she spoke, everyone else simply accepted what she said – no questions asked from any quarter."

"So, who do you reckon she is? Home Office?"
"Definitely. Probably a Permanent Secretary."
"Surely not?"
Moll dips her head slightly and arches her eye knowingly. "Not probably, Josh – definitely."

I make a whistling sound to acknowledge her confirmation that, while The Almighty might not have been in our presence, He had sent an archangel. There's a hell of a lot to process. What started out as a police matter now involves the intelligence services, the justice ministry, the military and a senior government adviser. The government have sent a civil servant so that the Minister involved has the shield of plausible deniability – pretty standard practice I imagine. One of the spooks has it in for me, but I don't know whether he's Five or Six.

"It's a lot to take in." Moll reads my thoughts and interrupts them. "But the most important thing is that you are still involved in this operation." She pauses and half-smiles, "*We* are still involved in this operation."

She's obviously gone right on a limb for me, as has the AC. "Thanks, Moll." I return her smile.

Chapter 22

The AC returns to the room, carrying a leather document folder under one arm, and sits back in the same position as before. She places the folder on the table in front of her, clears her throat, then looks up – firstly at Moll, then to me.

"DC Gray, a very great deal of trust…" she pauses on the word for emphasis and looks directly at me, "…is being placed in you."

She pauses again and I feel compelled to respond. "That trust is not misplaced, Ma'am."

She doesn't snap at me as before. "I hope so, for all of our sakes." She looks at me, meaningfully. "Developments are moving very quickly, DC Gray, with significant new information coming to light on an almost daily basis. Every data point, no matter how trivial it may seem in isolation, has to be reported back and then evaluated against the whole picture that is evolving."

"I understand, Ma'am."

"Actually, DC Gray, I don't think that you do – at least not fully. But you will develop a better appreciation over the next few minutes."

Her eyes give nothing away. I glance towards Moll, whose expression suggests that she is no wiser than I am. AC Carswell has the full attention of us both as she continues. "I have just concluded a conference call where the PS and I were joined on the line by our respective bosses. You are both aware that a basic tenet of undercover policing work is that the UCO should be briefed on a need to know basis – the logic being that, should their cover be blown, any information extracted from the UCO would be limited in its value. The consensus arrived at on the call is that, on balance, an appreciation of the broader picture would be of benefit to operational officers in this case."

As the AC pauses briefly, the silence in the small room is almost tangible. I am holding my breath, not moving a muscle – other than permitting my eyes to dart fleetingly towards Moll.

She too is still as a heron.

The AC opens the folder in front of her to reveal a stack of roughly half a dozen A4 sheets on top of a similarly-sized writing pad. She shuffles the loose sheets below the open pad, which I can see has today's date handwritten at the top of the front page, with three bullet points below in the same script.

"Both of you are aware that the political situation in the country is particularly febrile, even by the standards of a General Election campaign. The economy is in the doldrums and unemployment, particularly among the young, is at its highest levels in over four decades. Similarly, inflation appears out of control and the main political parties have each published manifestoes designed to appeal to the more extreme elements of their support in an effort to dissuade them from rallying to new fringe parties that have sprung up. There is also now compelling evidence that Russia is sponsoring Iran in a major social media campaign to foment discontent and undermine the electoral process. We also have reason to believe that Russia is the sponsor behind the group infiltrated by DC Gray, amongst others. The emerging evidence suggests that enemy states have identified our country as highly vulnerable and are making a concerted effort to destabilise it."

It's a long speech, delivered in a calm, matter of fact voice. It's clear that my operation, significant though it is, is just a subset of something very much bigger than I had imagined. I'm grateful for the context, but it prompts questions. There's no way I want to cross the AC again. "Ma'am, may I ask questions?"

"Go ahead."

"My understanding is that there is no military involvement in CTOC. Are you at liberty to explain the presence of the Lieutenant General earlier?"

"Downing Street believes that, until the exact nature of the threat is fully understood, the army needs to be fully briefed and on stand-by. The officer present earlier is in charge of the military involvement in the operation. Interestingly, he not only has a degree in psychology but also a lengthy spell in bomb disposal on his CV. His review of your psychological assessments – which was positive – did your case no harm."

So, Moll's view that he was on my side is borne out – and some. I wonder if my previous service as a squaddie counted in my favour. "Thank you, Ma'am. I understand that there were representatives present from the intelligence services, both MI5 and MI6."

The AC squints quizzically at Moll, but lets me continue.

"I can understand the involvement of MI5, but I'm confused by Six being involved."

"The involvement of Iran, and almost certainly Russia, had MI6 on alert. When we fed back that you had an interaction with Martin Jones, Lord Waterson, things escalated very quickly. Apparently he is an individual of particular interest. A significant proportion of his personal fortune is derived from his business interests in Russia. He was actually resident in Moscow for almost eight years when he was in his late twenties and early thirties, and his wife is Russian."

"Now that you say that, I remember she had a very faint accent."

"Another detail you omitted to report previously." The AC's acid tone reminds me that, while my questions are being indulged, I am still on thin ice. "Our intelligence services believe that he is working for the Russians. Whether it is for ideological reasons or simply financially driven is unknown."

"Why is he important, Ma'am?"

"For someone with such a low public profile, he is enormously wealthy, influential and well-connected. He has significant media and shipping interests, while his business success and political donations saw him ennobled. Unofficially, it's acknowledged that he is able to influence other peers serving on Select Committees, particularly in areas like foreign policy and defence. He also moves seamlessly in royal circles and, although not what might be called close, he is a friend of the monarch."

"Yet, despite all that wealth, he caught a train and a taxi to the funeral?"

"Quite – not at all what one might expect. Except that colleagues in the intelligence services advise that following someone in a private vehicle is actually easier than if they use public transport, particularly if the private vehicle is fitted with a tracker. Why Lord Waterson was quite so keen to mask the fact that he was attending the funeral of a friend's wife is a matter that is receiving some attention."

"So, has Waterson been linked to the operation?"

"Apparently not – yet. But there is a strongly held view that somehow he is, and investigative work continues. But perhaps now you can understand how, when it came to light that you had shared a taxi journey with him and failed to report it, you came under some suspicion yourself."

I can see that, particularly when taken together with my other perceived 'misdemeanours'. The thought crosses my mind that Amelia said she is investigating Lord Waterson and I wonder whether she is actually what she purports to be, or if she's actually involved in all of this in some other way.

The AC is one step ahead of me. "On top of that, DC Gray, you then met socially with Amelia Harris, a journalist who claims to be investigating Lord Waterson – albeit there is no clarity as to what it is she is investigating about him, or why. Given so many coincidences, it is hardly surprising that our intelligence colleagues had their suspicions raised."

I can absolutely see that. I'm surprised that, when the AC mentioned Amelia's name, my heart missed a beat. I make a conscious effort to pose my question calmly. "Yes, indeed, Ma'am – I can see that very clearly. And has Amelia Harris been identified as something other than how she has presented herself? Is she involved with the intelligence services?"

There must have been something in my voice that betrayed me, as both Moll and the AC give me inquiring looks, before exchanging a glance. "As far as I understand it she isn't aligned with the intelligence services. I believe that they are currently conducting discreet investigations, including light surveillance, to determine whether she is what she claims to be."

"I see, Ma'am. Thank you." Before I have the opportunity to ask anything more, I feel my phone vibrate in my pocket. The caller ID shows it's Ryan. "Ma'am, it's Ryan Watson – I should take this." The AC nods approval.

"Hi, Ryan."

Where are you? Ruthie and I called round at the flat earlier and got no answer.

"Sorry, mate. I pulled a double shift at work. One of the guys on the back shift called in sick and they asked me to cover."

Hmmmph.

"So, what can I do for you?" I can tell he's irritated.

We need to catch up. When will you be finished?

"Not until 10.30. Do you want me to come over when I'm done here?"

Nah. It can keep until morning. Can you be here by eleven tomorrow?

"No problem."

By the way, remind me of the name of the hotel where you work.

"The Aitchison Garden Hotel. Why do you ask?"

Oh, nothing. Just thinking we might bomb it after this is over. Teach them a lesson for working you so hard.

"That's not a bad idea. Okay, then – see you tomorrow morning."

Yeah. See you.

Ryan clears and I look up at Moll and the AC. The volume on my phone was sufficiently loud that they have heard both sides of the conversation. Moll looks at her watch. I know she's calculating when I'll need to leave here to be able to be seen exiting the Aitchison Garden at half past ten. "We will need to head off in the next twenty minutes to be sure we can drop you near the hotel in plenty of time."

The AC looks apprehensive. "Has Watson ever asked about your whereabouts before? Has he checked up on you?"

"He's always suspicious, Ma'am – always asking questions. But no, he's never checked up on me like this before."

"I presume that you have a way of entering the hotel unseen, so that you can be observed leaving it at 10.30?"

"Yes, Ma'am. I have an arrangement with a member of the management team, and I'm on good terms with a couple of the porters. They think I have a suspicious wife and are glad to do me a favour."

The AC seems satisfied, and wraps up the meeting with a further sermon about the importance of me toeing the line, and of keeping Moll fully briefed on everything. A car is arranged and I am soon speeding my way back across the city.

Chapter 23

It's 10.40 am and I'm already approaching Ryan's front door. I was ambivalent about arriving early. There's the off-chance that he might say something useful if it's just the two of us there. On the other hand he might see it as an opportunity to share his wisdom with me and prattle on interminably about his political theories.

Ryan answers my knock on the door by only opening it quarter way and eyeing me suspiciously. "You're early."

"Yeah, the buses all fell perfectly for me – saved me quarter of an hour."

He beckons me in and closes the door behind me before heading towards the kitchen. In the absence of any instruction to the contrary, I decide to follow him. The kitchen is immaculate and the thought crosses my mind that Ruthie is probably the one responsible.

"Isn't Ruthie here?"

"She doesn't live here, Josh." There's irritation on his voice. "She stays overnight when I want, but I don't want her getting the idea that she can live here permanently." I'm trying to appear contrite for having provoked him and, seeing my demeanour, his tone softens. "She's due here at 11.00, along with the others. Actually, she spent last night up west with her mother." He quarter-fills the kettle at the sink, returns it to its base and switches it on.

"I didn't realise her family were from London. I thought she had a bit of a midlands accent."

"Her mum is visiting, and staying at a hotel. Twin beds apparently, so Ruthie was bunking down there for the night." He collects a mug from the cupboard to his right then spoons in instant coffee and sugar from the two eponymously labelled jars on the work top. As the kettle boils he flicks the switch off and pours the steaming liquid into the mug, stirring with a teaspoon as he does so. "Pass us the milk from the fridge."

I do as I am bid and he pours himself a splash of milk before passing the bottle back for me to return to the fridge. The idea of him saying please or thank you is as remote as the possibility of it occurring to him that he might offer me a coffee at the same time as he makes himself one.

If I'm going to chance my hand, now is as good a time as any. "Ryan, once we've detonated the devices – what happens then? Will that be us finished, or do we go on to the next mission?"

He's holding the coffee mug to his mouth with both hands, eyeing me over the top of it. He takes a long, slow mouthful and swallows, all without breaking eye contact, before eventually lowering the mug. "You know why we're doing all this, don't you, Josh?"

"I think so."

"Because the whole fucking state – the country – is rotten. It needs tearing down and starting all over. Have you heard of the historian, Robert Conquest?"

Shit! It's lecture time, again. "No."

"He has three laws of politics. First is that everyone is conservative about what they know best. Second is that any organisation that isn't explicitly right-wing eventually becomes left wing. But it's his third law that's most relevant." He looks right at me and I can see that my question has fired up the zealot in him. "The simplest way to explain the behaviour of any bureaucratic organisation is to assume it's controlled by its enemies." He pauses, as if he expects a reaction. "Do you understand?"

"I'm not sure." I'm telling the truth.

"Let me explain. When I was still naïve enough to believe in mainstream politics, I thought that the Labour Party under Corbyn would provide the answers. Then, when he was rejected by the party, I realised that it was in the hands of its enemies and that we could never win. That was the lightbulb moment when I knew that conventional politics would never achieve anything and that I had to take things into my own hands."

I've heard this kind of shit from him so often before. Sometimes there's a different slant, but ultimately it's the same message. He's got that slightly faraway look that signals his pontificating is about to morph into a rant. It's maybe worth one more attempt to bring him back to earth before he goes fully into orbit. "I think I get it now, thanks. So, after we use the bombs to stick it to the man, what next?"

My reply and question actually seem to cut through as he smiles at me. "You've heard of the Hydra, haven't you?"

Oh no – he's going to go off on one now. I feign ignorance by shaking my head.

My bewilderment only serves to enthuse him more. "The Hydra was a multi-headed monster that Hercules was sent to kill. In the end he had to chop off its one immortal head to finally defeat it."

He pauses, as if I should know how to respond. Fortunately he only seems to detect the confusion I feel, but not the contempt or pity. "So that's what we do next, Josh. We kill the beast by chopping it's head off." He smiles at me excitedly, but I'm spared any more of his lunacy by the sound of the front door being knocked. I follow Ryan back along the corridor until he gives me a hand signal to indicate that I should go into the living room.

I recognise both Nate's and Merv's voices, and then Ruthie's too, as they are ushered through to join me by Ryan. Ruthie is explaining that she bumped into the other two as they were parking Nate's car, and that they had walked the last couple of hundred yards together. Her comment reminds me that Ryan's paranoia extends to insisting that no-one parks any vehicle that could be traced too near his home, and certainly not on the drive.

As people are taking their seats I decide to engage Ruthie in conversation, mainly to avoid having to talk to the other two. "How was your mum?" I smile at her.

"Oh," she hesitates, "she's fine." She gives me a questioning look.

"Ryan mentioned she was in London last night and that you were visiting her," I explain.

"I see." She still seems slightly thrown that I know about her whereabouts last night, but recovers her composure quickly and switches the conversation. "And how is Vi doing?"

"I phoned the hospital this morning. No change. I'm planning to call by again to visit her later today."

Nate and Merv are listening attentively to my rather limited update on Vi's condition, obviously interested. Ryan's radar is sufficiently attuned for him to realise he should let the brief exchange play out but, as soon as I've finished, he takes control. "Right. Let's get on with things. The best way we can show respect for Vi – and for Jonno – is to make sure that we do our jobs properly." He pauses and looks towards me. "So, Josh, where are we actually at with the devices?"

"I've pretty much spec'd the devices themselves. It's the triggering mechanisms that I'm still working on."

Ryan's clenched fist hammers down on to the coffee table with an almighty bang, startling all of us. "For fuck's sake, Josh! The attacks take place on Saturday week – just twelve days away. We need these specifications now!"

I'm genuinely thrown by the ferocity of his outburst. There's an almighty temptation to flatten the arrogant bastard, but I know that would be counterproductive. "I'm sorry, Ryan. It's quite complex, and work has got really busy. You know that I pulled a double shift yesterday."

"I don't want to hear it!" The fist crashes down again. I can see the others shifting uncomfortably in their chairs. "No more excuses!" He leans forward to get his face as close to mine as he can without actually getting out of his seat. "*When* will the specifications be ready?"

"Forty-eight hours." I can read his eyes – it's not quite good enough. "Absolute maximum. Maybe sooner. I'll do my absolute best – I'll cancel work, everything 100% focused on this." I'm giving it my very best Uriah Heep, every sinew straining to communicate deference through my body language.

Thankfully, it's enough. Ryan shuffles back in his chair and adopts a posture that signals he is now addressing the entire group, rather than just me. "Okay, as I just said, we've got twelve days until it's showtime. There aren't going to be any second chances, so we need to get this right. We need to be on it."

It's amazing to be so close up and witness the transformation from the rambling madman of just a few minutes ago as he now assumes the mantle of clear, strong leader – and so convincingly.

"Here's what I want you to do. Nate, Merv and Ruthie – you each need to go and do a personal recce on each of the targets to the extent that you can. Obviously getting inside Pilton Community Centre might be asking a bit much, but you can at least get a feel for the local geography and the location of the place."

Merv is sufficiently other-worldly that he isn't really cowed by Ryan, so doesn't think twice about interrupting and asking a question. "Why do you want each of us to visit all of the targets?"

Surprisingly, Ryan seems to almost welcome the interruption. "A couple of reasons, Merv. The more different eyes that review every site the better we all understand each target and the more likely we might be to spot potential risks. Also, if all of you have visited each target personally it means that you will be familiar with whichever one is allocated to you for the 22nd. Is it reasonable to expect everyone to visit all three targets within the next week?"

Nate, Merv and Ruthie all nod or make affirmatory sounds. Ryan's smart – actually visiting the targets in question means the others *are* more likely to spot things I might have missed, and it will mean they are more familiar with whichever target they are allocated. It also means he has cover for not allocating targets to individuals before he has to, which is just common sense.

"Do you want us to visit the targets at 7.30 in the evening, or can we go any time? And do you want us to go individually, or can we team up?" Merv is asking sensible questions.

"Going at the same time as we plan to trigger the devices would be ideal, but if you can't make it then, any time is better than not at all. As for teaming up, I'm pretty relaxed if you want to do that – up to you guys."

"But I still get the target that lets me kill the most people." It's impossible to tell from his tone whether this is Nate's attempt at a joke.

Ryan chooses to smile it off. "Don't worry about that, Nate."

Ruthie's normally pretty quiet in these open discussions, but the fact that everyone else has spoken seems to encourage her. "So, what's next, Ryan?"

"Josh needs to get his finger out and get the triggering mechanisms specified, and you three need to check out the three target sites. I'll keep in touch regularly to check on progress and then we meet back here in a week, or sooner if we're ready."

"I meant what's next after the attacks." Ruthie's voice is tentative.

Ryan frowns at the suggestion he might have misunderstood the point of the original question. He casts a quick glance in my direction as if he's assessing whether Ruthie and I are in cahoots, and I've no idea how he will respond, although I'm braced for one of his furious rants. Instead, he sighs and smiles. "All in good time, Ruthie. But I will say this. On the 22nd, the beast is going to receive a number of grievous body blows. Then, when it is wounded and weak, will be the time to chop off its head and finish it for good." The slightly faraway look returns to his eyes briefly, before he snaps back into the present. "But that's not for now. What's important right here and now is that we execute our plan to perfection and make sure we deliver those body blows."

His tone suggests this particular discussion is over and the conversation moves on to politics and the pointlessness of voting in the upcoming election. It's largely Ryan pontificating and the others meekly agreeing. I judge that after twenty or so minutes I can engineer my escape without provoking his ire. I make the point that my time is probably best spent working on the triggering mechanisms for the devices and get Ryan's agreement that I should leave. I choose not to mention again that I will call in to visit Vi on my way home, as he would certainly regard that as time wasted.

Chapter 24

I close the door to the flat behind me, take off my jacket and hang it up, then make my way to the kitchen to put the kettle on. The visit to see Vi in the hospital probably wasn't a good idea as it's been playing on my mind the entire journey back. I question why I bother going – it's not like she knows that I'm there, and it isn't as though there's any change in her condition. *No change, I'm afraid* the nurse reported, deploying an expression that mixed sympathy with pity. It's probably a sense of duty – the feeling that if I don't call in no-one will. However, the nurse said that a young woman had visited briefly before me, at lunchtime. I would have defaulted to that being Ruthie but, as she was with me and the others at Ryan's place, I presume that it must have been Amelia.

While I wait for the kettle to boil I collect my safe phone and check to see if there are any messages – none. I'm just about to text Moll to see if she's free for an update on the meeting earlier, when the phone rings. Amelia.

"Hello."

Josh, It's Amelia.

"Hi."

Where are you? Are you free?

"Why?"

I need to see you.

"Why?"

Because we need to talk.

"What about?"

I'll tell you when I see you.

"Why not tell me now?"

Stop being such a shit, Josh. I need to see you. Where are you?

There's a note in her voice – fear, perhaps – that causes me to relent. "I'm at the flat."

Can I come over?

"Okay."

I'll be with you in twenty minutes.

The call ends without a goodbye, as if to emphasise how much of a hurry Amelia is in. Was it fear I detected in her voice, or is that something I'm imagining? Maybe I'm confusing it with the urgency that was clearly there. Whatever the case, she'll be here soon and I'll find out then. Meantime, I should update Moll. I drop her a quick text to see if she's free and the phone rings less than twenty seconds later.

"Hi, Moll."

Okay, Josh – what have you got for me?

"I was at a meeting at Ryan's house earlier, along with Nate, Merv and Ruthie. I think Ryan called it to make sure we were all focused on preparing for the attacks. He gave me a bit of a tough time for not having spec'd the trigger mechanisms. I've got a 48 hour deadline to get that done."

Okay, go on.

So I continue. I talk her through Ryan's instruction for each of the other three to conduct their own recces of the targets, and the rationale he gave for doing so. I give my view on the state of mind of all four of them – which is that I believe Ryan, Nate and Merv are all totally committed, but that I have just a slight uncertainty about Ruthie.

Why the question mark over Ruthie?

"It's a good question, Moll. To be honest, there's nothing specific that I can point to – it's just a feeling at the back of my mind. I don't know whether she's maybe beginning to have doubts as the prospect of actually killing people gets closer."

Okay. Worth keeping an eye on, maybe. Is there anything else? Anything else at all?

I understand what Moll's asking, and why. "This might seem odd, Moll, and it's probably nothing."

Go on.

"I arrived a bit before the others at Ryan's place today. I took the opportunity to try to engage with him about what the group might do next, after the attacks."

What did he say?

"He came out with some cock and bull mythological stuff about chopping the head off of a monster or a beast, or something like that. I wouldn't have bothered to mention it, given the sheer volume of tripe he bleats on about, but it wasn't the usual political garbage so it stuck out. Then, purely by coincidence, Ruthie asked him later on what would be next after the attacks and he gave her pretty much the same answer."

Pretty weird, as you say. Can you remember precisely what he said?

"He said something about delivering body blows to the beast, then cutting its head off. I think when he talks about 'the beast' he's referring to the state, or to society as a whole."

And you mentioned mythology?

"That was the first time, when he spoke to me alone."

And what was the mythological allusion? Was it anything to do with Hercules?

"Shit! That's right, he did mention Hercules. How on earth did you know that?"

As you know, Josh, I'm a lot more than just a pretty face. The second labour of Hercules required him to slay the Hydra. It had multiple heads and ultimately he had to chop off its immortal head to finally kill it. Why do you think Ryan would be mentioning such a thing?

"Honestly, Moll, I have no idea. He's completely barking mad sometimes. He also likes to show off his knowledge a lot, so it could just be that."

Maybe. Anyway, was there anything else?

"Not that I can think of."

Okay. I presume you'll be getting back to him with specifications for the devices and their triggers pretty soon. Make sure you update me on that, and on anything else important that comes up in the meantime.

"Will do."

Good. 'Bye.

She rings off without waiting for me to return the goodbye. A quick look at my watch shows I've got ten minutes or so before Amelia is likely to get here, so I pop a couple of slices of bread in the toaster, while I pour myself a mug of coffee. I fetch a tub of humous from the fridge, and when the toaster pops I spread it liberally on the crisp, warm bread. My first bite confirms how hungry I am and I wolf down the lot at a pace that can't be good for my digestion. As I lick the last crumb from my finger I hear the knock on the front door.

When I open the door, Amelia sweeps inside without waiting to be invited and heads past me into the living room. I follow behind, oscillating between anger at her presumptuousness and curiosity about what is so urgent. She turns to face me and, despite everything else going through my mind, I can't help but be reminded of how beautiful she is. She is already removing a thick, black hooded jacket to reveal a pink crew-neck jumper that looks like it's cashmere. Charcoal skin-tight jeans and black Cuban heeled boots complete the look. But, again, it's her eyes that are so mesmerising – like Sophia Loren crossed with Alexandra Daddario. She looks up at me as she tosses her jacket on to a chair, and I remind myself that I have to be on my guard.

"So, what is it that's so urgent?"

She nods her head in the direction of the couch. "Is it okay if I sit down?"

"Sure." Amelia positions herself on the edge of the couch, leaning forward. I park myself in the chair opposite her across the coffee table. Something's not quite right. It's hard to put my finger on, but this isn't the unflappable, sophisticated beauty that she's presented as previously. A million tiny non-visual signals that, for whatever reason, she's spooked. I recognise the signs – it's not something that's easily faked.

She takes a deep breath and holds it briefly, as if she's steeling herself. "Josh, I need to know if I can trust you."

She's looking directly at me, waiting. I return her gaze and hold it for enough time that she should begin to feel uncomfortable, but she just waits. She might be anxious about something, but she's tough. "How do I know if *I* can trust you?"

There's another silence, but much shorter. "I asked you first."

"This isn't the playground, Amelia. You obviously want something from me. I don't want anything from you." I'm hoping the professional truth masks the personal lie. "Whatever you want, you need to persuade me that I can trust you first."

There's yet another hesitation, and I know she's doing the mental arithmetic to weigh up the odds. "Okay, Josh – whoever or whatever you are." There's resignation, but still a spark of defiance in her manner. "You know that I'm a journalist for The Herald."

"A junior reporter, I think you said. It's important we stick to the facts."

Irritation flares briefly in her eyes at the barb, but she continues. "I know that you're not who you say you are, who you pretend to be. I have my suspicions, but you made it clear the other evening that you're not willing to go there." She watching me intently, looking for the faintest flicker of a reaction, but I'm not giving her anything. "So, I'm just going to have to go with my instincts and trust you. I'll tell you the truth."

"That sounds like a good idea, Amelia."

"I told you that I was at the funeral because I wanted to see if Lord Waterson would be there. I told you that I'd been investigating him for over a year."

"I remember."

"What I didn't explain was why. Lord Waterson and I know each other, or at least we knew each other – I'm not sure whether he'll remember me." Her head tilts slightly forwards as she's speaking so that she's looking upwards at me from across the table. Unfeasibly, her eyes seem even bigger. I can't imagine any man ever forgetting her.

She continues, "My father was on the board of a company where Lord Waterson was Chairman. Dad got me a summer job assisting Lord Waterson's PA in the gap between me leaving school and starting at uni. I only lasted five weeks before I had to get out."

She pauses, apparently finding it difficult to talk about. I'm intrigued, but wary that this is simply an elaborate performance for my benefit. "Go on."

She takes a deep breath and resumes. "The work was interesting, even fascinating. But the whole atmosphere was horrible. After the first two days it was clear Waterson was having an affair with Irina, his PA. Over the next few weeks he began passing remarks about me and my appearance, asking whether I had a boyfriend, that sort of thing. His comments became increasingly coarse, and finally he suggested that I might want to join Irina and him in a hotel room overnight."

She clocks my surprise. "I know, the sleazy bastard." I can see her eyes are filling at the recollection, but when she speaks again, her voice is surprisingly calm and measured. "I made it perfectly clear what he could do with his disgusting suggestion. He just laughed and told me that I had better accept if I wanted my dad to keep his job. I told him to ram it and he suddenly snapped and shouted at me that I'd regret it."

She inhales a mighty sniff and is clearly now struggling to keep herself from crying. "I was packing my things away when Irina came to see me. She told me that I had been very foolish to cross him and that she had already been instructed to begin the processes necessary to have my dad fired. I said that I'd tell everyone what had happened."

A tear escapes her left eye and she wipes it away from her cheek with her finger. "I'll never forget how cold she was. She said that my childishness – that was the word she used – had just cost my dad his job. She said to me that if I told anyone – including Dad – that I would have my father's blood on my hands." She pauses, as a mild shudder convulses her body. "It was just the way she said it. I knew that it wasn't an empty threat."

There are tears rolling down both cheeks now. "Dad was sacked that same week and didn't understand why. Although it was a huge company, it was privately owned and – as the majority shareholder – Waterson could have his own way unquestioned. Dad ended up with clinical depression and didn't work for a further three years, before he made a partial recovery. If I'd just gone along with what they wanted then he wouldn't have had to suffer so terribly."

Amelia's resistance has crumbled and she is no longer attempting to stifle her tears. Instinctively I rise and move towards her as she gets to her feet to meet me, and become enveloped in my embrace. Emotion and heart are waging war with logic and mind inside my head. I hold her tight, breathing her in and comforting her while simultaneously reminding myself that I barely know this woman, and that she could be using her charms to completely blindside me.

After holding her close all too briefly, I feel her body relax and I reluctantly let her go and step back. Her eyes are still moist as she smiles, almost shyly, at me. "This is becoming a habit."

I resist the temptation to tell her it's a habit I'd be all too keen to develop. Instead, I return to my chair and she goes back to her own seat on the sofa. "That's a pretty harrowing story, Amelia, but what does it have to do with the present."

Amelia's composure has returned. She clasps her hands in her lap and begins her explanation. "Even though I only worked for him in a very junior capacity for a few weeks, it was pretty clear to me that he was involved in something dodgy. I've always kept an eye out on what he's up to and for the past twelve months or so I've been trying to keep closer tabs on him. I stayed overnight at the hotel the night before the funeral. That evening I noticed the three men having dinner at the table adjacent to me were speaking Russian. My ears pricked up when I heard them mention Waterson's name. I knew from my time working for Waterson that some of the more questionable things his company was tied up in involved Russia. I was able to get photos of all three of them on my phone."

Amelia produces her phone and scrolls to a picture of a thirty-something, dark-haired, clean shaven man seated at a table, then on to another slightly older fellow with fair hair and pronounced teeth, clearly engaged in conversation with someone out of shot. Finally she scrolls to a picture of a fifty-something, paunchy fellow dressed in a dark suit with collar and tie. He has receding dark hair and face that resembles a squashed cardboard box. Her phone is state of the art, and that is reflected in the pin-sharpness of the photos.

"When I got back to the office…" she is still pointing to the final picture, "…I did a bit of rooting around. This…" she taps the picture again, "…is none other than Anatoly Kuznetsov – the Russian ambassador." There's a note of triumph in her voice as she turns to gauge my reaction. "I went back to the hotel later in the week and I was able to confirm from two different sources that these same three men had dinner with Waterson the evening after the funeral, although he didn't spend a second overnight at the hotel."

There's no point in disguising my interest. "Can you forward those images to my phone, please?"

"There you go." The ping from my phone confirms receipt.

I'm impressed that she doesn't ask me why I want them or what I intend to do with them. The evidence suggests that she does actually trust me – or perhaps that's simply wishful thinking on my part.

"Amelia, when you called asking to come over – and again when you arrived – I got the clear impression that you were worried, scared even."

The equanimity that has characterised her for the past few minutes evaporates as my question resurrects whatever spectre was haunting her previously. "It might be that what happened to Vi has put me on edge." There's a quaver to Amelia's voice. "And at first I thought I was imagining it, but…" she looks right at me, "…I've had the feeling for the last day or so that someone is watching me. I know that might sound mad, and I haven't actually seen anyone following me, but it's like some additional sense is screaming at me that I'm being monitored or observed. Being followed. I could feel it again all of this morning, which is what eventually persuaded me to call you."

"And what did you think I could do?"

There's a hurt expression on her face which stings me, almost as much as her reproachful words. "I don't know, Josh! Listen to me, maybe? Put my mind at rest? Tell me that it's just my imagination? Just provide some reassurance. Can't you see I'm scared?"

Again, unless she's putting on a bravura performance, I can see that she really is frightened, and my heart softens. Whichever spooks are conducting the surveillance on her are obviously good enough to stay out of sight, but have done something to put themselves on her radar. "Listen, Amelia. I don't think that you need to be worried. Honestly, I don't."

Her expression is one of hope mixed with doubt. "How can you know that?"

"You asked about trust when you first got here. All I can say is that you can trust me when I tell you that you're not in any danger."

Amelia's expression morphs into relief and gratitude and something more. She rises from the sofa, rounds the coffee table and leans in to kiss me fully on the lips. Every fibre of my being is tingling as the oxytocin surges through my system. All my defences are down and this alluring creature can do whatever she wants with me – then a phone rings. The spell is broken and Amelia has her phone pressed to her ear.

"Yes, just following up on a lead."

Pause.

"No problem." Amelia checks her watch. "I can be there in half an hour."

Pause.

"Okay then, let's say twenty five minutes. Text me the address."

Pause.

"Yes. Understood. 'Bye." Her phone pings, presumably the requested text arriving, and she looks at me with a smile and eyes even more beautiful than ever before. "That was my boss. They want me to interview some eye witnesses to a ram raid attack in Hoxton. Gotta go."

She has already grabbed her jacket as she leans back in to peck me on the cheek and whisper, "I'll call you later." I don't even have the chance to mumble a reply before she's gone from the room and I hear the front door of the flat slam behind her.

I sit numb on the chair for fully two minutes, trying to process what just happened. Did that phone call from Amelia's boss just ruin an almost perfect moment, or did it save me from making a catastrophic mistake? Whatever the case, what Amelia just shared about Waterson could be dynamite. I take out my own phone and ring Moll, who answers straight away.

Hello, Josh

"Moll, Amelia Harris just called round to see me at the flat."

For God's sake, Josh – what are you thinking of?

"Look, she just called round, okay? Now do you want to hear what I have to report?"

Fire away.

So I report everything that Amelia had to say about Waterson. The history of him propositioning her, sacking her father and threatening his life if she were to tell anyone. How she has nursed a grudge for years and has spent 12 months trying to find evidence that would prove her belief that he is involved in some kind of nefarious activity. I explain about the evening in the hotel and Waterson meeting with the Russians, including the ambassador. I tell Moll that Amelia has supplied me with pictures.

This could be gold dust, Josh. Can you forward the pictures? We need to verify the identity of the ambassador, and perhaps see if we can ID the other two as well.

"Will do."

Can you also remind me of the address of the hotel for the funeral? I'm sure the spooks would have checked it out after the initial report that Waterson had been there, but they wouldn't have known about the Russian connection at that point.

"Yes, I'll send it with the pictures."

Thanks. Now I need to update you from this end.

"Go ahead. I'm all ears."

Two big things, Josh – both relating to Amelia Harris. My heart trampolines. *The spooks have checked her out and she's clean as a whistle.*

"What do you mean?"

She is exactly who she says she is. She's a junior reporter at The Herald. Good, honest upstanding citizen, by all accounts. No criminal record, no suspicious activity of any kind.

I feel relief surge through me, as I realise how much I wanted this to be the case. "You said two big things?"

Yes. And this is really interesting, given what you've just told me. One of the two guys who attacked her was 'persuaded' to reveal why they had picked on her. He gave up a name, and when that guy was questioned he said he didn't know who it was that had paid him to arrange the attack, but he did say it was a man with an eastern European accent, maybe Russian.

"Shit! Do you think there's a link to Waterson?"

Impossible to say at this stage, but definitely worth looking into.

"Does Amelia know about this?"

I don't think so – that feedback only came through this afternoon.

"Ah, okay. There's one other thing, Moll. Given that Amelia's clean, I presume that the surveillance on her can be called off."

Already done, Josh. In fact, it was called off almost before it started. When you texted yesterday morning to say she'd called round the night before, I passed it straight up the chain. They had already been checking her out anyway, because you were linked to her via the attack. Apparently they went into overdrive yesterday morning – phone records, bank, online activity, social media, employment history, social circle all the usual stuff. By yesterday evening they were convinced that she's clean and had switched their resources elsewhere.

"So she's not under surveillance then? There's nobody tailing her?"

No, and to be honest I don't think she was ever under that close a level of scrutiny. Why?

"It's just that when she was here earlier she seemed pretty spooked. She seemed convinced that somebody was following her. I thought that if it was the case it would be our guys, so I didn't think there was anything to worry about."

There probably isn't Josh. Remember, it's less than two weeks since she was attacked. It's hardly surprising if she's a bit jumpy – maybe even a little bit paranoid.

"Yes, you're probably right." I'm saying the words, but I don't believe them. "Okay, I better get on with spec'ing the devices and triggers for Ryan. I'll keep you posted if anything else crops up."

Same here, Josh. 'Bye.

"'Bye, Moll."

I ring off and immediately dial Amelia. It goes straight to voicemail. I text her: *Hi Amelia, call me as soon as you get this. Josh.*

Shit, shit, shit.

Chapter 25

I fire up the laptop and the screen reveals the half dozen or so open tabs detailing the various options I've been considering specifying for the trigger mechanisms. I'm actually fairly certain of what I will be recommending to Ryan, and I've been stringing things out. But given our last exchange, I just need to finish some final research then press ahead and confirm what he needs to source. Except I can't focus on the task in hand.

I open a new tab and type *Hoxton ram raid today*. I get six hits – the local paper, two nationals, the BBC, LBC and Twitter. The local paper actually seems to have the most comprehensive coverage. A Range Rover, suspected stolen, reversed at speed through the front window of a jewellers. Three or four armed robbers attempted to grab as much as they could. A member of staff, not identified, is believed to have been shot by one of the attackers. The vehicle appears to have been damaged in the act of ramming the premises and the raiders were unable to drive it away. They are reported to have run off in different directions.

I switch to Twitter. It's full of the expected wild rumours and speculation, but lots of the tweets contains photos or video footage – and as it updates in front of my eyes, I know it's the most current source of information, albeit probably not the most reliable. One tweet, timed just three minutes ago contains some video. There's a shot of the car reversed into the smashed shopfront, and there are at least four squad cars on the scene. There are plenty of uniformed officers, some keeping the rubberneckers in check. And there's two seconds footage of Amelia, her back to camera but clearly identifiable, talking to one of the officers. An enormous wave of relief surges through me – she's safe, or at least she was three minutes ago.

I comfort myself with the realisation that she's clearly too busy working to have read and replied to my message. She'll call when things calm down. In the meantime, I should get on with my homework. The challenge is that, although Ryan is no expert, he's smart enough to be able to challenge the suitability of whatever I propose. And whoever is supplying the devices will certainly understand all of the pros and cons of what I specify. It's clear that the spec will be for radio controlled devices – the trick will be to ensure that the signal can be jammed in the unlikely event that Ryan actually gets to deploy the devices.

I'm musing over a couple of alternatives when I'm interrupted by my phone ringing. Amelia.

Hi Josh. It's Amelia. I just picked up your text – sorry I didn't spot it before. It's been pretty manic.

I can tell from her voice that she's supercharged, probably full of adrenaline. I need to make sure that what I say registers. "No need for you to apologise to me, Amelia. It should be the other way round."

Sorry, Josh. It's really noisy here. I didn't quite get that.

"Listen carefully, Amelia. Remember when I told you earlier that you're not in any danger?"

There's a pause at the other end. *Ye-es.*

"There's no good way to say this Amelia. I think that I might have been wrong. I'm not saying that you definitely *are* in danger, but there's a chance that you might be."

The pause this time is longer. *If you're trying to scare me, Josh, then you're doing a bloody good job of it.*

"I'm not trying to scare you. Being scared doesn't do anyone any good. I'm just trying to advise you that you should be on your guard." This isn't going well. "After you left here earlier, did you still have the feeling that you were being followed?"

No. No, not really. To be honest, after what you said, I was more relaxed. I wasn't even thinking about it. I was more concentrated on getting here to interview witnesses. Why? Am I being followed? Her voice rises an octave. *Is there someone after me? Am I in danger?*

"I'm not saying that, Amelia. I'm just saying that I might have been wrong to be quite so reassuring earlier."

For God's sake, Josh, can't you just tell me what's going on?

I don't think I have any choice. "Okay. Can you get back here?"

No way, Josh. I just got a cracking interview with the

inspector on the scene here. I need to get my story filed. I reckon I'll get a by-line for this piece.

"All right. I'll come to you. Where will you be?"

The Herald offices in Plaistow. Do you know the address?

"I'll find it. When will you be done there?"

I can be there on the tube in less than half an hour, so I should easily be finished in a couple of hours from now.

"Right. I'll give you a call when I'm outside. See you later."

'Bye.

"'Bye."

My phone had buzzed during the conversation with Amelia, so I check and see a missed call and a voicemail from Moll. The message is short – *Ring me when you get this, Josh.*

I'm checking the address for The Herald on my laptop as I dial Moll's number. Her phone rings out half a dozen times before switching to answerphone. I leave a message to let her know I've returned her call and start checking online for the quickest way to get to Plaistow from here. I reckon ten minutes on the bus and then two tubes will be quicker than a cab at this time of day. As I get to my feet to go for my jacket, Moll rings.

Is now a good time?

"As good as any."

When we talked earlier I was distracted by the main case. I didn't put enough weight behind Amelia Harris' concerns that she was being followed. Given the evidence that the previous attack on her wasn't random, we should be taking this seriously.

"Agreed – and I'm ahead of you."

What do you mean?

"I've agreed to meet her outside her office. I was just about to leave now."

Wouldn't it be better if someone else dealt with this, Josh? It's not as if you've got nothing else to be getting on with.

"Maybe. It could be that I hand her over to someone else, but I've already committed to meeting her – so I should follow through on that at least."

And what are you going to say? What will you tell her?

"She's smart, Moll. She already has me sussed and will have her suspicions that I'm involved in some covert or UC op. I reckon that sharing some of what's going on – without going into detail – might be our best bet."

Don't be a prick, Josh! She's a journalist, for God's sake. If you give her even a sniff of what's going on she'll probably have it online and in print before we have a chance to stop her.

"I'm not so sure, Moll. You haven't met her. I think her hatred of Waterson would override any journalistic instincts."

That's not your call, Josh. You cannot tell her anything that puts the operation at risk.

"Understood."

We end the call with me promising to update Moll on how I get on with Amelia. I get my jacket and leave the flat, headed for Plaistow.

Ninety-five minutes later I'm sitting on a stool nursing a decaf Americano. I'm at one end of a bar in the window of a burger joint, immediately opposite The Herald building in Plaistow. There's a thirty-something man, dark-haired, clean shaven, wearing a smart navy suit playing with his phone at the opposite end of the bar, by the door. Between us, slightly nearer me, is a late-teenage girl in school uniform who appears to be in an intense text exchange on her smartphone. The seating area behind us, between the shop frontage and the servery, consists of a series of sparsely populated tables where individuals and one couple are consuming their chosen heart attack fuels.

I know it's a bit earlier than arranged, but I reckon I'll call her now on the off chance that she might be ready. "Hello, Amelia?"

Hi Josh, You're early. But it's okay, I'm....

Shit! "Sorry, my boss is trying to get hold of me. I'll ring you right back." I ring off without waiting for an acknowledgement, and immediately pretend that I'm taking another call. Shit, shit, shit! As soon as I said Amelia's name I clocked the barely perceptible change in the demeanour of the guy by the door – straining to hear what I was saying, whilst straining even harder to appear not to be listening. "Hi Mark." Pause. "Just finished the drop off in Plaistow and having a coffee." Pause. "Oh, yeah. I was trying to call that girl I was telling you about – the one I met at the club last Saturday." Another pause and a snatched look in the direction of my eavesdropper. "Okay. If it's that urgent send it to me now and I'll look at it straight away." Pause. "Fine. Goodbye."

I quickly scroll to my photos and confirm what I already know. The guy in the navy suit is one of the Russian speakers that Amelia photographed at the hotel. I suspect he's a pro and will be likely to have clocked me. I pretend to be engrossed in something on my phone as I text Amelia and Moll jointly. *Russian photographed by Amelia at hotel is now seated in restaurant opposite The Herald building in Plaistow, clearly watching the place. Suspect he is on to me. I will enter Herald building, meet Amelia and escort her to safety.*

I press send and see that the FSB or GRU guy, or whatever he is, is pretending to play with his own phone, while squinting beyond it to try to study my reflection in the window. My phone vibrates. Amelia texts *Come into reception and turn left. I will be there out of sight from the front. There is a back entrance we can use. Two minutes.* I text her back an okay.

I'm about to put my phone away when a text flashes through from Moll. *Sit tight and do nothing. Will have back up with you in nine minutes.* The text fades and I don't bother to open it. Moll will know it's been delivered, but can't be sure I've seen it. Good old plausible deniability. I put my phone in my pocket, slide off my stool and make my way past Boris and out the front door. If I cross the road and go straight into The Herald building it will confirm to him that I'm going for Amelia, but I reckon he already knows that. I cross over and get to the door before turning to look back. He's followed me out and is standing at the kerb on the other side, looking right at me. I touch my forelock and smile, then make my way into the reception foyer of the building.

The uniformed man behind the reception desk is on the phone and continues his conversation as he fixes me with one eye. I'm spared the decision of whether I have to approach the desk to sign in by Amelia hissing my name and beckoning me round the corner to the left of the entrance vestibule. The receptionist glances towards Amelia and then me, waving me through with a dismissive flick of the fingers of his free hand.

"Josh, what's going on? Why is this man following me?" Her eyes, almost impossibly, are even larger than ever, magnified by her obvious fear.

"First things first, let's get you away from here to somewhere safe. Your text mentioned a back entrance?"

"This way." She indicates a wooden double-door behind her and turns to lead the way. We travel along a surprisingly long corridor – I hadn't appreciated how deep the building was – then down a flight of stairs, before arriving at an anonymous blue door. Amelia presents a card to a reader and pushes the door outwards. We exit into a narrow service road that runs along the back of the building, turn right and then left down a narrow passageway that eventually opens out on to a secondary retail parade. I'm pretty confident that we're neither being followed nor observed – in fact I suspect that Boris probably cleared off once he knew that I'd clocked him.

Nevertheless, there's no point in running any risks. I wave at a cab driving past on the opposite side of the road. As it waits for a break in the oncoming traffic so that it can turn I beckon Amelia closer. "Do you trust me?" Her nod prompts me to continue. "Good. Please don't ask questions until I tell you it's safe. And please do everything I ask. Are you okay with that?" There's another nod followed by a fearful glance around as we climb into the taxi that has now pulled up beside us.

I instruct the cabbie to take us to Kings Cross St. Pancras and he pulls back out into the traffic. "Can you pass me your phone, Amelia?" Her hand feels for it in her pocket. "But can you unlock it first, please?" She does as requested and hands over the device. I open *Settings*, tap on *Security & location*, then tap *Location* and turn off *Use location*. Amelia watches exactly what I'm doing and I sense she understands. I return the phone and she slides it back into her pocket. She shuffles along the seat so that our two sides are pressed together and leans her head against my shoulder. But she can't settle and is soon fidgeting and looking out of the windows, obviously still scared. We make the rest of the journey in silence – aside from the odd oath muttered by our cabbie when another driver or pedestrian does something to rile him.

After I pay and we get out of the cab Amelia pushes me gently towards the side of the building that the cab dropped us outside. She moves sufficiently close for it to constitute a clear, albeit welcome, invasion of my personal space. "Did you genuinely think there was a chance the taxi was bugged or that the driver might be eavesdropping on us?" Her voice is calm and assured, as though the cab journey has allowed her to regain her composure.

"No. Not really. But there seemed no point in running any risks."

"And you brought us to Kings Cross because there are more underground lines here than anywhere else, didn't you?" She is a really smart cookie. "Do you honestly think we might still be being followed?"

"Again, no – not really. But it's sensible that we take every precaution possible."

She smiles acknowledgement and then follows my lead to the ticket machines inside the station, where I purchase a pair of one-day travelcards. We catch the Circle to Notting Hill Gate and then the Central line to Tottenham Court Road, where we resurface and go to an anonymous electronics shop and buy a pre-paid super-cheap smartphone and sim card. I'm aware that Amelia has noted my use of cash to pay for these, just as with the taxi fare and travel cards earlier. We take a further two tubes to Southwark. I've tried to ensure that we avoided surveillance cameras since we got out of the cab, and now I'm on really familiar territory and know exactly which route to follow to guarantee that we won't be observed.

After twenty minutes walking, including doubling back on ourselves twice, we arrive at the 80's-built block that I still think of as home. We take the lift to the fifth floor where Amelia follows me to the front door and through into the flat. I'm not particularly houseproud, but I feel pleased with myself that I've left it in such a tidy state after my last visit here. Amelia is looking around the place slowly, drinking in detail and that quick mind of hers computing, assessing.

"I'm safe here, aren't I?" She fixes her attention on me. "This is where you live when you're not being Josh, the gay ex-squaddie who is friends with Vi and her weird mates – isn't it? This is your real home. So, who are you? What's your real name?"

"Amelia, there are things I can tell you and things that I can't. I know that's frustrating, but that's how it is."

"Do you have any idea how clichéd and cheesy that sounds? Do you, Josh?" She's looking at me with defiance radiating from every pore. "I suppose that I have to keep calling you Josh?"

"The attack on you wasn't random. It was commissioned, indirectly, possibly by someone with a Russian accent. Your instincts told you that you were being followed and it turns out to be one of the Russians you photographed the night before Vi's mum's funeral."

I've got her full attention now. The anger has subsided, replaced by a total focus on what I'm saying.

"It's fair to assume that you are in some sort of danger. You need to disappear – go somewhere that nobody will be able to find you. You need to call your employer and make up some excuse – maybe a family bereavement – that gives you a reason for not going into work. You need to lie low until it's safe."

"How long do I need to hide?"

"Honestly, I don't know – maybe the best part of a fortnight. But I can't be certain." I'm weighing up the risks to her. If I hand her over to Moll and the AC then our spooks will know where she is, and I have zero confidence that they can all be trusted 100%. "If you know some place where you think that you could go to ground, where no-one would find you, that would probably be best. I can get you some cash – you mustn't use your bank cards or online banking – nothing that could be used to trace you. And you mustn't use your phone – only the burner we bought earlier."

She's still looking right at me, those mesmerising eyes part frightened rabbit and part ice-cold poker player. She's weighing up her situation and not liking it one bit. Even as I say it, I know how rash it is, and how those further up the chain of command would view it. "Or you could stay here, if you like."

She still hasn't broken eye contact, although her eyes have narrowed. I know she's weighing this new option and I'm suddenly desperate for her to choose it. "I can't stay here with you, Amelia. I have to be based at Vi's flat – for a whole host of reasons. But I can call in here regularly – bring food, fresh clothes and the like." I stop myself as I realise that I sound like a really shit junior salesman screwing up his first ever pitch to a customer. There's a pause of several seconds as neither of us say anything. I feel a compulsion to fill the vacuum. "There's no pressure, Amelia. You can stay here or go elsewhere – whichever you prefer. You should go where you will be safe."

She takes a step forwards, toward me. "I trust you."

There's another pause, briefer this time. Again, it's me who breaks the silence. "There's one more thing."

"What?"

"My name really is Josh."

She catches me completely unawares as she springs forward towards me, and I'm suddenly enveloped in her embrace, her lips firm against mine. It's as though the entire voltage of the national grid is surging through me, my tongue responding instinctively to the insistent probing of hers. It take less than three minutes for us to wrestle and strip our way into the bedroom and on to the bed.

Chapter 26

A surprisingly good night's sleep at Vi's place, despite the baby crying briefly in the flat downstairs. Now it's 5.50 am, so my body clock auto-wakes me. I reach across and switch off the bedside alarm, set to go off in five minutes, as there's no risk that today of all days I could fall back to sleep. Inventory time.

Today is the big one – the day of the attacks.

I'm due at Ryan's house at 3.30 pm to meet the others for our final briefing.

I also need to liaise with Moll for the latest instructions from her, and to see what additional intel she might have picked up.

Today is also the twelfth day since Amelia took refuge in my flat. I reported that she'd told me she was going to ground somewhere that no-one would find her, and that she didn't tell me the location of. Moll was furious – absolutely blazing mad. But there was nothing she could do. Since then I've managed at least a few hours every day except two at the flat with Amelia. I'm careful – as always – to ensure that I'm not followed or monitored by anyone every time I go there. Amelia is smart, quick-witted, very funny, as well as compassionate and kind, and I savour every second in her company. We cook together, talk and laugh lots. But mainly we have sex – passionate, adventurous, prolonged and deeply, deeply satisfying sex. I'm lying here smiling just at the thought of it. Once this operation is over we can move in together. If that means I need to leave the force then so be it. If we both have to disappear to make sure she's safe from Waterson and the Russians then that's fine too. After Moll finished with me I believed I'd never trust another woman. I've barely known Amelia five minutes, but I already know what I want. We just need to be together.

I swing out of bed and head towards the bathroom where I perform my morning ablutions, including shaving and showering. I return to the bedroom and dress, then make my way to the kitchen for breakfast. I casually flick on the radio, before fixing myself a bowl of muesli and putting on the kettle to make a cup of tea.

Instead of the interminable election coverage, the radio is focusing on a major incident that must have occurred overnight. It appears that there's been an explosion in a gay nightclub in small hours of the morning. The reporter explains that there are unconfirmed reports of fire exits being blocked and that the death toll is believed to be in excess of fifty.

My interest is sufficiently piqued that I switch off the radio and take my breakfast bowl into the living room, where I switch on the TV. The same story is being covered on the BBC breakfast channel. The cameras are positioned well back from the scene, which allows them to capture the fact that several vehicles and personnel from the fire, ambulance and police services are still present and active. The woman doing her piece to camera repeats the suggestion that fire exits might have been blocked and that over fifty people are feared dead, although she takes care to stress that neither of these details have been confirmed by anyone in authority.

She is just about to turn to interview someone she introduces as a local resident when the picture switches back to another woman behind a desk in the TV studio. *I'm sorry to interrupt, Andrea, but we are just receiving news of another breaking story.* The woman presses her hand to her ear and frowns as she focuses on whatever she is hearing. She nods, presumably an acknowledgement to whoever's voice is in her ear, then looks straight to camera with her serious professional face on full beam. *We are just getting reports of some kind of missile attack on Conservative Party headquarters in Mathew Parker Street in London. Eye-witness reports state that a dark coloured or black Range Rover drove down Mathew Parker Street at speed, stopping some fifty metres short of Conservative HQ at number four. Apparently two men exited the vehicle and one took aim at the building with a shoulder-mounted rocket launching device and fired a missile through a window on the first floor of the building. The attack took place barely quarter of an hour ago, at 6.20 am. We hope to bring you a live report from the scene very shortly.*

There's clearly as issue with the autocue or the feed to her earpiece, as the anchor woman pauses and a frown darts briefly across her features. Her face is a study in concentration, and the unexpected interruption to the flow of the programme simply serves to heighten the tension. She holds her hand up to someone off camera in a gesture that seems to suggest she needs more time, but that the camera mustn't cut away. Eventually, after almost a minute, she has digested whatever she is hearing and is ready to address her audience again.

We are now hearing reports of a further attack, this time on the United States embassy, only five minutes ago. It appears that a similar vehicle, perhaps the same one, has carried out an identical attack on the US embassy building. We are getting reports that the missile struck a wall rather than a window, but that the building appears to have suffered little damage. There is speculation that…

My safe phone is ringing and I mute the TV. "Hello, Moll."

Are you watching the news?

"Yes."

This isn't anything to do with your group, Ryan's lot, is it?

"No. Definitely not. What are you able to tell me?"

I've been in since half past five. There's a strong suggestion that the attack on the Manchester club last night might be linked to a group of extreme right-wing nutters based in the Oldham area. Now these two attacks in London have got us wondering whether it's all part of the big plan, and how many other groups there could be out there that aren't on our radar.

"Shit. The fact that these attacks are happening today is just too unlikely for it to be a coincidence. These aren't random."

Definitely not the assaults on Conservative HQ and the US embassy. The CCTV footage from the first of those captures the guy with the rocket launcher in HD, and it's been identified as an RPG 26. That's kit developed by the old Soviet Union and its been around long enough for virtually anyone to have been able to get hold of it. But given our belief that the Russians are co-ordinating a series of attacks, the provenance of the weapon looks like it probably has been supplied by them.

"I presume the Range Rover is being neutralised?"

There's a team working on that.

"Of course. The bigger worry is what other attacks are imminent that we aren't prepared for."

Exactly right. Including Ryan's group, we are aware of seven different cells who are planning a variety of strikes today. But we had no visibility of the Manchester and London attacks.

"What do you want me to do?"

Just continue as planned. If you hear anything from Ryan – or anything that would be useful from anywhere – you'll obviously let us know. Meantime let's assume we'll catch up again later, before you head off to meet up with the group.

"That's fine. Ryan wants us at his place at half past three, so I'll get back in touch with you around one."

Okay, Josh. Look, I need to go – it's a bit crazy round here. Speak later. She hangs up.

I flick the sound back on and finish my muesli as the TV hacks try to manage their way through what is turning out to be anything but a slow news day.

The next few hours are spent checking the schematics for the explosive devices and the trigger mechanisms. I know them off by heart and could probably draw them from memory. But I also know the value of being totally prepared, especially when the stakes are as high as they are. I occasionally take a break from the laptop to check if there are any further developments on the TV news. They are still majoring on the nightclub attack and on the two RPG assaults in London. Police have confirmed that the Manchester incident was definitely caused by an explosive device, rather than a gas leak, and that escape routes had been deliberately blocked. The death toll is now being reported as 67, with an expectation that it will rise, and over two hundred casualties are still detained in hospitals across Greater Manchester. Representatives of the LBGTQ community are prominent in their demands that the perpetrators be brought to justice.

The Range Rover believed to have been used in the London attacks was found abandoned near Battersea Park railway station. Grainy CCTV footage from inside the station shows four men, identified as suspects, making their way on to the platform. They are obviously rank amateurs to have planned such an easily traceable escape route. It's no surprise when later bulletins report that four arrests have been made.

Politicians are prominent on all channels, each trying to seem more statesmanlike than the other – condemning terrorism, national security of greater importance than party politics, yadda yadda yadda. Unsurprisingly, it is reported that the Home Secretary has followed the advice from JTAC and raised the threat level to critical, which each newsreader seems to revel in explaining means that further attacks are highly likely in the near future.

My phone rings, and I'm pleased that caller ID shows it's Amelia. "Hello, Gorgeous."

Hi Josh. How are you? Are you busy?

"I'm great, and no, I'm not busy. Are you feeling a bit stir crazy in the flat?"

I'm actually watching the news and it's just so depressing.

There's a note in her voice that hints she wants to say more. But she doesn't. "Is there something else?"

I was just wondering... She hesitates again before ploughing on. *You said you wouldn't make it over today because you'd be busy at work. Then all this stuff in the news got me wondering – is that what's making you busy? Are you involved somehow?*

"Look Amelia, you know I can't go into any detail about my work – we've discussed it. But you don't need to worry about me. I'll be fine."

Okay. Just one word, laden with disappointment that I'm still being secretive but also with relief at the reassurance provided. *It's just right from the day you let me stay here you've said everything would be cleared up by Saturday, the day after tomorrow. And now, with everything going on today – and you being busy – your friendly local reporter here is putting two and two together.*

One of the things I love about her is that she's smart, and there's no point in pretending otherwise. That's why I just take the line that there are certain aspects of what I do that I simply won't discuss. I know it frustrates her, but she seems to be willing to accept it on the basis that I've promised to be more open after the weekend. "Look, Amelia, I…"

I know, I know. I understand it's not something you're able to talk about, which pisses me off. But I can't help thinking about it, Josh. Promise me that you'll be careful.

"I'm always careful. And I promise that I'll be careful today."

Good. And is there any chance you might make it over here later? Even if I have to wait up really late?

"I'd say the chances are slim to none. If I am able to make it I will, but don't hold your breath." The conversation moves on to life's banalities – what each of us plans to have for lunch, what she's going to have for dinner, the new miniseries she plans to binge on Netflix this afternoon. The trivia of day to day existence for someone cooped up in a small flat is completely fascinating to me because it's *her* day to day existence. We are at that stage in our relationship where absolutely every single detail about her is profoundly interesting. It also helps that talking to her provides a welcome distraction from anticipating how events will unfold later today. Eventually the small talk runs its course and we say our goodbyes, along with another promise from me to be careful.

The rest of the morning passes without the news reporting any further major incidents. I scramble a couple of eggs and have them with tomatoes on two slices of toasted sourdough bread for lunch, washed down with a mug of Earl Grey tea. I make a duty phone call to the hospital to confirm the daily 'no change' status with regard to Vi's condition. Once this is all over I am going to make it my business to sort out whoever is responsible for the assault on her.

It's only quarter to one, but I decide to ring Moll anyway. She picks up straight away.

You're early, Josh. Is there anything wrong?

"No, all okay here. I did say I'd call around one, so I'm not all that early. Is there any new intel? Anything I should be aware of?"

It's been pretty crazy here, as you can probably imagine. The Manchester and London attacks caught the top brass flat footed. An awful lot of shit hit the fan and I suspect there will be a lot of bloodletting once everything is done and dusted. Meantime, there have been a number of changes to what was planned.

"What kind of changes? Do they affect this operation?"

No to your second question, at least for now. On five of the other operations the decision has been taken to act pre-emptively. Go in and neutralise in advance – they've already done so in Glasgow and Southampton.

"What about the other three?"

They are scheduled to go in, but in each case they are waiting for the right moment depending on the circumstances of the particular op.

"So, if the bosses have decided to strike pre-emptively against five groups, why aren't they doing the same with the other two? Why isn't that the strategy for this op and the other one where they're hanging back?"

I don't know about the other op, Josh. The AC didn't share any details, and I suspect that she's probably told me more than she should about the wider strategy and all the fallings out between agencies after the earlier attacks.

"Okay. But what about this op? Why haven't we decided to neutralise it pre-emptively?"

There's some concern that we don't have the full picture on this one, Josh.

"What? What a pile of shit! What don't we know? We know the individuals involved, we know they're meeting this afternoon, we know what the targets are and we know what kind of devices they are going to use. What the fuck don't we know?"

It's twofold, Josh. First, there are five individuals in the cell, including you, but there are only three known targets. There's a question mark there. What if there are more than three devices? Might there be additional targets?

"That's a crock of shit, Moll. Even if there are additional targets and devices it wouldn't matter if we neutralise the whole cell pre-emptively. I'm not buying it." I'm in control of my temper, but I'm angry.

You need to stay calm, Josh. You're assuming that everyone will assemble at Ryan's house at 3.30 pm. But what if there's a fourth target and Ryan meets one of Ruthie, Nate or Merv separately – at a different time and location?

"Moll, I know these people. There isn't a fourth target, and even if there was it could be neutralised like all the others if we just swoop on the whole cell when they're gathered at Ryan's house later." A thought flashes through my mind. "Where has this come from? You said before that some of my intel had been corroborated by another agency. Is this coming from them?"

Honestly, Josh, I don't know. I don't know if it's coming from anywhere. I told you that things have got pretty manic. I'm not sure how much joined-up thinking is taking place, or that people are thinking everything through properly.

"That's not good enough, Moll. Lives are at risk – lots of lives. And just because the higher-ups are chasing their own arses we are being handed down really poorly thought through instructions."

I already told you, Josh – you need to stay calm. This is a very, very dangerous day and you know how vital it is for the chain of command to be respected. If the people at the top can't rely on the rest of us to follow instructions then we really are screwed.

She's right, of course. The decision makers have had hours to process data, evaluate options and make decisions. I'm simply reacting in the moment, without having had the chance to reflect properly. Every good soldier knows the importance of following orders – I just hope this isn't a case of lions being led by donkeys.

I've been pacing round the flat with the phone pressed to my ear for the last couple of minutes, the expenditure of energy helping me control my frustration. "You're right, Moll, I need to follow orders. Now what was the other thing?"

Sorry?

"You said 'it's twofold' a moment ago. What's the second thing?"

Right. There's a belief that Ryan might be a really good conduit to help us nail whoever it is that's working him, the people who are sponsoring this entire terror campaign. Taking him and his cell out pre-emptively would compromise the ability to land a much bigger fish.

I resist the temptation to observe that it must be a hell of a fish to risk hundreds of innocent lives. "Okay, Moll. Understood. So we are sticking with Plan A for this op."

Yes.

"Fine. I had better head off soon. Obviously I won't have this phone with me, but I've got your number memorised so I can ring you from my other phone if there's an emergency.

OK, Josh. Good luck.

"Thanks." I finish the call.

Chapter 27

Despite being five minutes early, it turns out that I'm the last to arrive at Ryan's place. Ryan greets me like a long lost brother. At first I think he must be on something, and he might well be, but it soon becomes apparent that he is jubilant about the carnage that has already occurred and the chance we have to add to it. He ushers me through to the living room where the other three acknowledge my arrival with silent nods before returning their attention to the television screen.

It quickly becomes obvious that while I have been travelling there has been another incident, this time in Dudley, in the West Midlands. A bomb has exploded in a civic centre which had been hired to host the reception for a Hindu wedding. As stunned and injured guests staggered their way out of the building they were cut down by a hail of automatic gunfire. The on-screen reporter explains that the attack is believed to be the work of a single male and that the individual in question has taken cover in the wrecked building and has exchanged gunfire with the armed response unit at the scene. The reporter advises us that there were believed to have been over three hundred guests at the reception.

I'm processing all of this as the horror on screen almost hypnotises me. I realise that identifying and neutralising the threat of lone individuals today will be a task that is probably beyond the resources we have available. Identifying cells like the one Ryan has assembled is more straightforward than locating which known lunatic individuals have been primed to cause mayhem today. The horror at this wedding is unlikely to be the last such atrocity reported today. The newsfeed from Dudley is interrupted by a solemn-faced male presenter in the studio who sombrely advises his audience that reports are being received of a petrol bomb attack on a synagogue in Cambridge. Details are sparse, but updates will be provided as more details become available.

Ryan seems unable to contain himself and claps his hands

together like an excited child at their own birthday party. It's the same behaviour he exhibited when we brought the crane down – delight at the chaos and not a thought for Jonno. He picks up the remote from the coffee table and switches the TV off, thereby assuring his audience's full attention. "It's happening." His voice is shot through with undisguised glee. "Manchester, London, the midlands, Cambridge – and there will be plenty more. And all building to the crowning glory of our multiple strike this evening."

He pauses to gauge his audience. All four of us are almost entranced by his performance, waiting to see where he's going with this. I imagine that this must be what it was like to be up close to Charles Manson, Adolf Hitler, Jim Jones or Pol Pot. Evil incarnate, but with an uncanny ability to influence those around them. I say uncanny but, in truth, Ruthie, Nate and Merv have the collective intellectual depth of a car park puddle and are incredibly biddable.

Ryan is off on one. "Social media is on fire! Different sections of society are blaming each other. People are demanding retribution, urging others to take the law into their own hands. And this is just the beginning. There are others like us, poised ready to strike and up the ante even more. Opposition politicians are blaming the government, and government ministers are blaming their critics. The voices calling for calm are being drowned out. The whole house of cards is on the point of falling down, and we have the chance to speed it on its way."

The whole social media frenzy has been building for a fortnight. Moll said that intel from CTOC and GCHQ was that there is a co-ordinated campaign by malign states to foment unrest and spread disinformation in the run up to the election. It sounds like it's now gone into overdrive. I'm looking at Ryan and thinking that he's the maddest bastard I've ever seen up close, only for Nate to leap to his feet and whoop, "Let's fucking go kill people!" Before staring at us manically.

His lunatic outburst seems to bring Ryan back to earth. He smiles and puts a hand on Nate's shoulder. "All in good time, Nate. First we need to run through who has the honour of hitting which target. Let's sit back down…" he nods towards the empty armchair that Nate just evacuated, "…and I'll explain who is doing what."

Everyone was already hanging on his every word, but there's an extra level of hush across the four of us and I realise that, like the other three, I am leaning forward in my seat – as if being closer to the words means that I'll hear them sooner.

"All four of you are familiar with each of the targets, so now it's time to learn who has been allocated to which. Merv, you get Drayton Park railway station. Josh, you get Pilton Community Centre. And Nate, you get North Greenwich tube station." He pauses, before continuing to address Nate. "Obviously you've got the star prize, Nate. Given its layout, you are virtually guaranteed to kill more people at the tube station than the other two." He smiles at his fellow psycho who responds with a demented grin.

I can tell from her manner that the allocation of targets isn't news for Ruthie. I presume that she's going to hang back here with Ryan while we three are deployed on our separate missions. I imagine that I've been allocated the hustings at the community centre because I'm the least obviously crazy looking of the three of us. The other two would probably be reasonably anonymous in throngs of people moving around busy stations, but would stick out more seated in a hall filled with political activists and journalists. My height makes me somewhat distinctive, but to a lesser degree than Nate and Merv's – how shall I say this – idiosyncratic appearance.

"Right, follow me." Ryan is on his feet and leading us into the hallway and through the door that connects to the attached garage. There's a Mini parked in there that I've never seen before, but it's the trestle table against the rear wall that takes my eye, and which Ryan directs us towards. There are four identical rucksacks in a row, each with a basic Nokia mobile phone placed in front. "Nate, Merv and Josh, pick up a rucksack each, along with the mobile phone in front of it, and bring them back inside the house."

I deliberately nod in the direction of the fourth rucksack and throw Ryan a quizzical look. "Don't worry about that, Josh, It's just a spare – a precaution in case one of the other three has a fault." He gives me a reassuring smile. Shit! There *is* a fourth device, and God knows where he plans to deploy it.

We dutifully troop back into the living room, three of us carrying our rucksacks and phones, and resume our positions in the same seating arrangement as previously. Ryan talks us through the plan yet again. Each of the three of us should time things such that we place our devices in situ then remove ourselves a safe distance and detonate at 7.15 pm precisely, or as close to that time as circumstances permit. My mission is arguably more straightforward as I can leave my device on or under my chair in the hall on the pretext of going to the toilet, and then trigger it once I am in a safe position to do so. The other two will have much greater time pressures as they will need to exit the immediate location of their bomb drops at speed because security is likely to react within seconds. They will have to trigger their devices the instant they believe they are far enough removed not to suffer injury. Each of us should ensure that we are not followed after the attacks and make our way back here.

It's a pretty shit plan. The likelihood of all three devices being triggered successfully has got to be questionable. And the lack of detail around the plan for evacuating the target sites and returning here is laughable. But then Ryan isn't particularly concerned with that. I'm sure he plans to trigger the devices remotely and therefore doesn't expect any of the three of us to be coming back anyway.

Ryan instructs me to arm the devices and watches me intently as I do so. It's not a complicated process and, once he's observed it three times, I realise that he will be competent to carry out the same process on the fourth device. Ryan reminds each of the three of us that once we are in situ and ready to trigger our devices, we simply need to access the only number stored in each phone's memory and then press dial. Then he asks each of us to hand over our own personal mobile devices on the pretext that we ought not to run the risk of those accidentally triggering our bombs at the wrong time. It's utter horseshit of course, but a sensible precaution by him to ensure that we don't have the ability to phone or message anyone else.

After enquiring to ensure that none of us have any questions, Ryan checks his watch. "Just about time for you to go, Josh." As my target is south of the river and further away than the other two, it's sensible that I leave first. As Ryan also pointed out earlier, it's much better that we each leave individually, rather than have three men with identical backpacks marching along together. He takes my right hand in his and shakes it firmly. "Good luck, Josh – you'll be a hero after this. Remember to come back safely." The faux sincerity is as polished as any line delivered by a politician. With nods and muttered wishes of good luck from the others, I'm quickly out the front door and en route.

This is the most dangerous stage of the mission. I have a live device strapped to my back and the so-called trigger mechanism – the Nokia supplied by Ryan – is a useless piece of kit provided to give me a false sense of comfort and control. I have no doubt that Ryan has phones containing the correct codes with which he can trigger the devices at will.

But, once Nate, Merv and I reach our respective targets we – and everyone else – will be safe. Each target zone has been flooded with powerful stationary jamming devices, set to block mobile phone communication signals. I spec'd sophisticated RF tech that transmits radio interference signals that spread out and saturate a spectrum of frequencies that block trigger devices from activating the explosives. I also spec'd sufficient power and additional antenna arrays to effectively ensure a substantial "dead" zone at each target site. I'm confident that our tech boys will have got the set-up right, perhaps even improved on my spec. There will also be appropriately trained personnel at each location to ensure the devices are made safe.

The danger is that, for whatever reason, Ryan decides to trigger the devices early, while each of us is en route to our targets. That way he would still inflict serious damage and likely kill a number of commuters. But I'm gambling that he does actually want to strike against the identified targets. The biggest risk is that he spots something is wrong. I have absolutely no doubt that I am carrying a tracker along with my device, and that the same will be true for Nate and Merv –

Ryan's paranoia will guarantee that he is monitoring each of us to ensure we are taking the expected route to our targets. The presence of such tracking devices precludes the possibility of intercepting the devices before they reach the targets – any interruption or deviation from the plan would prompt Ryan to trigger the devices early.

The critical point will come when each of us approached the "dead" zones. At the point where the trigger signal is blocked, so too will the tracking signal. Loss of one or more tracking signals might alert Ryan that he has a problem and cause him to trigger the other devices early. An alternative could have been to locate a jamming device near to Ryan's house to cut any triggering signals off at source, but if he drove elsewhere – for example to plant a fourth device – that wouldn't have worked. So we are left with this approach. Nate, Merv and I should all arrive in our respective "dead" zones within seconds of each other. The gamble is that, by the time Ryan registers that there is an issue, all three bombs will be blocked.

As I make my way away from Ryan's house and around the corner I clock my shadow. I recognise him as a fellow UC officer that I've met briefly once before. He is memorable for an appearance and a manner reminiscent of the kind of bloke you see in certain pubs, trying to sell shoplifted sausages and aftershave from a holdall. A hundred metres further, as we pass a local parade of shops, I acquire my second shadow – a woman in her late twenties who had honed her blandly anonymous appearance to perfection. The pair stay with me on foot, on the tube, on the train and back on foot for the final approach towards Pilton community centre. They're good – if I wasn't trained I'm pretty sure I wouldn't have registered their presence at all. I'm confident that both Merv and Nate will be oblivious to their respective shadows.

It's a 400 metre walk from the station to the community centre, and I can sense my heart rate increasing. My mouth is dry. This is crunch time and my life – and those of many others – is out of my hands. There's much more of a buzz around the place than on my previous visit – the fact that Mary Montgomery is speaking at the hustings has brought a bumper turnout of both voters and media. I can see five huge outside broadcast lorries from various TV channels in close proximity to the centre.

My heart freezes and I almost miss a step. What a complete fucking idiot I am! I completely forgot to factor in the huge media presence, and what the implications might be for the jamming technology. I'm trying to think it through but I have neither the knowledge or the time, and each passing second brings me a couple of paces closer to my destination. Shit! Shit! Shit! I'm across the road, immediately opposite the main entrance to the centre. Do I turn back or go ahead?

There's a man outside the building who's waving at me. As I try to figure out what is going on I feel a hand on my shoulder. "Okay, DC Gray. Well done – you're safe now. There's no signal possible here." A bespectacled man in a navy bomber jacket and jeans is holding my eyes with his – talking me down in a calm, assured and massively reassuring voice. "It's worked, DC Gray. Now let's get your rucksack off and disposed of." Two more men materialise from behind a van and come towards us.

"How do you know it's worked? How do you know what's happened at the other two targets? If there's no signal here or there, how can you know?"

The hand is still on my shoulder, now reinforcing the reassurance rather than to get my attention. "Old fashioned land lines and hand signals." He smiles. "My name's Doug. It's Josh, isn't it?"

"Yes, that's right. Nice to meet you, Doug." The light is beginning to dawn, but I feel the need for clarification. "So talk me through it."

"Sure. There are a series of landlines linking the three target sites, Ryan Watson's house and various points on the routes to the sites. We were advised of when the two station devices were neutralised. Drayton park was 65 seconds before you reached here, and North Greenwich was just a few seconds before your arrival. That's what the wave was signalling – that we'd had phone confirmation that North Greenwich was safe."

The other two are helping me off with my rucksack as the

discussion takes place and, unsurprisingly, are handling it with great care. "These fine fellows will disarm the device. The quicker the better, eh chaps?" His friendly prompt is met with reassuring nods – it's easy to see that these guys are real pros. "It's not just public safety that's at stake here, Josh, the broadcasters have been going apeshit for the last quarter of an hour – unable to do their jobs or to contact their HQ's. Quite amusing really, if it weren't all so serious. Anyway, it looks like your folks are here now, so I'll let you have a debrief with them." He smiles and turns to follow the pair who have taken the rucksack.

My two shadows step into his places. The shifty looking fellow speaks first. "DC Gray, I'm not sure if you remember – we met once before. DC Hamilton. Johnny."

"I do remember DC Hamilton, Johnny. I'm Josh." I shake his hand and then that of the nondescript woman, who introduces herself as DC Karen Woodley.

"Who was that you were with?" she asks.

"To be honest, I'm not sure. He's either a spook, or he's military. But the key point is that he seems to have things under control."

Karen smiles, "Almost certainly a spook, from what I understand of this op. Well, at least everything has come up smelling of roses."

"Not quite." My unexpected response causes both of them to frown. I explain about the fourth device and Johnny immediately hares off to get outside the dead zone to phone it in. Karen and I shout to the spook, run over to appraise him and suggest that he get the message passed upwards via the landline. I ask if there's a vehicle available and within a couple of minutes I'm being driven back north of the river and calculating how soon I can arrive back at Ryan's place without raising suspicions.

Before I get the chance to knock on Ryan's door, I can hear shouting coming from inside. I was pretty sure he'd still be here – given that the place is under surveillance I'm sure they'd have got a message to the car if he had left. The shouting is just Ryan, there doesn't seem to be anyone else shouting back. I hammer on the door.

A few seconds later and Ryan pulls the door open aggressively, his face thunderous.

I need to be on the front foot. "What the fuck happened? What went wrong?"

Meeting fire with fire seems to catch Ryan off guard, and he takes a pace backwards. "You better come in." He nods me through then closes the door behind me, after having a quick look out in both directions to see whether there is anyone outside.

I can hear voices in the kitchen and head in that direction, to find Ruthie and Merv whispering together. It's not obvious whether they are conspiring, or have simply been cowed by Ryan's fury.

Ryan follows me in and is back on the offensive. "How the fuck did you get back so quickly," he demands.

"I jumped in a fucking cab! When the fucking bomb didn't go off I just wanted to get away as fast as I could. Where's Nate? Did his device work?" I look towards Merv. "And what about yours?" Merv shakes his head.

I turn again to face Ryan. "So mine didn't work and Merv's didn't work. I think if Nate's had detonated we'd know about it via the news by now – so safe to say it didn't fucking work either." I take a step towards Ryan, whose eyes narrow as they focus on me. "So what the fuck went wrong, Ryan?"

He surprises me by pirouetting away and in one surprisingly graceful movement, drawing a huge kitchen knife from a wooden block on the work surface beside the sink. He brandishes it in front of him, and the madness in his eyes signals real menace. "What went wrong?" He mimics my tone. "What the fuck went wrong?" He waves the knife and I have little doubt he's willing to use it. "I'll tell you what went wrong!"

Ruthie, Merv and me are three or four feet apart from each other on one side of the table, with Ryan on the other. "What went wrong is that we were betrayed." He spits the last word and his features are contorted by fury. "Somebody in our team was a plant. A fucking spy." He's swaying ever so slightly as he shifts the weight from one foot to the other and then back, repeatedly. "Somebody who was working for the security services all along."

Shit! Shit! He's rumbled me. God knows how, but he's on to me and his face, his whole demeanour, is a study in vengeful, murderous intent. Just as I'm trying to anticipate his next move he lunges forward, diving across the table. There simply isn't time to react as he plunges the blade deep into Ruthie's chest. She falls to the floor under the weight of the blow and the momentum of Ryan's body. He is on top of her stabbing repeatedly at her chest, neck and face in a mad frenzy, screaming about her being a spy and a traitor. Merv is between me and the grounded pair, backing away in horror and preventing me from intervening. By the time I get past him I know that Ruthie is dead. As I pull Ryan off of her his hand releases the knife, which remains upright, embedded in her left eye socket.

"It was her. The bitch. She was fucking spying on us and reporting back all the time." He chokes up some phlegm and spits violently on her prone body, then takes a deep breath. When he speaks, it's as if a different entity has taken control of his body. He is calm and measured, his voice clear and well-modulated. "It looks like Nate isn't going to make it back. I suspect that both of you will be top of the most wanted lists, so I suggest you probably want to go to ground for a while."

"What about Ruthie? What about her body?"

"Fuck her!" He spits in her direction again.

"What about you? What will you do?'

"Don't worry about me. I'll make sure that this wasn't all for nothing." He makes his way out of the kitchen and through the door to the garage. I hear the sound of the main garage door opening. Just as I decide to chase the murdering bastard and dispense some justice, Merv shrieks, "She moved!"

I crouch down by Ruthie and take her wrist, feeling for a pulse. Nothing. Absolutely nothing. The only movement is the slowing seep of blood across her blouse. Then the sound of a car engine alerts me that Ryan is getting away.

Chapter 28

Merv froze the instant Ryan began his assault on Ruthie, but the sound of the car engine jolts him back to life with a suddenness that takes me by surprise. He sets off like an Olympic sprinter from the kitchen and has ten metres on me before I get up to speed. Opening the front door slows him and I halve the gap between us, although I lose momentum as I dodge the door, which Merv has flung back aggressively on his way out. By the time I get to the threshold I see the Mini turning left out of the driveway and Merv sprinting to the right. He's easily twelve metres ahead of me now. I'm a very fast runner, but I can see that this skinny bastard is much quicker than me.

There's no point expending energy pointlessly and I pull up. There's surveillance on the property so both bastards will get caught anyway. I make my way back into the kitchen and check Ruthie again just in case I missed something before, but she is stone dead. I go through to the living room where Ryan had placed Nate's, Merv's and my phones on a shelf below the television when he'd collected them earlier. I pick mine up and phone Moll.

Josh. Are you okay?

"I'm fine Moll. I thought you might appreciate a sitrep."

Absolutely. Let me put you on speaker. I've got the AC with me and two colleagues from the security services. There's a brief pause. *Okay. Go ahead.*

"I am at Ryan's house. He has escaped in a blue Mini and I believe he has a fourth device with him."

Please clarify DC Gray. AC Carswell's tone is business like and urgent.

"There is a fourth device, identical to the other three. I saw it earlier, when Nate, Merv and I were being briefed on our targets. As I say, Ryan Watson has escaped in a blue Mini and I suspect that he has the device with him." I can hear indistinct whispering between two male voices at the other end. "It's imperative that he is apprehended before he can carry out whatever attack he has planned. Equally, there is a danger that he might decide to detonate the device if he becomes cornered."

Understood. The AC pauses and I wonder what glances or signals might be being exchanged on the other end of the call. *Continue with your sitrep please, DC Gray.*

"When I returned to the address, Ryan, Ruthie and Merv were there – no sign of Nate. Ryan was going apeshit, clearly furious that our mission had failed. He had us all in the kitchen and was ranting. He was screaming about being betrayed and somebody being a spy." There's another muffled male whisper. "Then he grabbed a kitchen knife and launched a frenzied attack on Ruthie." There's total silence on the other end. "I'm afraid that she's dead. I couldn't intervene in time to save her."

Oh God! No. A male voice, clear as day. There's what sounds like movement of some sort at the other end.

The AC resumes control. Please continue, DC Gray.

"Ryan Watson raced from the scene and departed in the Mini. At virtually the same time Merv decided to make a bolt for it – I'm not sure why. I pursued him to the front door, but he was too fast for me. I observed the Mini turning left out of the drive, presumably driven by Ryan, and Merv dashing off on foot to the right. I had already checked Ruthie's body and found no pulse, but I decided that I'd go back and try again. Not that there turned out to be any point."

Thank you DC Gray. Could you hold on just for a minute, please?

The minute turns out to be more like a minute and a half, to the extent that I'm starting to wonder whether I've been cut off rather than just put on mute.

Sorry about the delay, Josh. It's Moll's voice, and she does sound apologetic. *There's a team on its way to you – it'll be less than twenty minutes. Someone from the surveillance op will be with you imminently, if he's not already there. We want you to come in for a proper debrief. The team that's en route has a spare car and a driver to bring you here.*

"That's fine, Moll. Thanks." A loud banging on the open front door and a shouted enquiry signal the promised arrival of the surveillance guy. "That's one of our guys here now, Moll. I better go to him. I'll see you in an hour and a bit."

'Bye, Josh.

I shout to the new arrival to come in. He enters the room and introduces himself as Tom Hartley. He's only an inch shorter than me, a bit broader and well-upholstered, without it running to fat. Late 30's, cropped greying hair, five o' clock shadow and the exhausted appearance of someone who's spend too many weary hours on an obo.

"Sounds like you've had a helluva day, mate." He gives me a tired smile and I feel grateful to him that he's making the effort.

"I like being busy – it keeps me out of mischief."

"There's a team on its way. They're bringing a car and a driver for you."

"Yeah, I was just on the blower to my gaffer and she said the same."

"D'ya wanna talk about it?"

"No, to be honest. I've already had to debrief on the phone and then I'll probably have hours of it tonight."

"Fair enough. I understand."

"I am interested in how your op is going. What about the two suspects that bolted from here? Have you got them yet?"

Tom Hartley has taken a seat in one of the armchairs which he looks too big for, particularly as he looks uncomfortable, shuffling his position. "Well to be honest, mate, it looks like a right royal fuck up."

"What do you mean?" I don't try to disguise the ice in my voice.

"Well, when everything kicked off over here, I had gone for a piss. That meant there was only George, my partner on the obo, actually in situ, so to speak. All of a sudden, the garage door is open and then, just as a car starts to emerge, the bloody front door opens and matey-boy is doing a runner up the drive. George is screaming for me while I'm trying to do up my flies."

Tom is recounting this as if it's a funny story to share with his pals at the pub. I clear my throat aggressively and fix him with a look that I see helps him realise that I think this is far from a laughing matter.

"So George has to decide. We've got an unmarked car just two streets away. Send it after the motor or the geezer who's doing a runner? George sent it after the geezer."

"What about the Mini?"

"George's thinking is that it'll easily be picked up on CCTV and traced, whereas the bloke who's on foot could jump on a bus or a train, maybe catch a cab and then we'd have lost him."

"So, he's been picked up? You've got Merv?"

"Not yet, at least not when I left to come over here. The squad car's been joined by two others doing a sweep of the area. He's a pretty distinctive looking guy, so it's only a matter of time."

I wish I shared Tom's confidence. "And the Mini? I presume you've got the registration number?"

Tom sucks his teeth and pulls a face as he shuffles on the chair again. "'Fraid not, mate. Our obo is set up three doors down to the right on the opposite side of the road. When the car arrived the other day we didn't realise it was going to the address until it started reversing down the drive. From our angle it was impossible to read the number plate or get a good camera shot."

"For fuck's sake! Well what about tonight? When it came out? You must have got the plate on camera."

"George focused the camera on the bloke who was running. Only shot of the car is side on."

I know it's not his fault, and I know I have to resist the temptation to chin him. But this level of incompetence is catastrophic. "You and your fucking clown mate had one job to do, and you totally screwed it up. You useless fucking arsehole!"

Tom is on his feet now. "Come on mate, it could've happened to anyone. You know what it's like. When you need a piss, you need a piss."

"Tell that to the woman in the kitchen with a knife sticking out of her eye, you fucking great waste of space."

I think that we both reach the same point simultaneously, where we realise we either have to let it go or take it up a notch. Common sense and maybe professionalism prevail. Tom sits back down forcefully and pointedly stares at the blank television screen, while I walk out of the living room and into the garage. Silence reigns in the house for the next twelve minutes until the team promised by Moll arrives.

Fifty minutes later I'm dropped off at the same location where I had my 'interview' with the various interested parties almost a fortnight ago. It's twenty past ten, but there are lights blazing on every floor and more cars parked than I can count. My driver has called ahead and Moll is waiting, holding open the door that I remember needed a card reader to enter when I was here previously.

"Hi, Josh." Her voice sounds as tired as she looks.

"Hi, Moll. Looks like you've had as busy a day as me."

She responds with a weak smile and a nod to indicate that I should follow her. We make our way upstairs and along corridors, passing various open doors to rooms where people are working at screens, on phones or engaged in conversation. There's a quiet buzz, but not the electricity that I imagine must have been a feature earlier in the day. I get the sense that the atmosphere is similar that I experienced after my regimental HQ came under mortar attack in Afghanistan, people busy clearing up after the worst is over, but still wary of unexploded shells.

Moll slows to half-pace as we approach a door at the end of the latest corridor. "Just a heads-up, Josh. The AC is pleased with you – you did yourself a lot of good in her eyes today. She'll lead the debrief. I'll be there, obviously, and a couple of people from the security services."

"Okay. Thanks."

Moll opens the door and leads the way into a three metre square meeting room, illuminated – like much of the building, by a slightly too bright strip light. A closed blind covers the window on the wall opposite the door, otherwise the décor is extreme minimalist – as in there is no other feature, except the rectangular brown melamine table with three matching chairs along each length and another on each end. AC Carswell is seated at the far end and to her right is a dark-haired, bearded man in his fifties and a petite, birdlike thirtysomething woman with manly short brown hair.

"DC Gray, thank you for getting here so quickly." She indicates that I should take the seat to her left, and Moll positions herself on the chair beside me. "These are colleagues from the security services." The man and woman opposite me both nod, the woman with a hint of warmth in her expression.

"I know that you've had a testing day, DC Gray, so I'll keep this as concise and focused as possible."

"Thank you, Ma'am."

"You are aware that there was a large programme of attacks planned against a wide variety of targets up and down the country today. You also know that, despite our best efforts, some of those attacks were successful."

"Yes, Ma'am."

"Unfortunately, while you were engaged on your own op, we became aware this evening of another attack that had not been on our radar. There was a mass poisoning of residents of a care home for former military veterans in the North East. Over one hundred and thirty residents and staff died, and others were injured in a subsequent arson attack. A left-wing extremist has been arrested. He claims he wanted to send a message to people in our armed forces to let them know that they would never be safe in their own country."

"I'm very sorry to hear that, Ma'am."

"You're probably wondering where I'm going with this, DC Gray. I'm describing that atrocity so that you have some sense of the wider context. There were a number of successful attacks on our society today. There was a much larger number – including those in your operation – that were thwarted. The agents involved in these attacks were right-wing, left-wing, anarchists, racists, religious zealots – a complete kaleidoscope of disparate groups and individuals, many of whom hold completely contradictory views from one another."

I'm aware that the two spooks opposite, while listening politely enough, are focused completely on me. The AC seems to be warming to her theme, and leans forward in her seat. "Colleagues from other agencies..." she shoots a sideways glance to her right, "...are convinced that this diverse range of extremists were groomed by the Russians to form part of a co-ordinated campaign designed to destabilise our country in the run up to the General Election." She pauses. "They believe that, while the Russians are clearly the puppet masters, they are being helped by some prominent members of our own establishment – in particular by Lord Waterson. The issue they have is in securing evidence that would prove his involvement."

The AC pauses again, this time holding it sufficiently long enough for me to feel compelled to make some sort of comment. "I understand, Ma'am".

"I know that you queried with DI Leishman why we didn't strike pre-emptively against Ryan Watson's cell and one other cell today. The reason is that we believe that Watson and the leader of the other cell might be able to give us the link to Waterson that we are looking for."

This isn't a development I'd seen coming. "Go on, Ma'am, please."

"Unfortunately, the leader of the other cell was killed in an exchange of gunfire earlier today. So that means Ryan Watson remains the only viable option we know of that could provide a link to Waterson. And of course the botched surveillance job means that we don't know his whereabouts." The last comment is accompanied by an accusatory glance at the pair opposite me.

"I take it that he hasn't been tracked down?"

"We were able to identify the Mini he was driving from CCTV footage, but it was found abandoned in a side road in Camden. Apart from that we've found neither hide nor hair of him. Of course there's a massive search going on, ploughing through more CCTV footage from bus, train and tube stations, as well as from the vicinity where the car was found."

"Ryan's smart, Ma'am. He'll change his appearance and disappear. He will have had a number of alternative escape routes researched and planned. It's worth continuing the search, obviously, but I wouldn't be confident of finding him quickly."

The AC nods, and leans back slightly on her chair. "That's what we fear too. And it's why it's so important you tell us everything you possibly can about him. Don't spare any detail. Tell us exactly what he said and did on both occasions you saw him today. Take your time."

So I do. I relay details of what happened when the five of us got together at 3.30 pm in Ryan's house before three of us set out with our devices. I strain to remember every word that Ryan uttered and report it faithfully. I realise that no-one is taking notes, and that no-one is recording this session. I assume that it will be written up sparingly afterwards. When my throat becomes dry I ask for some water. Moll leaves the room and returns with tray containing five glasses and two carafes of water. I am the only one who takes a drink.

As I start to describe the events when I returned to Ryan's address for a second time, there is a palpable change to the atmosphere in the room. Subtle, slight shifting of positions on seats, barely perceptible adjustments of body positions, clearing of throats – all signal a ratcheting of the tension. It peaks when I describe the assault on Ruthie.

"What exactly did Ryan say?" The AC's words are spoken very deliberately.

"Watson was ranting, Ma'am. He had clearly lost the plot and was waving a large kitchen knife around. He said that we had been betrayed, that somebody in our team was a spy. A plant."

The tension in the room is enormous. I think that I might be only person actually breathing. I continue. "He said that somebody had been working for the security services. I thought he had discovered my identity and was bracing myself for being attacked when he suddenly launched himself at Ruthie. Next thing he was on her, stabbing furiously and screaming words like spy and traitor. By the time I realised what was happening it was too late for me to save her."

The man opposite flinches and the woman swiftly places the back of her hand across his chest. She's clearly his boss. She looks to the AC, receives a nod of approval and looks back towards me. "Did Watson mention what reason he had to believe the accusations he was making about her."

"No, he didn't."

"Ruthie's real name is…was…Val Hope. She was one of my officers and was working on the op undercover."

The man beside her can't contain himself. "She's got a severely disabled eight year old son in a care home. Orphaned now." The emotion in his voice turns angry. "And you just stood there and let that bastard murder her. And after her covering for you."

The back of the woman's hand is once again against his chest, this time pressing more forcefully than before. "Enough, Malcolm! Stop!" The ferocity in her voice mellows in an instant as she looks back to address me. "Please accept my apology, DC Gray. My team – and me – are all very upset about what happened to Val. I'm sure you can understand."

"I do understand, and there's absolutely no need for any apology. I'm truly sorry for your loss." And I am, as well as being completely taken aback. I'm now racking my brains to see if there were any clues to Ruthie's true identity.

The AC takes back control. "DC Gray, have you got any idea where Ryan Watson may have gone, or what possible target he could have in mind."

"Sorry, Ma'am. It's a no to both of those. I'll keep thinking about it, but I don't expect I'll have any flashes of insight."

"All right. If anything – and I do mean anything – occurs to you, please let us know immediately."

"Will do, Ma'am. One question, if I may?"

"Go ahead."

"The involvement of Waterson – is that something that Amelia Harris knew about? Might she be able to shed any light on things?"

When I mention Amelia's name the pair opposite me stiffen virtually microscopically, but just sufficient for it to register. The AC's response is pointed. "That's a question that we would very much like to know the answer to. However, since she was allowed to go to ground we have been unable to put that question to her." The frown that accompanies her words signals that the AC holds me responsible for Amelia's disappearance, and that she is not exactly pleased about it. "Now, if there are no further questions, I suggest we conclude this debrief." She gets to her feet, as do both spooks, and the three of them exit the room together, leaving me alone with Moll.

"You made a bit of an arse of it at the end, Josh, reminding her that you screwed up by letting Amelia Harris do a runner."

"Yeah. I guess I didn't exactly think that through."

"Don't sweat it. I reckon you earned enough brownie points today for her to overlook that – and to help you when it comes to your disciplinary procedure. You've done well, Josh."

"Thanks. Can I ask about what that spook said? You remember he said that Ruthie – sorry, I can't think of her as Val yet – had been covering for me?"

Moll closes her eyes for a few seconds and sighs quietly. "When you called with the news earlier about her, that was the first time the intelligence services confirmed that she was one of them. The spook that was in here and another of his colleagues we listening in on the call. You could see that they were crushed. The other guy – the one you've not met – was in tears."

"Shit. And what about her covering for me?"

"Apparently Ryan had some suspicions about you. He asked her to check you out on three separate occasions, which she did. She had obviously clocked the fact that you were a UCO, so fed back to Ryan the answers he needed to hear to allay his fears. Didn't you have any inkling that she was a spook?"

"No, not at all. God, that's terrible. I feel so sorry." And I really do.

"There's another thing that I need to update you on, Josh. Four people have been arrested in connection with the attack on Vi."

I'm all ears. "Go on."

"They've been charged with assault and bailed."

"Assault rather than attempted murder?"

"You know how it works. The CPS will have advised there's a better chance of making the assault charge stick."

I know she's right, but it's still sickening. "And what about motive? Were they put up to it by someone?"

"Too early to be certain, but it doesn't look like it. Apparently they were on a weekend visit to one of the men's brothers in London, got a bit bored and decided to have a bit of fun with the young immigrant mother. Then Vi got involved and it all escalated."

"God Almighty. It makes me fucking sick."

"It's been a long day, Josh. Time you headed home for some shut-eye. We can reconvene again tomorrow to plan next steps. Do you want me to arrange a car for you?"

"That would be great. Thanks."

Chapter 29

I'm just about to put the key in the lock when I realise that I can hear Amelia's voice, albeit sufficiently muffled for her actual words to be impossible to distinguish. It's ten past one in the morning so I'm surprised that she's still up, and utterly astonished that she's got company. As I press ahead and unlock the door I hear her say *I've got to go.*

When I get to the living room she's rising from the table to greet me, her face a mixture of 'caught with hand in cookie jar' and warm greeting. The thought flashes through my mind that the latter is being forced to disguise the former.

"Josh!" She throws herself towards me, wraps her arms round my waist and squeezes. "I didn't think you would be here until tomorrow."

"Who were you talking to just now?"

"Oh, eh, just a guy called Harry Chisholm about work stuff."

"Isn't it kind of late to be talking to anyone about work?"

Amelia tilts her head slightly to the side, arches her eyebrows and smiles. "Why Josh, I do believe that you might be a little jealous!"

I feel myself bristle at the suggestion. "Not at all. It's a perfectly reasonable question."

She's still smiling as she gestures to the table behind her with a flourish of her arm. "I hope you don't mind, but I've been using your printer to print out photos from my phone." I can see the desk is largely covered with images of varying sizes alongside a pair of large kitchen scissors. Amelia continues. "I was playing around with how they might be laid out on a page – I find it easier to do with physical copies than on a computer screen."

"That's all well and good, but it doesn't explain phone calls in the small hours of the morning."

"I'm coming to that. I just thought you'd appreciate a little bit of context first, my favourite green-eyed monster." Her eyes are sparkling and a smile plays across her lips. "Harry lives and works in California, so he's eight hours behind us. We've been friends since we did a journalism course together. He was always exceptional at graphics and lay-out – he has a natural eye for it. I was just picking his brains, asking advice from an old pal."

"Sorry, Amelia. It's been a long day."

She puts her arms back around my waist, pulling me close as she looks up into my face. "Do you want to talk about it?"

"Maybe tomorrow, in the morning?"

Her beaming smile confirms I've given the right answer. "Good. This is the first night we'll have spent together, and I can think of much better things to do than talk."

Any tiredness I might have felt disappears, and I follow her deliberately teasing sashay towards the bedroom.

It's 5.50 am and I'm awake, whether I like it or not. I can feel Amelia's skin against mine and hear her gentle, shallow breathing. There's a subtle hint of her perfume that's been captured by the bedclothes, mingled with the delicious smell of our sex. Actually, I think I do like being awake, despite the fact I've had less than four hours sleep. I believe that what I'm experiencing is contentment. That might not sound like something desperately aspirational, but it's something I've not felt since before Moll and I split – and the ache I've had in the meantime means I really appreciate what I've got now all the more. This is a time to savour.

Except that it's also a time to get work done. Ryan is out there somewhere with that device. I presume Merv is still at large. And God knows where Nate is. We've been working on the assumption that yesterday was the biggie in terms of what the Russians had planned, but what if there's even more on the cards for today or tomorrow? What do we need to do to nail Waterson? Then there's the matter of checking on how Vi's doing, not to mention what to do about her evil bastard of a father.

The intrusion of such pressing realities means that my brain is now engaged, and the chance of luxuriating in relaxed contentment beside Amelia is gone. There is too much to do and

I need to get up. I ease out of bed gently so as not to disturb her, collect fresh clothes quietly from the wardrobe, and make my way to the bathroom. It's the first time I've properly registered that my toothbrush and shaving kit have been relegated to a lesser shelf in favour of Amelia's own toothbrush and toiletries. Similarly, my shampoo and shower gel are now in a corner of the shower tray, replaced on the shelf beside the pressure and temperature controls by her more feminine versions. Given that I bought all of Amelia's stuff and brought it to her here I can hardly be surprised by its presence. I suppose it's just interesting to see how quickly someone can establish themselves in a particular place, making it their home. In truth, I'm pleased by it.

Once I've shaved, showered and dressed I go to the kitchen and put on the kettle to make myself a coffee. I check my phone and I'm glad to see that there don't appear to have been any further attacks overnight. I make my way to the living room and go to the table covered with the prints of Amelia's photos. The same pictures she's already forwarded to me from the eve of Vi's mother's funeral are there – Anatoly Kuznetsov, the Russian ambassador, plus the two other Russians, including the one who tailed her to The Herald building. But most of the pictures feature Waterson. There are pictures of him alone, with his wife, and in snaps with others that I can't identify. The pictures seem to cover at least a few decades, given how young Mallingford appears in some of them. There are fourteen pictures where he appears with other men which all appear to have been taken on the same day, at some sort of shooting party.

"Reviewing my homework?" I flinch, only just managing to avoid spilling any coffee, as Amelia's arms envelope my waist from behind.

"Did I wake you? I tried not to."

"The sound of the shower did it."

"Sorry."

"Not a problem." She squeezes me gently. "What do you make of my handiwork?"

"Honestly, I'm not too sure. Why don't you explain it to me?"

Amelia releases her hold and steps forward to move alongside me. "The truth is that there's not that much to tell. In front of you is every single photographic image I've been able to track down of Waterson, plus the recent images of the Russians. You can see that there are less than forty photos featuring Waterson – remarkably few, given how prominent a figure he is. The man actively avoids the camera."

"Where did you find these?"

"Since I started researching him I've scoured all the normal sources, going back some thirty-odd years. You can see…" she gestures with her hand, "…that some of them are old and poor quality. Those portrait shots, for example were lifted from early company reports, before he became Chairman and stopped all mugshots of directors appearing. Some are more recent, like that one after his introduction into the House of Lords. Even this one with his wife at their wedding isn't particularly sharp."

"But what about these? They're obviously all taken on the same day, at some sort of shooting party."

"Ah, yes. There are fourteen of those, and they're not in the public domain." There's a real note of pride in Amelia's voice. "These were taken by my dad. He's actually in two of them himself, there…" she points, "…and again there. He obviously got someone else to take those two."

"It's obviously a shooting party – what's the context?"

"Waterson is crazy about shooting, even in the short time I worked for him there was a shoot being arranged for the next week – and that took precedence over anything to do with the business. Apparently his estate is famous amongst the shooting fraternity and an invite there is a hot ticket. Dad said that cabinet ministers, royals, foreign dignitaries have all shot there. This was the only time Dad was ever invited – apparently he wasn't very good. It was just work colleagues and business contacts on that occasion, but I think these might be the only pictures from a Waterson shoot in existence." That note of pride in her voice again.

"So, what's the plan with all of these photos?"

"I was kind of hoping you'd tell me that."

"Okay, Amelia, now you've got me. You're going to have to explain that one."

She fixes me with those big eyes, slightly widened to suggest incredulity, with a hint of a smile playing across her lips. "Come on now, Josh. You know what's going on, and now you're free to share it with me."

"Nope. Still not getting it."

A mild flicker of exasperation flits across her face. "Josh, you are MI5 or MI6, or an undercover cop, or a spy of some sort. We both know it." She dismisses my protest face. "There's some sort of major operation to undermine the UK driven by the Russians that somehow involves Waterson. It came to a climax yesterday. We both know that too."

I've got my poker face on. Best to hear everything she has to say.

"I've been working for ages to put together the story that will discredit Waterson, and now is that time. Why else do you think I downloaded all of these pictures..." another flourish of her hand over the table, "...from the cloud yesterday? You said when I first moved here that everything would be cleared up by Saturday – tomorrow. So you clearly knew about the plan for all those attacks yesterday. And I bet there were even more attacks planned that didn't go ahead. Attacks that you and your colleagues stopped."

She catches my eye for a split second before I have time to divert my glance. She's seen enough. "I'm right, aren't I? There were other atrocities planned that you guys prevented. And you can prove Waterson was involved. Can't you?"

I'm torn between keeping schtum and confirming what I can for her. She reads my hesitation. "Come on, Josh. Fill me in on what you know. If I can get enough copy I can run an exposé on the bastard – *The Lord Who Betrayed Britain*. Then I can run a follow up timeline feature charting his life and career. There's mileage to be had from highlighting every famous person who's ever had links to him. Just tell me what proof you've got and I can do the rest. Good journalists never reveal their sources, Josh, and I'm a good journalist."

"Is that what this is all about for you? The headlines and the stories?"

"I'm not going to lie to you, Josh. If this story breaks and it's got my byline attached to it than that would be great for my career. But that not what it's all about. I want that rat exposed and destroyed." The fire in her eyes and the note in her voice brook no debate as to her sincerity. "In all honesty, if the only way to bring him down was to hand the entire story to another journalist, I'd do it in a heartbeat."

Her passion is ferocious. She pauses, staring right into my eyes. "Well?"

"Amelia, I can't give you what you want."

She takes half a step backwards, still maintaining eye contact. "Can't, or won't?"

"It doesn't matter whether I would or not, because the answer is that I can't. I don't have any evidence that links Waterson to the Russians and what happened yesterday." I can see her eyes narrowing as she weighs up whether I'm being straight with her, or spinning her a line. "I don't have any evidence, and nor does anyone else."

Amelia's expression darkens, but she's still listening. "Although…" her eyes flare as I say the word, "…your theory that he's involved is one that is widely shared. There's a real effort to uncover the evidence, but it just hasn't been found yet."

As I let the words land I'm trying to read her. Confusion, relief, anger, frustration and disappointment all appear to vie with one another for supremacy. I wait quietly for her to think it though.

Eventually, after several seconds have elapsed, Amelia delivers her judgement. "I believe you, Josh. But by God am I frustrated that it looks like he's going to get away with everything. It just isn't fair." She pauses. "I understand that you can't tell me something that you don't know. But you can tell me what you do know. So come on, Josh, spill."

I make the calculation and decide that I will. I confirm much of what she already suspected, particularly that there were other planned attacks that were thwarted. I play down my own involvement, but she is – as she said a good journalist, and she keeps mining away until she wears me down. She is taken aback that Ryan, Merv and Nate are all still at large. She seems particularly fascinated by Ryan, and once again demonstrates her forensic questioning as she persuades me to repeat what I can remember of everything he has ever said or done, and of conversations he had with me or others. Eventually, the inquisition comes to an end, and I realise that it's almost quarter past eight. I explain to Amelia that I need to get back to work which she understands completely. I'm just about to ring Moll to ask where she wants me, when she pre-empts me by calling first.

"Good morning, Moll. How are you?"

Where are you?

"And a very good morning to you too."

I asked where you are. There's an edge to her voice that immediately has me on guard.

"I'm at the flat."

Which flat?

"My own flat. I didn't see the need to go back to Vi's as the UC op is over."

And are you alone?

"I am alone."

Right. Well get your arse over to Bolton Street nick pronto. I'll see you there in thirty minutes.

Moll rings off without any of the normal formalities. Someone or something has clearly rattled her cage. I'd better get there ASAP, otherwise she's only likely to be even more arsey when I get there.

Amelia has overheard one side of the short conversation and has gleaned that my boss doesn't seem too pleased with me. "Why do you think she asked if you were alone?"

"No idea."

"And did I detect that you and she were once more than professionally involved?"

"No flies on you, eh, Sherlock? Ancient, ancient history. Nothing for you to worry about."

"Don't flatter yourself that I'd be worried." She says it with a smile, but also a feistiness that gladdens my heart. I grab her in a passionate embrace and we kiss.

"Gotta go, or I'll just make things worse with the boss. Catch you later."

"Okay. 'Bye."

It's at least couple of years since I last visited Barton Street and the reception has had a recent lick of paint, although nothing else seems to have changed.

I announce myself to the officer on the desk, who I don't recognise. "DC Gray here to see DI Leishman."

He looks up at me and smiles. "Been here before?"

"Yeah."

"She's in Interview Room C, just along the…"

"I remember Interview Room C, thanks." I nod to him as he buzzes me though.

I make my way down the familiar long corridor and hang a left towards the interview rooms. The doors to A, B and D are open, revealing themselves to be unoccupied. I turn the handle to open the door to C and as I enter Moll is getting to her feet from a chair behind the table. "Close it behind you." She looks red-eyed.

I close the door and turn back to face Moll. The back of my head crashes against the glazed panel in the door, thrown back by the force of the first punch. Two more fierce blows connect with my face, and another to my neck, before I am able to grab hold of her wrists.

"Let go of me, you bastard."

"For fuck's sake, Moll. What's got into you?"

"Don't you Moll me, DC Gray. You will address me as DI Leishman." The use of our formal titles seems to remind her where we are, and what sort of behaviour is acceptable. I can sense the tension in her body ease and I release her wrists. She returns to the chair she was in before and nods for me to take the seat opposite.

"DC Gray, I know that you are not one for protocol, so let me explain the purpose of this meeting. In short, it is for you to be advised of your immediate suspension from duty."

"Sorry, Moll. What's going on?"

"If you insist that we do follow protocol I can arrange for another officer to attend, along with your Fed Rep."

"You know I don't care about that crap, Moll. Just tell me

what's going on – for God's sake."

"Our colleagues in the security services seem to have had a pang of conscience overnight, and decided to share a little secret that they'd been keeping from us."

"Cut the cryptic shit and tell me what you're talking about."

"Amelia Harris."

"What about her?"

"She's with Five."

"What? Don't be ridiculous."

"Don't talk to me about ridiculous, you fucking clown. Apparently she's been a "contact" of theirs for well over twelve months. They've had suspicions about Waterson for a long time and apparently there was some issue between Waterson and her. Subsequently she has been investigating him with a view to getting some revenge."

I feel sick to pit of my stomach. This all chimes with what Amelia has told me. I already sense that my hope that this is a mistake isn't going to survive. "Go on."

"Five took the view that my enemy's enemy is my friend, and contacted Harris. She's not an agent or actually employed by them – more of a contact or informant. She's been on their books in that capacity for over a year."

"And the attack on her?"

"Five believe that her investigations were getting under Waterson's skin and that he commissioned the attack. It simply reinforced their view that she was a useful asset to be nurtured and better looked after. But I presume that you know all of this already, Josh."

"Eh? What are you talking about? Why would I know all of this? How?"

"Cut the crap! While we were going apoplectic that Harris had gone to ground, the spooks seemed pretty laid back about it. Turns out that's because they knew exactly where she was." She stops and looks at me, her face a mixture of fury and loathing. "They knew she was at your flat, because she told them. She's been in contact with them on a daily basis, letting them know when you've been to 'visit' her…" she makes quotation marks in the air as she says visit, "…and anything useful or interesting you might have said."

My stomach is knotted tight and the palms of my hands clammy. I can't believe Amelia would play me like this. I can't believe I've been such a fool. "Why would the spooks do that? Why wouldn't they be open with a fellow agency?"

"The spooks were never satisfied that you were reliable. They weren't sure that you could be trusted, and then you offered them the ideal opportunity to keep you under surveillance. And they were obviously right, weren't they? You can't be trusted." There's a crack in her voice, but she keeps going. "I backed you, Josh. I trusted you and the AC backed my judgement. Now you've totally wrecked your career. I'll survive, but I'm damaged goods. And the AC and the Commissioner have massively lost face with the Home Secretary and the PM. All because you couldn't turn down the chance to screw some journalist." She almost spits the final sentence, contempt dripping from every word.

"Moll, that's not how it was. I need you to…"

"Save it! I'll hear no more from you, DC Gray." She takes a deep breath and composes herself, before continuing in a calm voice. "One positive outcome is that, now we've confirmed that you are being removed from the case, MI5 are being much more forthcoming with us. Apparently they feel confident that they can establish Waterson's involvement in all of this. They have managed to secure photographs of a third party, probably a go-between, with Waterson and then separately later the same day with Ryan Watson. Their chums in MI6 have secured credible advice from a source in Moscow that Waterson was turned when he lived there and that he is utterly loyal to Russia."

"Why are you telling me all this?"

"Because I want you to realise what a total fuck up you've made. Just as things are coming together and we have the chance to get those responsible, you decide to screw it all up by disobeying orders and undermining our credibility."

The steel in Moll's eyes matches the flint in her voice as she continues to twist the knife. "Both Nate and Merv have been picked up and are in custody. Ryan Watson remains at large with a bomb designed by you, determined to do whatever damage he can with it. And we need to find him and stop him without you, DC Gray, because you simply can no longer be trusted. You are suspended with immediate effect. You will remain on full pay until the disciplinary process is complete. Whilst suspended you will be available on your mobile phone 24/7 in case we identify a question we believe you might be able to help us with. Otherwise you are no longer to have any involvement in this operation. Now, if you will excuse me, some of us still have serious police work to be getting on with."

I bow my head slightly to avoid the possibility of eye contact, although I suspect Moll has no intention of looking at me. Not now, and probably never again. She gets to her feet and a couple of seconds later I hear the door close behind her.

Chapter 30

I'm back at the flat barely two hours after I left. Two hours in which my world has turned upside down. I know as I turn the key and push the door open that she'll be gone. And I'm right. The feeling of emptiness in each room is almost tangible. A superficial inspection indicates that all of her stuff is still here, which might indicate an intention to return. That said, she turned up here with her handbag and the clothes she stood up in, so all that she's left here is of no great importance to her.

I feel like a cliché from a bad movie when I finally spot the note. It's on the table beside all of the printed out photos.

Dear Josh,

Sorry. I couldn't stay cooped up any longer when there's so much to do.

See you soon.

Love,

Amelia

x x

That's it. Not a single clue as to where she might have gone. And she's signed off with the word love. Ha! There's clearly never been any love on her part. Lust maybe, but not love. I presume she must realise that I know about her links to the security services, and that's why she's cleared off. My own op, and probably my career, are over – so I'm no longer of any use or interest to her. Maybe at some point in future I'll appreciate the irony of her having been undercover reporting on me, but now it is too raw. All I feel is anger.

I need to keep my mind occupied, otherwise I'll go mad. I go to the kitchen and check the fridge. There's plenty of food in, so no need to go shopping. I go to the bookshelf and select the novel I bought two years ago and never found time to start. I settle into an armchair and open the first page. Twenty minutes later, I return the book to the shelf. I've always found concentrating on fiction difficult and today is no exception – maybe even more difficult than normal.

I wander round the flat from room to room, looking for little odd jobs that might need doing. It doesn't take me long – it's not that big a flat and there aren't any outstanding tasks that are obvious. It's too early to start making lunch, and I'm not particularly hungry anyway. Moll didn't specify how long this suspension would last, but I suspect I'll go insane with boredom long before it's over. In fact, I'll probably go mad before the day is out.

For want of anything better to do, I pick up the remote and switch on the TV. I check the listings and see the usual daytime crap – soaps, game shows, property porn, z-list celeb chat shows, lifestyle magazines. I flick on to a news channel, although I suspect that I'll find it sufficiently boring or irritating that I'll switch it off in pretty short order.

Unsurprisingly, the news is full of yesterday's incidents. There's a review that covers all of the separate incidents at a summary level, albeit with sufficient detail for it to be informative and satisfying. The anchor woman reports that the Home Secretary has confirmed that sixteen separate planned attacks were thwarted by security services and police. She also reports that he refused to be drawn on speculation that such a massive programme of terrorist activity, albeit involving widely disparate groups, must have been co-ordinated in some way. Instead she reports faithfully the bland assurances about ongoing investigations and the primacy of public safety that are to be expected from a politician less than a week away from polling day.

The picture switches to the Prince of Wales and the Duchess of Cornwall visiting the scene of the attack on the veteran's care home in County Durham. The pair are being shown round the site by a senior uniformed officer, all three wearing appropriately sombre expressions. The reporter voicing the piece advises viewers that the couple will be visiting survivors in hospital later today, where they are expected to be joined by the Duke and Duchess of Cambridge, who had been enjoying a family holiday at a location in Cumbria. When the picture switches back to the anchor she advises that the Queen has sent messages of condolence and support to people affected by all of yesterday's atrocities, and that it is expected that she will address the nation live on television tomorrow evening. When the anchor moves on and invites the political editor, elsewhere in the studio, to provide some insight into how yesterday's events are likely to affect the result of next week's election, I switch off.

I go to the kitchen, fill the kettle and put it on. Rather than wait for it to boil, I wander back into the living room and go to the table. I pick up Amelia's letter and read it again, before placing it back down. My eyes wander across the pictures arranged neatly on the table and are drawn to those depicting the shooting party. I pause for a moment as I sense the germ of an idea meandering through the byways and B-roads of my mind, before arriving in my consciousness as a fully formed thought. A lightbulb moment.

I grab my laptop and fire it up. I curse my decision to delay upgrading to a new model as the machine clunks slowly to life. Eventually I'm in and straight on to Google. I type in *Martin Jones Lord Waterson Shooting* and hit enter. I'm rewarded with the jackpot immediately. The third article on the first page, from a country pursuits magazine, talks about the almost mythical status of Waterson's shooting parties at his Aldingworth Estate's remote location in Northumberland. I type in Aldingworth Estate and find it on a map – it really is remote.

When the page of search results first came up the link to this page was purple rather than blue, indicating it had been clicked on before. I go into search history to see that someone – Amelia – had searched *Lord Waterson Shooting Estate* a couple of hours ago. She had also been searching *Royal Itineraries*. She's been thinking along the same lines as me, but is ahead of me. I think she's made an educated guess about where Ryan has gone, and I'm willing to bet she's gone there too.

It's a hunch, but the stakes are too high to ignore it. I take out my phone and dial Moll. *The number you have dialled is currently busy. Please try later.* Shit! I ring off and return to the laptop. I plug in my address and Aldingworth Estate. Shit! Five hours and fifty minutes by car. It's two hours and fifty-one minutes from King's Cross to Newcastle by train, and then another hour by car from there. By the time I get to King's Cross and wait for the next train it'd be no quicker than driving.

I dial Moll again. *The number you have dialled is currently busy. Please try later.* Bloody hell, Moll! I leave a voicemail and send a text asking her to contact me urgently. Then on to the app to check the availability of a Zipcar. I'm in luck, there's one available in a bay less than four hundred metres from here. It's a bigger, faster model than I'd usually select, but that suits me. I'm familiar enough with the site to make the booking quickly.

I scroll through the contacts list on my phone 'til I get to my old friend Andy Cheeseman's contact details and hit dial. *The number you have dialled is currently busy. Please try later.* I don't believe it! I leave a message asking him to call me back. I make sure I have my jacket, keys, portable signal jammer, wallet and phone, then head out the door.

I've been driving three and three quarter hours now and everything has been jam side up so far. The car had a full tank of fuel, so I should have enough to make it without stopping, despite the fact that I'm hammering it. I've made incredibly good time and the satnav shows that I've made up over twenty-five minutes on the anticipated journey time. I'm due to arrive in an hour and forty minutes. The only fly in the ointment is that I'm flying solo. I've tried Moll's number twice more and got the same busy message as before. I'm pretty sure she's blocked me. I also tried Andy Cheeseman again and got a busy message there too.

Almost as if thinking about him invokes a magic spell, my phone rings with caller ID showing that it's Andy.

"Andy! Thanks for calling back."

No problem, mate. Sorry it's taken so long. Been having a bit of a manic day. I'm guessing you want something. A phone call out of the blue after all these years can only mean one thing.

"Well, as it happens…"

Sorry, mate – you'll need to speak up a bit. There's a lot of background noise.

"Yeah, I'm driving. Is that any better?"

Much better. Look, I can call back later if it's more convenient – once you've finished driving.

"Don't worry. I'm on hands free. It's not a problem. Anyway, you're right. I am looking for a favour."

Go on then. What can I do for you?

"I was just wondering, are you still assigned to royal protection?"

I certainly am, squire. I look after 3, 4, 5 and 6.

"Sorry, you've got me there. What does that mean?"

There's a note of joy in Andy's voice as he explains, presumably for the thousandth time, his idea of a joke. *Her Majesty is Number 1, obviously. And the Prince of Wales is Number 2 – no laughing at the back.*

"So you look after the Duke of Cambridge plus his three kids. Numbers 3, 4, 5 and 6. Is that it?"

Got it in one. I always said that you're not quite as thick as you look. Anyway, how is it I can help you?

"I need to know where the senior members of the royal family are going to be tonight and tomorrow."

There's an ominous pause before Andy replies, all levity gone from his voice. *Why do you want to know that?*

"I wouldn't be asking if it wasn't important."

Josh, I can't answer your question – I'm paid to protect the royals, not go blabbing their whereabouts and itinerary to every Tom, Dick and Harry. And anyway, you didn't answer my question. Why do you want to know?

"Andy, please – can't you just tell me?"

Honestly, Josh, it's a complete non-starter. There's no way I can tell you.

"Okay, I understand. And I'm sorry for putting you in an awkward position. How about if I tell you where I think they're going to be?"

You can try.

"Okay, I think that either the Prince of Wales and the Duchess of Cornwall, or your lot – William and his family – are going to be at Aldingworth Estate."

There's a prolonged pause, before he replies. *Right, Josh – this is serious. How the hell do you know about Aldingworth*

Estate, and what is going on? There's a real tension in his voice.

"I can tell I've got it right. So who's going there – I presume it's Charles and Camilla? You need to get a warning to their protection team that they're possibly in danger."

Okay, Josh. We can't keep talking in riddles to each other. I'll level with you on the basis that it's mutual. Deal?

"Deal."

You're right about Charles and Camilla. But it's also the Cambridges too – all five of them. Shooting doesn't go down well with a large slice of the general public, so the fact that they'll be there tomorrow for that purpose isn't something that gets widely publicised. Prince William and his family were on holiday not far from here, and the plan was always that they'd round things off with a shoot at Aldingworth tomorrow morning, before heading back south in the evening.

I don't want to interrupt, but my curiosity gets the better of me. "And the plan was for the Cambridges to meet up with Charles and Camilla, to go shooting together? Even with the kids in tow?"

Prince Charles and the Duchess were scheduled to open a new building at Newcastle University before heading to Aldingworth this evening. So they and the Cambridges were both in the area following yesterday's shenanigans. That's why they're all here now.

"Where's here?"

Monkswell Hospital. They've been visiting some of the survivors of yesterday's attack on the veterans' care home. You wouldn't usually get two royal parties at the same venue, but the size of this atrocity and the fact that both were nearby make this an exception. We're virtually done here now and about to head off to Aldingworth. Now, quit bullshitting me and tell me what this is all about.

So I tell him. I go through the detail of yesterday's op and Ryan's escape with the fourth device. I explain Ryan's strange description about chopping the head off the beast, and my theory that he means the Queen, as the head of state, or possibly other royals. I also explain about the link between Waterson, the Russians and Ryan. I explain the fact that I'm suspended and that's why I'm having to approach him in this manner, rather than through official channels. I also explain that I'm en route to Aldingworth. As I recount everything I realise how utterly fantastical it would all sound, were it not for the evidence of yesterday's attacks.

Andy asks a few questions of clarification as I go, but largely he remains in silent listening mode. He stays that way for fully three or four seconds after I finish, before finally responding. *So you think this Ryan Watson character might try to attack the royal party at Aldingworth, or possibly Her Majesty herself at Windsor?*

"Being honest, I hadn't even considered he might attack the Queen. It just all looks like it's set up to be at Waterson's estate."

I suspect you might be right, but I will need to alert her PPO. The fact that she's at Windsor rather than BP means that she's automatically better protected. There's a moment's hesitation before he continues. *Listen, Josh, don't take this the wrong way – but you are on the level here, aren't you? You've not gone crazy?*

"I've made some mistakes, Andy, but I don't think I'm wrong on this. You know that feeling in your gut when you work something out? Well that's how I feel about this."

Okay. I'm going to get a message to Windsor and I'm going to divert the party here to a different destination from Aldingworth. I'm going to have to go now, but I'll get back to you ASAP.

"That's fine, Andy. Thanks, mate."

No problem. Speak later. 'Bye.

"'Bye."

I've been on the phone to Andy for the best part of half an hour and the satnav tells me I'm only an hour and ten minutes from my destination. The traffic is relatively light and I put my foot to the floor.

I'm only thirty minutes' drive from Aldingworth when Andy calls back.

Windsor has been advised and is on high alert. The royal

party I'm with has been diverted to two separate addresses. We need as few of them in one place as possible until this threat is properly assessed and neutralised.

"Thanks for the update. Any other news?"

Plenty. But first things first. We need images of Ryan Watson to send to Windsor and to our people in situ at Aldingworth.

"You need to contact DI Leishman at the Met – she can let you have everything you need."

Will do. I hear him relaying Moll's name to someone else to get the contact expedited. *That's Molly Leishman, isn't it? I thought you and she had a thing going, you dirty hound.*

"Ancient history now. Let's just say I'm not her favourite person. What's this other news, then?"

Major screw up, mate. We have two officers already in situ at Aldingworth and let them know about the change of plans. They started to pack up and were asked by the local security team what was happening. Our guys explained that the royal party had been diverted on account of credible reports of a possible attack on Aldingworth. Just five minutes later Waterson vamoosed out of there in his private helicopter.

"For fuck's sake, Andy! If he knows we're on to him he's going to high tail it to God knows where. What sort of shit-for-brains morons do you guys employ?"

Sorry, mate. Breakdown in comms. We were 100% focused on ensuring the safety of the royals.

"It's done now. Can the chopper be tracked?"

Dunno. I'll get someone on it right away.

"And what are the names of your guys on site? I'd rather deal with your people than with Waterson's."

Denise Wilson and Hannah Boyd. Denise is the more senior. They've been instructed to stay put and assist you when you arrive.

"Thanks. Can you let them know that I'll be there in…" I have a quick look at the satnav, "…twenty-five minutes?"

Will do.

"Is there anything else? I need to concentrate on driving."

No. Catch you later.

"'Bye."

It's ten to six and darkness is falling as I pull into the Aldingworth Estate car park. Before I can get out of the car my phone rings again. Moll.

Josh, what the hell are you up to?

"How lovely to hear from you, DI Leishman."

I've had SO14 chasing me for images of Ryan Watson. And I've just had the AC on to me. She's had a call from the Commissioner, who's been getting an ear bashing from the PM? What the hell are you up to?

"I had an idea of where Ryan might be and what his possible target was."

You were told that you were suspended – off the case. You were instructed to stay available at home if we needed to get in touch with you.

"I was instructed to be available by phone, not to stay at home. And I'm available now. I did try calling you. I left a voicemail and a text."

I'd blocked your number because I was so furious I couldn't stand the thought of having to speak to you. I wouldn't get the alerts to let me know about the text or the voicemail. She actually sounds a bit sheepish. *Tell me what's going on.*

"I don't have time, Moll. If I'm right and Ryan is here, he's soon going to realise that his plan is screwed – if he hasn't already. I've got to find him before he disappears again. I've got to go." I hang up without giving her a chance to speak.

Before I have the opportunity to open the car door there's a loud, insistent knocking on the window. I lower the glass and an earnest looking woman lowers her head to address me. "Are you Josh Gray?"

"Yes."

"Good. I'm Denise Wilson. Let me in, please." She doesn't wait for a response, but darts round the front of the car, opens the passenger side door and parks herself in the seat next to me. She takes her phone out and holds the screen towards me, showing a mug shot of Ryan. "This is your man, isn't it? Ryan Watson?"

"Yes."

"He's at The Lodge." She points towards an unlit tree-lined road stretching off into the darkness. "About two miles down this way. My colleague has eyes on him."

I put the car into gear and head in the direction indicated. "What's The Lodge?"

"It's a lot grander than it sounds. It's the original shooting lodge for the estate, but it's been extended so much that it's actually bigger than the main house. It's got 22 bedrooms, a gym, swimming pool, dining hall – the whole works. The royal party were scheduled to dine there this evening and stay overnight before tomorrow's shoot."

"And that's where Ryan is now?"

"Yes. The place was buzzing earlier with all sorts of staff and contractors preparing things for the guests. Watson was using an alias and had ID that showed he was a member of one of the catering firms drafted in. The ID was pukka, so it seems obvious that his presence was well-planned. The fact that he knew about the royals being here also implicates Waterson. We had no idea that he was anything other than he claimed to be until we got a call from Andy Cheeseman."

The road bends to the right then twists sharply to the left, and I realise that I need to slow my speed. "And what's happening at The Lodge now?"

"A lot of confusion apparently. The Estate security people went back to the main house as soon as the cancellation was advised, and we think that most of them went off with Lord Waterson in the helicopter. There are still some of his staff there, managing the caterers mainly. Some of the food can be put in the refrigerated vans and returned, but a lot of the cooking was pretty advanced. Hannah – that's my colleague who's in situ – says that the plan is to serve the food up to the caterers and other staff, rather than let it go to waste."

An adult hind darts across the beam of my headlights, not more than ten metres ahead, and I'm glad I reduced my speed earlier.

"It's just along here, round this next bend. There's a big parking area on the right, immediately beside The Lodge."

We pull up and get out of the car. There must be at least a

couple of dozen other vehicles parked. Although it's dark, there are sufficient lights on for me to gauge the scale of the building – or buildings, as it turns out. I have the sense that in daylight this would look like a medium sized upmarket hotel development.

Denise leads the way towards the main entrance, which is unguarded. She has her phone pressed to her ear, talking to Hannah, confirming her location. I hear her curse quietly. We navigate what feels like a never-ending series of corridors before arriving in a large, modern kitchen, bustling with activity. A slim black woman with close-cropped hair and a flustered expression approaches.

"How did you lose him, Hannah?"

"I was distracted by that bloody journo. It looked like she was about to take a picture of him on her phone – trying to be discreet, like, and then she bumped into a waiter and made him drop a big, heavy metal tray. There was a huge clanging noise and when I looked back, Watson was gone. But he won't be far away."

"Journo?" I intonate it as a question, although I already know the answer.

"This is Josh, by the way." Denise reminds me of my manners.

"Nice to meet you, Josh. I'm Hannah." She hold her mobile phone screen towards me, showing a full length picture of Amelia in profile. "She arrived here about an hour ago, just after the Aldingworth security team had pissed off. Waltzed right in, unchallenged. I clocked her pretty quickly as a face I didn't recognise. Then I overheard her asking someone if they knew where Ryan Watson was. When no-one recognised the name she asked if anyone new had arrived yesterday or today. She pretty quickly sussed that he was here, albeit using an alias."

"Journos." Denise sniffs. "Bane of our lives. We can usually spot them a mile off."

I realise that Amelia made the same deduction as I did. She had grilled me about Ryan to extract every possible detail she could, including his enigmatic comments about cutting off heads. She worked it out more quickly than me. Is she here as a journalist or as MI5? Has she tipped off her contacts at MI5? Why didn't she know what Ryan looks like – if she's with MI5, surely they would have supplied her with his image?

Denise shakes me out of reflective mode when she addresses Hannah. "You said Watson won't be far away. I don't understand why he hasn't already cleared off out of here."

"I think I know why." Hannah has our full attention. "He keeps going into the dining hall, which is about as busy as this kitchen. It's like he's waiting for an opportunity when there's no-one around. I think he's placed his explosive device below the table where the royals would have been seated, and he's looking for his chance to retrieve it."

"That would make sense. If this plot has been foiled, he wants the means to do damage somewhere else." Denise looks thoughtful. "Let's check out the dining hall. If he's not there, we can station one of us there while the other two look for him."

Denise is obviously as familiar with the layout of this place as Hannah, and leads the way through the double swing doors at the far end of the kitchen, and along a relatively short corridor to an impressive large teak door. The brass sign stating *Dining Hall* saves me having to guess. "Okay, let's go." She turns the handle and leads us through.

As I follow the two SO14 officers the world seems to go into slow-mo. The hall is grand, a perfect forty by twenty metres rectangle, with eight foot high teak panelling all the way around. The high vaulted ceiling reinforces the sense of space. Along the wall to the right are a series of arched windows, the same height as the wooden panelling below them. The other walls are plastered above the panelling and decorated with hunting trophies, guns, shooting sticks and other similar paraphernalia. There are three doors evenly spaced along the left hand wall, and another in the middle of the wall opposite, directly mirroring the one through which we have just entered.

There is a long table in the centre of the room, draped in a white linen tablecloth and set for sixteen places. Half way along the left hand side of the table a chair has been pulled out and Ryan is hunkered down, staring directly at me. The door at the opposite end of the hall opens and Amelia enters. She squints at me as though she can't believe what she is seeing, then calls out my name. Her shout breaks the slow-mo spell. Ryan looks in her direction, then back towards me before stretching under the table and retrieving the familiar looking rucksack hidden there.

Hannah and Denise take a step to the right and left respectively and stop. I move between them and continue to walk slowly towards Ryan. "It's done, Ryan. It's over. You need to come with us now."

His face tells me that he's worked it out. He knows that his earlier suspicions about me were right. Loathing leaches from every pore as he looks me in the eye. He holds the back pack at shoulder height in his left hand and waves a mobile phone at me with his right. "That's far enough, soldier boy! Take one step closer and I'll blow the lot of us to kingdom come."

I slow my pace by half, but continue walking towards him. "Don't be such a drama queen, Ryan. I know that you are a complete coward. You don't have the balls to detonate that device."

"I'm not fucking bluffing!"

His voice has risen an octave and I can see the madness in his eyes. I take another step forward. And another.

Ryan screams. His thumb is repeatedly pressing a button on his phone, which he is waving manically at the rucksack. He looks toward me, then towards the jamming device I'm waving at him in my right hand. He screams again and hurls the rucksack at me, causing me to duck.

Then the world switches back to slow-mo. Ryan reaches on to the table and grabs an enormous carving knife, pirouettes back to face me and launches himself forwards. I see murder in his face. I hear Amelia's scream. I hear the crack. I hear and feel the rush of air by my ear. I see the perfect small circle in the centre of Ryan's forehead. A second bullet zings past and lodges in Ryan's sternum. I see the blade fall to the floor as his body crumples.

I look over my shoulder. Hannah's arms are outstretched in front of her, hands clasping a 9mm Glock 17.

Amelia's arms are tight round my waist, her body pressed hard against me, shaking. Denise darts past, crouches by Ryan and fires two shots from her own Glock in quick succession into the nape of his neck to definitively deactivate him, a standard precaution to prevent any automatic spasms that might trigger the device. Then she kicks the phone away from his hand. Just following procedure.

Chapter 31

It's 10.00 am on Wednesday the 28th, five days after Ryan was killed. I'm in a quiet corner of a coffee shop just round the corner from the nick where my disciplinary meeting will be held in half an hour's time. Technically I'm allowed five days' notice of the hearing, but I was happy to forego that to get the matter resolved. My Fed Rep will meet me here in ten minutes to needlessly run through my defence one last time.

I usually rely on my phone or the TV for news, but today I've bought a copy of The Herald to read with my cappuccino. It's Amelia's big splash today and I was interested to see what she has written. She certainly didn't miss Waterson. She's outed him as an ideologue, totally committed to Russia, and willing to do anything in his power to damage Britain. It appears that, despite denials from the Kremlin, Waterson and his wife are now safely ensconced in Russia, living a very comfortable exile in the desirable Moscow suburb of Arbat. I'm sure she'll have her contacts in MI6 to thank for that juicy titbit.

She's clearly covered by the Official Secrets Act, which has prevented her from publishing everything that she might have done otherwise. Nonetheless, it's a pretty good bit of journalism and achieves her aim of taking Waterson down. The only thing that she needs to be careful of is the Russians. She will have right royally pissed them off, and they have become increasingly bold when it comes to settling scores with those that live outside their borders. Still, that's no longer my concern. I explained to Amelia face-to-face that we were finished. She's called, left voicemails and texted over twenty times since. I will keep ignoring her until she gets the message.

Amelia's story gets the first two pages, plus another double page spread inside, forcing the politics to page three and beyond. Given the election is just two days away I have to go pretty deep into the paper to find news that doesn't relate to the terrorist attacks or politics. On page 17, which appears to be a digest of crime stories, I find what I'm looking for.

Triple Tragedy

It was reported late last night that Viscount Mallingford, aged 57, had been found murdered at his home in Wantwell. Mallingford, best known for his extensive property development interests, was found by a cleaner yesterday morning. He had died as a result of a single bullet wound to the head. Police officers have launched a full investigation.

The news comes as a further devastating blow to his extended family and friends, following the death of his only daughter just two days before, and the death of his wife earlier in the month.

Further down the same page is an even shorter snippet.

Suspicious Deaths

Police are investigating the deaths of two men and two women found in a flat in South Shields. Tox reports indicate that all four had consumed contaminated drugs. Police are urging anyone who has information relevant to the investigation to come forward as a matter of urgency.

I fold the paper and place it on the table in front of me. The police investigation into Mallingford's death will reveal no signs of forced entry, and will further discover that the security CCTV recordings have been wiped. Similarly, the investigation in South Shields will not identify any signs of forced entry to the flat where the bodies were found. In any case my phone would prove that I was at home in my own flat at the time both of those crimes took place. Not that I expect to have to prove anything.

Acknowledgements

I'd like to thank the following people.

John Ballam for his wisdom, encouragement and advice.

Maureen O'Neill, Audrey Slade, Theresa Black, Viv Moaven, Jo Pike and Chris Wilson for their help and support.

Zoë Govan for contributing a couple of ideas and being more constructive than I expected.

The friend who provided technical consultancy on the basis that he remain anonymous.

My wife, Chris, for her patience, love and support.

Printed in Great Britain
by Amazon